THE BEAULIEU VANISHING

by *Vicki Gwilliam's sister*
K. E. Martin

Grosvenor House
Publishing Limited

This book is published by
Grosvenor House Publishing Ltd
28-30 High Street, Guildford, Surrey, GU1 3EL.
www.grosvenorhousepublishing.co.uk

A CIP record for this book
is available from the British Library

ISBN 978-1-78148-465-4

To all my sisters, the living and the departed, with love

PRINCIPAL DRAMATIS PERSONAE

At Middleham Castle

- **Richard, Duke of Gloucester**, youngest brother of King Edward IV; also known as Dickon, Gloucester and my lord of Gloucester
- **Anne, Duchess of Gloucester**, wife of Richard, youngest daughter of the Countess of Warwick and her late husband
- Francis Cranley, close friend and foster brother of Richard of Gloucester; sometimes known as Frank
- Matthew, Cranley's personal servant
- **Sir James Tyrell**, a loyal adherent of the Duke of Gloucester
- John Knewstubb, one of Tyrell's most useful retainers
- Tom Brankin, another of Tyrell's men, very handy with a bow

At York

- Margaret Pennicott, lovely young widow of a wealthy merchant

At Beaulieu Abbey

- **Anne Neville, Countess of Warwick**, widow of the great Earl of Warwick and mother of the Duchess of Gloucester; occasionally known as Proud Nan

- Eleanor Vernon, attendant to the Countess of Warwick and orphaned daughter of a Derbyshire gentleman
- Father John Piers, abbot of Beaulieu
- Brother Martin, the abbey horse master
- Brother Christopher, the abbey cellarer

At Netley Abbey

- Father Marmaduke Draper, abbot of Netley
- Brother Walter, novice master
- Peter of Keverne, a novice monk

At Southampton

- Bernard Gover, taverner at The George
- Old Stumpy, innkeeper at The Mermaid
- Maurice Berkeley, Keeper of Southampton Castle
- Andrew Coterel, a port official
- Nicholas Bonvylle, the town's most prosperous merchant
- Agnes Bonvylle, Nicholas's luxury-loving wife
- Jane Bonvylle, a poor relation

Elsewhere

- Ralph Abney, a Derbyshire gentleman down on his luck
- Dick Chapman, a pedlar
- Alys Aldis, a carpenter's daughter
- **John de Vere, Earl of Oxford**, a nobleman with traitorous tendencies
- Jigger, Oxford's trusted henchman
- **Sir John Arundell**, Sheriff of Cornwall and Tyrell's father-in-law

- **Sir Henry Bodrugan,** a leading Cornish gentleman
- William Kylter, a minor Cornish gentleman
- Albrecht Giese, an influential Hanseatic merchant living in London
- Steffan Kornherr, a Hanseatic merchant living in Rostock
- Karl Warsitz, a seafarer
- **Hans Duringer, a clockmaker**
- Isolde Duringer, daughter of Hans

Names in bold denote real historical figures.

Portsmouth, April 1471

The women huddled close to the fire, anxious to claim as much warmth as possible from the tavern's meagre blaze.

"This dismal place is unfit for you, my lady," the younger of the two protested, casting wary glances at the uncouth clientele.

"You should not set foot in such a place, nor break bread with these ruffians! Heaven help us, why ever did Ralph have to bring us here?"

"Abney is not at fault," her companion replied, pitching her voice low to prevent the tavern's inquisitive customers from eavesdropping. "There was no other option, as you well know. Until the outcome of the battle is known, we dare not seek shelter where we might be recognised. Come now, Eleanor, what do we gain by complaining? Here we are and here we must wait until Abney returns with news. In the meantime, no more grumbling while those we love face danger and discomfort far greater than ours. Instead, let us offer silent prayer for their safety."

Compunction replaced irritation as the girl heard the trembling in the noblewoman's voice. Though it was cold, Eleanor knew it was not the unseasonable weather that made her poor mistress shiver.

"Do not fret, my lady," she said, rubbing the older woman's hands in an effort to impart both warmth and reassure. "Ralph will return soon enough, and he's sure to bring news of a great victory. Of a certainty he will. How could it be otherwise with your noble husband in command?"

In answer, the woman managed nothing more than a bleak smile. While grateful for her young friend's attempt to raise her spirits, she was unable to share the girl's optimism. She felt no conviction that the tidings they awaited would be good and, if truth be told, she no longer knew what outcome she desired. Since her husband had switched allegiance from King Edward and thrown in his lot with the Lancastrian Queen, she found herself wishing for the impossible, the turning back of time.

Through long habit and personal inclination she had always been loyal to the House of York. She had remained so even when her husband began railing against the King's folly and the limitless rapacity of his beautiful consort's family. But he had not sought her opinion when he formed an alliance with the King's deadliest enemy, for she was nothing but a woman and therefore of little account, even though she had been the means by which he gained his title, wealth and power.

Yes, she had been horrified by his betrayal of the King but nonetheless had accepted it without dissent, for such was her duty. Only when she learned of his plan to wed their youngest daughter, her namesake Anne, to Edward of Westminster, the Lancastrian heir, had she spoken out, begging her husband to reconsider the match. She had reminded him that the lad was said to be haughty and cold, and that disturbing whispers clung to his name like murky cobwebs. Even as she reminded her husband of these things, however, she had recognised the futility of her words. He had made a king once before and now, as he stood on the threshold of making another, he meant to ensure that his own blood shared the crown. This time there would be no mistakes; no interlopers would be allowed to drive a wedge between him and the throne as the hated Woodvilles had done after he had placed Edward upon it. Set against this, it mattered little that young Anne feared her future bridegroom, or that the marriage placed her life in jeopardy. It was a high stakes game that he was playing and he was willing to risk all – his own life and the safety of his family – on this one last throw of the dice.

"Jesu save us all from his ambition," the woman whispered, barely moving her lips so that Eleanor would not know she had spoken.

Her sombre thoughts were disrupted as the door opened and a dishevelled Ralph Abney stepped inside, a chill wind following him as he hastened to her side.

"All is lost, my lady," he blurted as he fell to his knees in front of her, sick despair contorting his features.

"A messenger was searching for you," he continued between gasps as he gulped steadying air into his lungs. "I found him, half-dead of battle wounds and fatigue. He brought word that your lord husband had met with the enemy near Barnet. They had brought to the field a great host but despite this, at first it seemed that your husband would win the day. Victory was within his grasp until a poisonous fog descended upon the field, rendering it nigh impossible to know friend from foe. The messenger told of great confusion then, with Neville men mistaking the Earl of Oxford's banner for that of the King. They attacked them, my lady, causing Oxford to cry treachery and flee the field. With him and his men gone King Edward was able to turn the tide and win the day."

"Tell me the rest," the woman commanded. "I see it in your face yet I must hear it from your lips if I am to believe it."

Abney flinched but did as he was ordered.

"The Earl is slain, my lady, and his brother Montagu also. Our cause is lost, though the messenger says the Lancastrians mean to fight on."

Eleanor cried out at these words but her mistress made no sound. In that moment she realised she had been waiting for this news throughout her married life. She had learned to love her warrior husband but had always known him marked for a battlefield death. Now that his fate had claimed him she found she could not regret it, at least not until she knew that her daughters were safe.

Before she could voice her concerns for them, Eleanor spoke up.

"Ralph, did the messenger bring word about my father and William? Do they yet live?" she asked, her pretty face twisted with fear.

Abney hung his head, even more reluctant to destroy the girl's hopes than he had been to inform the Countess of her husband's death.

"There was no direct word of them," he mumbled, "but there is no doubt that they too have perished, for with his own eyes the messenger saw the Earl's body-guards slaughtered as they sought to protect him. Eleanor, I am so sorry. Your father was a fine man. Your brother, too; God knows he was the best friend I ever had."

He reached for her hand but she jerked it away and turned her face so that neither he nor the Countess could read her expression.

"Well then," she said with brittle cheerfulness, "so now I am alone in the world."

"Not alone, Eleanor, not so long as I live," Abney declared. "For your brother's sake, I swear I will never leave you unprotected."

"Noble words, but I fear you have little choice," the Countess interjected. "Whatever fate awaits us, I doubt Eleanor and I will suffer physical harm. It is not Edward's way to wage war on women. But for you, Ralph, it is a different matter. If you are caught now you will be dealt with as a traitor, for you are known as my husband's loyal follower. Your best hope is to flee to France. From there you must write to Edward seeking forgiveness. In the fullness of time it may become possible for you to return to your estate but for now you must assuredly go."

"Am I a craven beast to abandon you to save myself?" Abney glowered. "My lord entrusted me with your care and until you are safe I cannot think of my own hide. I shall stay with you come what may."

The Countess sighed, too weary to resist the sacrifice the young fool was willing to make of his life. Not so Eleanor, who was sparked to anger by his reckless words.

"Just go, you dolt!" she spat at him. "How do you think we will feel if you are slain protecting us? Do we need to see you with a sword run through your belly, your innards roiling in the dirt or your thick head hacked from your shoulders? It is bad enough for me to know that my father and brother perished thus, without looking on as you meet the same fate! For the love of God, Ralph, put aside your stupid pride for a moment. Consider instead the feelings of those that care for you and do not wish to see you die."

When she stopped, panting with exertion from her outburst, the Countess stared at her young companion in surprise and admiration. She had known Eleanor had spirit but never before had she heard the girl speak with such passion.

Abney also stared at her, though for a different reason. He had paid scant attention to her angry eruption, choosing instead to concentrate on how well her complexion looked when she was animated, but he had heard enough to know she had said something or other about caring for him. And what was caring but a word used by maidens too modest to proclaim their love? His spirits soared at the thought. Even to himself he had never dared admit how deeply he loved her, this joyful, good-natured girl he had known all his life, for always there had been the nagging knowledge that she was too clever and fine for a dullard such as he. Yet now that did not signify for had she not said that she cared for him? Perhaps after all, staying alive was a better option than dying for a lost cause.

"Aye, I will leave," he announced abruptly. "I will do as you command, my lady, and head for France. But, before God, I swear I will return as soon as I am able."

Rising to his feet, he bowed briefly to the Countess and then clasped Eleanor in an awkward embrace. Too affronted to speak, she batted him away with a gesture he mistook for virginal delicacy.

"God be with you," the Countess called as he strode from the tavern. Dutifully, Eleanor echoed her words before putting all thoughts of Ralph Abney far from her mind as she turned to a more pressing matter.

"So now, what must we do, my lady? Do you know of some safe place that we can make for?"

In answer, the Countess shrugged her elegant shoulders. She knew she should take control but the searing anxiety she felt for her daughters, particularly Anne whose present location was unknown, made rational thought impossible. After a long, expectant silence, the unwelcome realisation hit Eleanor that her mistress was not going to provide the answer she sought. Very well then, she thought, clasping her hands together so tightly that her knuckles drained of colour. Very well. She would shoulder responsibility for their safety.

Summoning the shifty landlord, she slipped him her last coin and told him to ready their horses.

"And whereabouts do you go now, young mistress?" he asked, displaying a curiosity that might have been innocent but most likely was not. Belatedly it dawned on Eleanor that he and the other tavern occupants must have overheard Abney's every word. So much for remaining incognito.

She feigned thought before making her reply.

"I think we must find a ship without delay. It is imperative that I get my poor lady to her friends in the Low Countries."

Outside, she was relieved to see their palfreys standing ready by the mounting block, their reins held by an undernourished stable lad. As she helped her passive mistress onto horseback her gaze was caught by a small, vicious-looking blade stuck into the boy's plaited leather belt.

"Hand me your knife," she ordered the startled youth.

It had occurred to her that two unescorted women would be easy prey for the robbers and vagrants known to plague the area. At least with a knife she would be able to mount some sort of defence, should they be attacked. For a moment emotion choked her as she remembered William's playful lessons in armed combat; without a younger brother to train in the arts of war, he had been forced to make do with his little sister and she had been a willing student. Now he was dead but perhaps his lessons would help to keep her alive.

When the boy hesitated to obey her command, Eleanor reached out and removed from her cloak a bright, heart-shaped brooch made from twisted gold. A thing of exquisite beauty, it had been her father's betrothal gift to her mother. Parting with it would cost her dearly but it was the only item of value in her possession and, in any case, this was not the time for sentiment.

"Look," she said, proffering it to the inquisitive lad, "I have no money but I will trade you this brooch for your knife. It is very precious, worth more than your master earns in a year. Take care he does not steal it from you; he looks the sort that would."

At this the youth grinned and, eyes alight with avarice, handed Eleanor the knife hilt first, outstretching an open palm for the brooch. She waited until she was seated on her palfrey before dropping it onto the grubby hand with a small sigh of regret.

"Come, my lady," she called as she rode with the Countess from the tavern, "we must make haste if we are to catch the tide."

Only when she was certain they were out of sight did she check her mount and reveal their true destination to her dazed mistress. Several hours later, bone weary and cold almost beyond endurance, the women rode up to an imposing stone gatehouse. Relief surged through Eleanor, imbuing her with new strength as she pounded the door with her balled up fists and demanded admittance. Roused by the commotion, a peevish porter raised a candle to spy on the noise maker through the peephole in the gatehouse door.

"You must state your name and business if you've a mind to shelter here this night," he grumbled, unimpressed by the bedraggled visitors and minded to turn them away.

"Very well then," came the reply in a clear, young voice that rang with authority.

"I am Eleanor Vernon, only surviving child of Sir William Vernon of Derbyshire, lately slain at Barnet field. With me is my mistress, the most noble Countess of Warwick, whose husband the Earl of Warwick is also lately slain in that same battle. We are come to Beaulieu to claim sanctuary so do your duty, churl, and admit us without more ado."

Chapter One

Every morning when I awaken I wonder if this day will be my last. Every day I pray it will be so, though I know our callow village priest would name that prayer a sin. He would have me give thanks to God for granting me a generous life span but I balk at this, having lost too many that I loved. Brainless cleric, he does not understand that when all those a man holds dear are in their graves, a long life is more a curse than a blessing.

I was not always alone, nor am I now, in truth. I have servants to see to my needs and civil company when I care to summon it. This I do infrequently since it is not and never can be the company I crave. I was blessed to share friendship with the very best of men, and to know the love of a woman who made each day I spent beside her a taste of paradise on earth. Both now are gone. Well-meaning fools tell me that as long as I remember my loved ones I can never truly be alone, unaware that memories are no substitute for living flesh.

Besides these two, my noble lord and my dearest love, there were others – friends, lovers and comrades-in-arms – who touched my life and left their mark upon it. They too are long gone but their faces crowd my memories; sometimes they visit me in my sleep and then how merrily I wake until the cold dawn tells me I have been dreaming. Of late, my slumbers have been teeming with the people I met when I went about the King's business at Beaulieu, seeking to discover the fate of pretty young Eleanor Vernon.

†††

It was the middle of May when my lord of Gloucester returned to his castle of Middleham from Nottingham where he had gone to speak with his brother, King Edward. With his young Duchess newly delivered of their firstborn, a son, my friend had been sore at heart to leave but he returned in high spirits, bearing news that was sure to gladden her. Pausing only to impart these tidings to her and to kiss the brow of his precious heir, he had hastened to his privy chamber and sent word for Sir James Tyrell and me to attend him without delay.

"His Grace has seen fit to grant my request at last," he told us, his eyes ablaze with a secret joy. "The Countess of Warwick is given leave to quit sanctuary. She will not be fully at liberty, for the King fears what mischief might ensue should she fall into the hands of our brother Clarence. For my part I cannot believe George would do her real harm, though I know him well enough to know that he could not suffer her to live in peace. Therefore she is to come here to Middleham, to live out her remaining years with Anne and me."

Now I understood my friend and master's jubilant mood. For many months he had endeavoured to secure the liberty of his wife's mother, writing often to Edward to plead her case. He argued that she should not suffer for the treachery of her husband, the late Earl of Warwick. Thus far his appeals had achieved only vague promises to consider the matter. That the King loved and valued his youngest brother none could deny and ordinarily he was happy to prove his affection by granting Richard's rare requests. This made his continued refusal to end the Countess' two year sojourn in Beaulieu sanctuary all the more remarkable, as did the fact that Edward tended to gentleness when dealing with his enemies' womenfolk. It was my belief that his unusual obduracy regarding the Countess sprang from the bitter grief occasioned him by her husband's betrayal.

Happily for my lord and his wife, the King's delight on hearing of the birth of his nephew and namesake, coupled with his gratitude for the stability Gloucester's wise rule had brought to the north, had at last moved him to allow Anne of Warwick her freedom, albeit a restricted version of it.

"Hah! And this prospect brings you joy, my lord?" Tyrell snorted when Richard had finished recounting his news. "By Jesu, given the choice I'd sooner share my home with a flatulent friar than with the cabbage-breathed hag who spawned my lady wife." I winced at Tyrell's blunt remark but my friend Dickon smiled and let it pass without comment. A cheery, well-made man a year or so short of his thirtieth year, Sir James was famous for his candid speech and he made no secret of his indifference to his child bride, nor of the strong aversion he felt for all her kin, contriving to spend as little time among them as possible. He had entered Gloucester's service some two years since. Some folk whispered that he came from tainted stock, his treasonous father having been executed by the King, but I knew my lord liked and trusted him. As yet I was not sufficiently acquainted with him to form an opinion of my own but for now, the knowledge that he had Dickon's good opinion was enough to incline me in his favour.

"So you require us to bring the Countess north?" I ventured, at which my lord nodded his assent.

"Aye, Frank, that's the nub of it. I would have you deliver the news to her at Beaulieu and then bring her home to us. Give her a few days to arrange her affairs. The poor lady is in great want, she tells Anne in her letters, having long since expended the little money she had about her when she entered sanctuary. Much as I have desired to, I have been unable to send her more without going against my brother's express wishes, and though the monks keep her warm and well fed their hospitality does not extend to having her accoutred according to her rank. I will give you a fat purse to take to her, to enable her to obtain whatever is needful. She must be made comfortable for her journey.

"I give the charge of this mission to you, Tyrell," he continued, "but Cranley will accompany you, for he is known to the Countess where you are not. Otherwise, take only so many men with you as you think necessary to ensure her safety. A larger number will delay your progress and that I cannot countenance, for Anne will be counting the days until she is reunited with her mother."

"My lord, it will be as you desire," Tyrell intoned with humble solemnity. Glancing at him, I could see that beneath his smooth gravity he was gratified to have the task entrusted to him, and no wonder. Escorting the Countess of Warwick to Middleham would stand him in good stead with the Duchess and we all knew that

Gloucester's special favour fell on those that pleased his wife. As for me, I already basked in that sweet lady's high opinion and daily thanked the Saints for it, aware that it was little enough deserved.

Begging leave from the Duke to make an immediate start on his travel preparations, Tyrell exited the chamber and I made to follow but was halted by a gesture from my noble friend.

"Francis, you comprehend why I am desirous for you to accompany Tyrell?" he questioned me.

"I believe so, aye, my lord. The Countess knows me from the years I spent here with you under her husband's tutelage. You think my familiar face will serve to hearten her, and reassure her that Middleham is to be her home and not her prison."

At this, Gloucester flashed a grateful smile at me. "As ever, Frank, you know my thoughts."

None better, I thought, remembering the days of our shared boyhood. I had been raised alongside Richard and his brother George following the death of my father in service to theirs, the late Duke of York. Though I had been his only son, illegitimacy debarred me from claiming my father's modest estate and as for my mother, for reasons unknown she had chosen to abandon me when I was scarce one month old. Had it not been for York's intervention I should have perished; had it not been for Dickon, throughout my boyhood I should never have known what it was to matter to another living soul. For this he had my eternal allegiance and I had long since made it my business to read his moods and thoughts in order to better look out for his interests.

"And yet you are uneasy, Dickon," I ventured, addressing him informally as he preferred whenever we were alone, "for you imagine that in giving Tyrell charge of this matter you slight me, but it is not so. I understand that it would scarce be fitting to consign Proud Nan to the care of a bastard nobody. Why, the good brothers at Beaulieu would be outraged, and rightly so. All honour and dignity must be accorded the noble lady, and if that means I must be Tyrell's lackey then so be it."

My friend grinned at my foolishness and at my use of the name we had as impudent youngsters bestowed in secret on Warwick's lady on account of her queenly bearing.

"Scarce his lackey, you knave!" he laughed. "But let me speak plain for a moment, Francis. I believe it will profit you to leave Middleham for a spell. There has been a pall about you of late and I know it stems from that dismal Plaincourt affair."

I grew grave at these words which alluded to a mission the Duke had sent me on last December and from which I had returned damaged both in body and in mind. Though my official position at Middleham was personal minstrel to the Duke and Duchess few took this seriously; certainly not once they had heard me play since my passion for music far exceeded my ability. Those close to the Duke understood that my true function was to be his trusted man, going wherever necessary to enact his wishes and protect his good name from calumny. In this at least I had so far always succeeded but the recent Plaincourt Manor affair had cost me dear. It was bad enough that I had been unable to bring to justice the murderer I had uncovered there. Worse still was the fact that I had failed to save the life of a woman I had since discovered was my own kin, and close kin at that. Added to these bitter memories was the misery caused by another misfortune which had befallen me during Gloucester's recent absence from Middleham, though he knew nothing of this and I had determined never to burden him with it.

"I grieve for your lack of spirits," Dickon continued, "and do believe the journey south will do you good. And it will serve to better acquaint you with Tyrell, who is a good, true friend of mine. It would please me to know that you and he were also friends."

"I see no hardship in that," I replied honestly, "for I like him well enough already and will endeavour to like him the better for your sake."

So saying I made my exit and went directly to my chamber to instruct Matthew, my servant boy, to ready my belongings for a long journey.

†††

I set out the following morn with Tyrell and two of his retainers, John Knewstubb and Tom Brankin, who hailed from his manor of Gipping in Suffolk. Knewstubb was a broad, hard slab of a man with an everyday air of cheerful menace. Though smaller, his companion Brankin was lithe and wiry and, according to Tyrell, a bowman of no mean accomplishment. Matthew pulled faces and muttered obscenities when he learned he was not to come with me but his mood had brightened when he realised that my absence would give him a respite from his daily duties. To help him feel useful I entrusted to his care my beloved lute, knowing I would have no need of it on this journey.

Spring was a pleasant season to be riding south in genial company, all the more so since as Gloucester had discerned, my spirits were in dire need of a tonic. While he had been meeting with the King in Nottingham, I had donned my finest apparel and hastened to the Pennicott house in York, intent on persuading Margaret, the woman I loved, to forgive my shortcomings and become my wife. I see now that I acted too swiftly. Her worthy old husband was barely settled in his grave yet I had dallied once before and lost her to another. This time there could be no hesitating; I was resolved to prove my love and ardour to Margaret by pressing my suit most urgently.

An initial refusal I had anticipated, since I knew how deeply I had hurt my beloved with my ill-concealed misgivings over her low birth. Her father was Smithkin, the rough-spoken sergeant-at-arms at Middleham Castle, while her long dead mother had been a shepherd's daughter. Though I loved Margaret I had been ashamed of her parentage and could not envisage her as fit company for the Duke and Duchess. A churlish dog I had been, aye, and a benighted fool also, but I know that in time I would have come to my senses and seen that set against a life without Margaret, my qualms about her background were of no significance. Yet she had despaired of me err I reached this conclusion and wed Master Pennicott, a wealthy merchant whose generosity and kindness she took as compensation for his lack of youth and vigour. Thus when I set out to woo her some months after his unexpected demise I was fully prepared for a refusal. Womanly pride would prevent Margaret from accepting me immediately, I could see that, but in my youthful arrogance I was certain that an hour or two of remorseful pleading would suffice to rekindle her feelings for me.

I failed, of course I failed, for in my self-absorption I had not allowed for the Widow Pennicott being one single whit different from the sweet-natured virgin I had known as Margaret Smithkin. I discovered my error at once when she received me with great hauteur in the lofty hall of her comfortable house and dismissed my suit almost before the words had left my mouth.

"Tie myself to you?" she had scoffed. "Why in the name of Our Lady should I do that? Be assured Master Cranley, that I'd far sooner wed my pigman, stinking and toothless as he is, for at least I know him to be honest."

At this I had made to remonstrate but she silenced me with an angry gesture.

"Oh, spare me your pretences! Had you been sincere in your love for me you would have made me your wife when you had the chance. But you did not, and we both know why. You lusted for me, I grant you that, but your lust was not strong enough to blind you to the inconvenience of my humble birth. Yet though I come from common stock, at least I am not baseborn!"

This allusion to my bastardy startled me, for the Margaret I remembered had always been too much in awe of my friendship with the powerful Duke to recognise the dubious nature of my own background. Nor was this my only surprise, for this new Margaret had abandoned the rich Wensleydale dialect of her girlhood in favour of the careful, studied address of a prosperous merchant's wife.

My confusion must have shown on my face for she paused a moment and then continued in a gentler manner.

"Francis, knowing your mother was a whore made no difference to the love I bore for you, though you despised me for being my father's daughter."

"Only give me a chance to make amends, Margaret," I had begged, catching her small hands and folding them within my own. "I was a fool, I know it; indeed I knew it the moment I learned that you had wed Master Pennicott but then it was too late. Now you are free and we can begin again.

"I have changed, dearest Meg, I swear I have. I have learned that life without you has no savour. Forgive me and become my wife and you will see how much I have changed. For now I know that I can never be truly content without you by my side."

Though my words could not have been more heart-felt, I knew even as I spoke them that they were not enough to erase the deep hurt I had done to Margaret. Like laying a poultice upon a mortal wound, my speech was wholly inadequate and in any case came far too late. Still I clung to hope, convinced that somehow I would find a way to win back my beloved until she shattered that idea with an embittered accusation.

"Once there was a time when all I craved in the world was to be your wife. But it was a time of madness and the madness passed when you rejected me. Then I wed good Master Pennicott who did not despise me for being low born. With him I found a measure of contentment and in due course I even learned to think of you with composure. Now here I am, a respectable widow with wealth and property to my name and all at once here you come, eager to take me to wife as you never were when I had nothing. For shame, Francis! However bitterly I have thought of you in the past,

I never imagined you would stoop so low as to court me for my fortune!"

Too mortified by this false accusation to defend myself, I released her hands and stepped away from her, intent on ending the interview before she could sting me further. Even here, however, I fumbled matters for she had time to speak again before I reached the door.

"That was unworthy of me, I beg your forgiveness," she said with stiff dignity. "I see you believe you love me and I pity you for that. But I cannot allow you to leave with even the smallest suspicion that I will ever consent to wed you. Even supposing I could teach myself to love you again I would demand of you an impossible promise. I would make you swear to place my interests above all others, even above those of Richard of Gloucester, and that I know you never could do. Your loyalty to your friend is truly admirable, Francis, but it is also the reason I will never be your wife."

There was such awful finality in her voice that I knew it would be futile to dally a moment longer. Besides, though I had barely flinched when those barbed words about Dickon left her sweet lips, they found their mark all the same and left a lasting wound. In affairs of the heart, nothing wreaks more injury than the truth.

I had headed home to Middleham so black of countenance that for once Matthew had been moved to hold his tongue. This was regrettable, for as we rode in silence I realised that his customary prattling impertinence would have made a welcome distraction from the bleakness in my soul. As it was, I found I had little to occupy my thoughts save the knowledge that Margaret was assuredly lost to me forever. It struck me then that despite the ease with which I was able to secure comely bedfellows, where it mattered most my luck with women was the very worst. Deserted by my mother as a babe in arms, I had discovered my sister too late to save her from a terrible death. Now the woman I loved had rejected me in such unequivocal terms that only a simpleton would cling on to hope.

Well then, I decided, enough of pining for a woman's fickle heart. There were several saucy pieces amongst the Duchess's ladies who would, I reckoned, be glad to take a tumble with me and one day, God willing, one of them might even make me an amiable wife. In the meantime I would banish Margaret Pennicott from my thoughts and concentrate on serving to the best of my ability the one person I cared for who had never let me down.

Such had been my mood when I returned to Middleham from my ill-fated wooing and it had altered little by the time Tyrell and I set out for Beaulieu.

Chapter Two

Mindful of Gloucester's injunction to accomplish our mission with all speed, Tyrell and I pushed hard, taking full advantage of the fair weather and long hours of daylight. Drifts of late bluebells edged the dusty roads, scenting the clement air with their fragrance so that my spirits could not help but rise. Though heart-sore still, I found myself responding as any young man must to the pleasure of purposeful occupation undertaken in agreeable circumstances.

As we progressed southwards I had time to gauge the character of my companions and was glad to judge them admirable sorts. Tyrell's men, Knewstubb and Brankin, were amiable souls, ready enough to laugh at my jests and intimidating enough to deter any but the terminally reckless from chancing their luck with us. Tyrell I found harder to read initially since he took care to mask his private thoughts with a surfeit of noisy good cheer. Nevertheless, as I have often observed, little encourages fellowship between acquaintances so much as sharing the travails of aching limbs, questionable lodgings and suspect food, and thus it proved with Tyrell. By the third night, when we took shelter at Kenilworth, we were sufficiently at ease with one another to speak of personal matters as we sat together in the Abbey guesthouse.

It was I that began it. Proximity with the holy brothers had caused my thoughts to turn, as they often did of late, to my unknown mother who had bought her way into a religious house in Caen when I was but a lad. I had discovered this only recently, together with the startling intelligence that I had been born a twin. What gnawed at my innards was the knowledge that Fayette, my mother, had deserted me when I was a swaddled babe yet had chosen to keep my sister. Throughout my boyhood I had never been much troubled by the fact of my abandonment but since discovering I had a twin, I found myself filled with resentment and confusion. Why had I been discarded and not my sister? Some months ago, driven by emotions I did not fully comprehend, I had made a solemn vow to search for my errant mother. Now, in part to distract myself from the dispiriting pottage placed before me by the Abbey hosteller, I sketched this story for Tyrell in a few brief sentences and finished by telling him of my determination to find out if Fayette still lived.

"And if she does?" he had prompted, his grey eyes alight with interest.

"Hah! No doubt she'll soil her linen when the nuns hand her a letter from her long-forgotten bastard."

Though I spoke lightly, Tyrell heard my resentment and gave me a searching glance.

"You show the world a merry face, Cranley, but you do not fool me. I think you are burdened by your ignoble origins. Well, I like you the better for it. You must know that I, too, make my way with a stain across my name. Yours is illegitimacy, mine is treachery.

"I was a strapping lad of seventeen when the King took my father's head for treason, leaving me to live with the shame of it ever since. My sire was a good man in his way and full deserving of my love and respect save for one thing. Try as I may, I could not shift his stubborn allegiance to Lancaster. I saw, as he could not, that England had for too long been torn asunder by this pestilential wrangling over whose head wears the crown. I knew that what we needed was a strong leader; a virile King able to succeed in battles, aye, but also to succeed in peace. I judged that Edward was that man but Father did not. He could not reconcile himself to York and the failure cost him his life."

Knowing the story well, I murmured bland sympathies as Tyrell buried his face in his ale cup. I thought he was done with his confiding but I was mistaken.

"Did you ever see a woman crazed with grief?" he asked unexpectedly. "I have, and it is an ugly sight, I tell you freely."

He closed his eyes, as though shutting out a painful recollection, before resuming.

"Throughout my boyhood my mother appeared to me as beyond emotion. Always she was calm, unruffled and dignified. Passionless, I thought her, but affectionate enough to me, and is that not exactly how a son would have his mother? But then came the day we received word of Father's beheading. After she had dismissed the messenger she doubled over and rent her raiment in distress. Then I understood that she was not passionless after all. Like a beast in agony she was, my dignified lady mother, shrieking and clawing at her skin until her sleeves were ragged and red with her blood."

He shuddered as he recalled his mother's anguish.

"Jesu save me from witnessing the like again! To that end, and to keep my own head lodged firm upon my shoulders, my loyalty is pledged most sincerely to the

King. And though some may look askance at me for the sins of my father, I know my fealty was proven to Edward's satisfaction at Tewkesbury."

As he spoke of that charnel house my mind shifted and for a hellish moment I heard again the despairing cries of the fallen as their pleas for quarter went unanswered, and breathed again the corrupting stench of terror, hatred and death. Many had fought with valour for the King that day, I amongst them, serving under Dickon's command in the vanguard of the attack. Yet Tyrell's reckless ferocity had been a thing apart and it had earned him a battlefield knighthood.

"If truth be told," Tyrell opined, calling me back to the present, "I believe our noble Edward knows me for a man of his own sort. We share an appetite for wine and women, though of late I have had to curb my appetites lest our pious little Duchess accuse me of licentiousness!"

I bristled at these words, as I was wont to do at any criticism of the Duke or his sweet lady, but I swallowed my anger and after a moment's contemplation realised that Tyrell meant no harm. It was but his way of lifting the fog of gloom summoned by recollections of Tewkesbury.

"So my friend, I would lay a scheme before you," he had continued, bringing his head of abundant red hair close to mine so that he might speak softly. "Whilst my lady of Warwick packs her shifts and else-wise prepares for her journey, what say you and I make for London in pursuit of some merriment? I find I like your company, Francis, so I am willing to share with you a close kept secret. It happens that in London I have a small house, in Hosier Lane to be exact, and in this house I keep a raven-haired temptress, Joanna by name.

Ah, my fair Joanna! I tell you, Cranley, she is everything my scrawny child bride is not – warm, womanly and well-versed in the arts of love.

"My friend, though Joanna is a whore I am unashamed to confess that I hold her dear and it grieves me that since entering the service of our good Duke I have had scant opportunity to enjoy her charms. But now, well, Beaulieu is not so very far from London, is it? Come man, what say you to this scheme?"

He grinned with such unabashed delight at the prospect of lying once again with his leman that I could not keep from laughing.

"I see no objection," I answered, "so long as there is time enough for such a pleasure jaunt."

"Aye, there will be!" he replied at once. "I am certain of it. From Beaulieu we can reach London in less than three days and then, why even if all I manage is one paltry night with Joanna, by all the Saints I swear it will have been worth the effort! And do not imagine I will suffer you to lie cold and yearning while I bask in my sweetheart's embrace. Joanna will know of a likely wench to warm your bones, Cranley, you may be sure of that."

This notion gave me pause; I was loath to offend Tyrell yet would not chance a tumble with an unknown trollop in case she was diseased. My answer, therefore, was that while I would gladly accompany him to London, while he dallied with his wench I would use the time to locate a ship's captain willing to make enquiries after my mother.

Though we did not give voice to it, Tyrell and I both knew when we rode from Kenilworth the following dawn that we left there the mutual suspicions that had impeded the start of true comradeship. Also left behind at the Abbey were our spent horses which were to rest in the care of the lay brothers until our return while we completed the journey on fresh mounts hired from the town. Refreshed in spirit, we continued to ride hard and were in Winchester as dusk fell on the seventh day after our departure from Middleham. With our destination now little more than a morning's ride distant, we took lodgings at a comfortable inn and rewarded our diligence with hot food and tolerable wine.

A strange incident occurred at the inn's stables as we were making ready to leave early the next morning. I was concentrating on securing my pack to the saddle of my hired mount while Knewstubb and Brankin waited, mounted and ready to leave. Of Tyrell there was as yet no sign and since his tardiness was unusual, we passed the time by guessing the cause of his delay.

"Knowing the master I'll wager he found a willing doxy to share his bed. At this very moment he is bidding her a lingering farewell," Brankin opined with a lusty wink.

"Nay, not likely," Knewstubb disagreed. "The only female we saw last night was the inn-keeper's wife and she is not the master's type. He prefers them with a tooth or two in their heads! No, if he's bidding farewell to anything I reckon it's those jugs of wine he was busy emptying last night."

"Whatever delays him," I put in, "he will have to make haste if we hope to reach Beaulieu by noon."

As I spoke I became aware of another figure readying his mount across the stable from where I stood. Though he had been there all the while, I had scarcely observed him before but some sudden tension about his person when I spoke of Beaulieu snagged my notice. Before I could think any further he turned to address me and I saw that he was a nondescript, weary-looking fellow. Probably no more than a year or two older than I, he was swathed in a cloak so patched and grimy my servant would have scorned to wear it. From the dust and straw clinging to this disreputable garment I deduced that lack of funds had necessitated he slept above the horses instead of in one of the inn's guest chambers.

"Pardon my intrusion," he began, scuffing the chaff-strewn floor with his muddy boots. "I would not trouble you, only I gather that you ride for Beaulieu. Pray forgive me, it was not my intention to eavesdrop; in truth I had not heeded you at all until my ears caught mention of your destination. You see, I too have business at the Abbey. Might I beg leave to ride with you? I have been alone on the road a long while and would welcome some company, should you have no objection."

Though shabbily garbed he spoke with a gentlemanly manner and seemed harmless enough to me. I saw no reason to deny his request though out of courtesy I glanced at Brankin and Knewstubb to determine their opinion. When they signalled their assent I ambled towards the man and held out my hand.

"No objection at all," I said, "so long as you are willing to ride hard and fast. Francis Cranley is my name, and these good fellows here are Tom and John. We await the last member of our party, Sir James Tyrell, and then we must away without delay."

As I mentioned Tyrell the stranger's mouth spasmed and then fell open for a heartbeat, his tired face flushing with some sentiment I could not read.

"Tyrell is among your party?" he queried. "Sir James Tyrell, of Gipping in Suffolk? That I did not know. Excuse me, sir, I have made an error. I cannot ride with you. That is, I find I do not ... I was mistaken about Beaulieu. My business there can wait. Forgive me, I must take my leave at once."

Tyrell's lads and I watched in silent bemusement as the nervous oddity scrambled onto his scraggy rouncey and made a speedy exit from the stable. So unexpected was his behaviour that there was a pause before any of us spoke. At length I broke the silence.

"It would seem the gentleman is reluctant to meet with your master."

Knewstubb made no reply save to spit and scratch his sizeable buttocks but Brankin gave me a keen look.

"Should I go after him, Master Cranley?" he enquired, his eyes narrowing with pleasure at the prospect of some sport. "Send a few arrows past him to encourage him to halt?"

He stroked his bow lovingly and for a moment I was tempted. Tyrell was full of praise for this man's skill as a bowman; a demonstration would be diverting though it would inevitably delay our departure.

"No, leave the fool be," I decided.

That the man feared an encounter with Tyrell was clear but he seemed such a trifling creature I could not think him a threat to us. Should our paths cross again, well then I would make it my business to discover why he fled from Tyrell but until then I had more pressing matters at hand. Later I was to wish I had given Tom Brankin leave to pursue the jumpy fellow but at the time I saw no call to apprehend him. In any case, as the Earl of Warwick was wont to say when I was a boy, there's as much sense in teaching a dog to curtsey as in crying over a path not taken.

The stranger was gone from sight when Tyrell at last appeared, full of regret for his tardiness which he ascribed to a brief but violent malady of the bowel. As we picked our way carefully through the town which was already alive with noise and bustle despite the earliness of the hour, I told him of the curious encounter. However, when it came to describing the peculiar stranger my efforts were hindered by the dreary blandness of the fellow's features. Try as I might, the best I could offer was that his hair had been thin and sandy, his stature medium and his complexion wan and tired.

"And this is all?" Tyrell had snorted. "Come Francis, I can think of a hundred or more such men. Surely there is more you can give me?"

Easier said than done, I thought, but attempted to oblige my new friend nonetheless, if only to forestall further derision.

"He was down on his luck," I ventured, "and his person and countenance had a battle-hardened look, for all that he took off like a startled stoat when he heard your name."

"What do you say, Brankin?" Tyrell demanded of his henchman. "Was this fellow a Gipping man?"

"I'd say not," Brankin answered, "for he did not speak like one. And, begging your pardon, but it is true what Master Cranley says. There was nothing remarkable about the bugger's looks, save perhaps that his nose is a mite bigger than most."

By now we had negotiated our way through the Southgate and were onto the open highway where we could at last put spur to flank. Riding at speed rendered further conversation impossible and when we pulled up our horses outside the great gatehouse of Beaulieu Abbey several hours later, the incident had vanished from our thoughts.

I had never before had cause to visit Beaulieu and knew little of it save that it shared with Westminster and Winchester the right to provide long-term sanctuary to serious miscreants, even those accused of treason. Those claiming this privileged sanctuary, which had been granted by charter in ancient times, were free to live untroubled by the law on any land belonging to the Abbey. Given that in Beaulieu's case this included more than eight thousand acres of land between the Solent and the New Forest, and additional property as far distant as Berkshire and Cornwall, this offered plenty of scope for ne'er-do-wells and traitors to evade justice. Or so it would have done, except that in order to be granted leave to stay beyond forty days, the sanctuary seekers had to persuade the abbot of their good character or else convince him of their intention to reform. For common felons this was nigh on as difficult as baking bread from sand but for the nobility it was a different story. For such a distinguished individual as the Countess of Warwick, sanctuary would have been granted the moment she claimed it.

Our arrival was greeted by the porter with tepid courtesy but, having announced ourselves as emissaries of the Duke of Gloucester, we were escorted with a notable increase in civility to a well-appointed audience room in the abbot's fine house set within its own small garden a short distance from the chapter house. There a servant bade us wait, telling us that his master was currently at dinner but would attend us the moment he had finished. Hearing this, Knewstubb and Brankin exchanged such hungry glances that Tyrell gave them leave to seek nourishment at the guesthouse. I envied them somewhat since my belly, too, felt empty and I feared it would be some while before I ate. However, I also knew that as official messengers from Richard of Gloucester, Tyrell and I would eat at the abbot's own table which would offer daintier fare than the guest-house had to offer.

There was little time to think much else for no sooner had he left us than the servant returned, in company with a man we identified at once as the abbot. In general I held a low opinion of monks and clerics for most of those I knew were either oily, self-serving toadies or joyless zealots. John Piers, the abbot of Beaulieu, proved to be a rare exception. A tall, substantial man aged some-where between forty and fifty years, he was possessed of a pleasing, open countenance and a creased mouth that hinted at a warmth uncommon in a Cistercian. I liked him from the very first, for without fuss he summoned hot water and cloths so that Tyrell and I might rinse the road from our hands and faces, and then he led us to his private dining room where he pressed us to share his meal of fish, coddled eggs and soft white bread.

"Come, eat your fill," he enjoined us, "for as you see the fare is plentiful. I ordered enough for four because I was expecting to be joined by our good Prior. He enjoys a hearty dinner, though it would mortify him to hear me say it. Alas, I just had word from our infirmary that the Lord has seen fit to visit the poor fellow with an ague and thus for once he has no appetite. It is a shame for him, Prior Baldwin does so relish coddled eggs, but at least his misfortune means my table can do justice to hungry visitors."

As we ate, Tyrell explained our mission and our liberal host beamed his approval.

"It is well, it is very well!" he exclaimed, refilling our wine cups himself and earning a reproving look from his servant in consequence.

"That poor lady has suffered much and pines greatly for her daughters. I rejoice that God has moved the King at last to show her kindness."

I thought, but refrained from saying, that credit for the King's change of heart belonged to my lord of Gloucester rather than the Almighty. Tyrell felt the same but was less circumspect.

"Aye, well, that's your view, my lord Abbot," he said, "but mine is that the Countess would be left here to rot for eternity, were it not for my master pleading on her behalf."

As my blunt friend spoke I took care to scrutinise the abbot's face, expecting it to register umbrage or annoyance. Instead, his eyes crinkled and he smiled broadly before taking a deep draught of wine.

"And who do you think prompted your master to plead for her?" he asked mildly. "His wife, you will say," he continued swiftly as he saw Tyrell poised to reply, "and of course you are correct. But why did he heed her?"

"Because he loves her," I offered, entering the fray for the first time.

"Indeed, Master Cranley, indeed! Yet who but God caused the great love between your master and his lady? That is why I say God moved the King to show clemency to the Countess, for His hand is to be seen in all things."

At this I met Tyrell's eyes and with the merest shake of my head discouraged him from butting in. It would be futile to argue the point further for we could win no ground on such a matter and in any case I was keen to put a question to the abbot.

"Where is the Countess?" I enquired. "I had thought she would surely dine with you."

"Ah," he replied, "and so she does from time to time. Of course, when she first came to Beaulieu and she was lodged here in my house, Prior Baldwin and I had the pleasure of her company every mealtime. At the time she was much distressed, being newly widowed and in bad odour with the King. I did what I could to comfort her though I fear it was little enough."

He sighed, as though genuinely regretting the inadequacy of his efforts to cheer his noble guest.

"Once it became clear that her sojourn with us was to be prolonged, we moved her and her waiting woman to our grange at St. Leonards, a little over three miles distant. It seemed more fitting that she should have a small household of her own. There she is able to live simply and quietly, with the conversi seeing to all her needs."

This was unexpected; I had thought to find the Countess sharing the abbot's comfortable lodging instead of being despatched to some rustic outpost of the Abbey. Yet I could see the arrangement made good sense from the abbot's point of view. In her youth Anne of Warwick had been a handsome woman and though she was now well into middle age, her figure had still been voluptuous enough to entice a man's lust the last time I had seen her. John Piers would have been a fool to invite such a woman to linger amongst his flock and, as I could see, he was very far from that.

Our hunger now assuaged, Tyrell and I were eager to present ourselves to the Countess without further delay and so, having thanked the abbot for his hospitality, we reclaimed our horses and rode south towards St. Leonards. During the short ride our guide, a lay brother named Martin, called our attention with proprietary pride to the fields rich with ripening oats and wheat. As we approached the grange the first sight we beheld was a vast barn into which these same crops would be conveyed come harvest-time. I marvelled that a building of such immensity should be needed, especially as I knew St. Leonards was but one of several granges supplying the Abbey. To the left of this great barn stood a house, modestly-sized but large enough, as Brother Martin told us coyly, to be divided so that the Countess might live in decency in one part and the lay brothers in the other.

As I followed Tyrell through the low door into the house, nothing could have prepared me for what I was about to see. The sound of horses' hooves had summoned Warwick's widow from her private chamber; as I learned later, so monotonous had her life become that she mined for interest even the smallest departure from the daily routine of the grange. She stood before us as we entered the hall, shabbily gowned yet standing proud as an empress, a piece of embroidery gripped tight in one hand. Behind her, partially enveloped in shadows yet visible all the same to my disbelieving eyes, stood Margaret.

Chapter Three

I have it on Tyrell's authority that I gasped like a startled virgin. Be that as it may, I saw at once that I had been in error. The figure standing behind the Countess was not Margaret, how could it have been? In truth, the young woman bore no more than a slender resemblance to Mistress Pennicott. They were of an age, it was true, and shared a similar height and shape but where Margaret's claim to beauty lay in a comfortable melding of honeyed warmth and earthy sensuality, the features of her unwitting impostor were a stark contradiction of fire and frost. Her abundant hair, worn loose since company had not been expected, gleamed furnace bright and her cheeks were hectic but beneath their rosy glow her skin was pale and smooth and her eyes were the blue of an endless frozen sky. My treacherous body reacted to her charms even as my mind determined to despise her for not, after all, being Margaret. Such is the folly of the human heart.

Happily for my reputation as a man of sense, Tyrell alone had observed my confusion and though he was unaware of its cause he came to my aid by presenting himself to the Countess with an unusual degree of pomposity. By the time he had concluded his longwinded introduction I had recaptured my composure. This was just as well since, having greeted Tyrell with amused dignity, Anne of Warwick turned to me, a smile of real pleasure briefly enlivening her careworn features.

"Francis!" she exclaimed. "It is Francis Cranley! I thought as much even though it has been some years since last we met. Well, this is a welcome surprise. It is so very good to see you."

The warmth of her greeting took me aback; in the past her manner toward me had been civil yet distant as befitted a great lady dealing with a person of no consequence. I was further surprised when she took my hand and squeezed it gently, in the manner of one dear friend to another, before returning her attention to Tyrell.

"Well Sir James, you had better present me with these important letters you carry, and whilst I attend to them Eleanor here will fetch you some refreshment."

As her name was mentioned the girl stepped into the light and dipped an uncertain curtsey in our direction. Tyrell responded with a grin and an appreciative stare which she withstood without flinching, though I saw a slender hand tremble as she smoothed a crease from the front of her threadbare gown.

"And Eleanor is....?" Tyrell enquired with a leering smile, his curiosity besting his manners.

"Forgive me, Sir James. She is Mistress Eleanor Vernon, of Butterton in Derbyshire. Her father and brother were loyal adherents of my husband. Foolish but loyal. They perished with him at Barnet and since then Eleanor has stayed with me, for where else is the poor child to go? Strange and sad, is it not, that her one true friend is a person with so little to offer? Yet so it is, for the King has seized her father's estate, as is his right, and thus she is rendered homeless and penniless. She has many Vernon cousins in Derbyshire, it is true, but none that are willing to open their home to a traitor's orphan with no fortune of her own."

I pitied the girl then, and willed Tyrell to stop tormenting her with his frank appraisal even though I understood full well why he stared. Eleanor Vernon was as pleasing to look upon as she was unexpected. We had known that a waiting woman attended the Countess in sanctuary but for no good reason we had assumed she would be the same age as her mistress, if not older. In no way had we been prepared for this fresh-faced beauty.

In his instructions to us before we set out, Dickon had decreed that we should bring the waiting woman home with us, so that she might see to the comfort of her mistress during the arduous journey. Once at Middleham, however, she would be at liberty to choose her future; if she so desired she could remain with the Countess but, if she preferred to return to her kin, she would be provided with a purse of money and an escort to see her home in safety. Whether she stayed or left had been a matter of supreme indifference to me when I had envisioned the waiting woman as a matron of mature years. All was different now I had beheld the lovely Mistress Vernon. From what the Countess had said about the girl's melancholy circumstances it was obvious that she would have to make her home at Middleham and I confess that the thought gladdened me.

As the Countess withdrew to a corner of the room to read her letters, Eleanor poured two cups of sweet wine and invited Tyrell and me to sit with her at the simple oak table.

"The honey cakes are all gone or I would offer you some," she said, speaking for the first time since our arrival. I found myself readily charmed by the clear, low-pitched timbre of her voice.

"But if you are hungry I can fetch fresh bread and perhaps some fowl?"

"Thank you, no. We dined heartily with Father John," Tyrell answered, eyeing the girl in a way that made it plain she was the only tasty morsel on his mind. In response her bright cheeks flushed even more becomingly than before. Seeing she was ill at ease, and understandably so since there had been none but chaste monks for her to converse with in recent times, I scoured my wits for a way to ease her discomfort.

"You and your lady have been well cared for here?" I ventured. "You have been given all that you need?"

"Thank you, yes! The abbot has been so generous, he has seen that we are provided with every comfort. We could not have asked for more."

There was sincerity in her words yet as she spoke her eyes travelled to her gown and I understood that grateful as she was, she regretted, as any gently bred maiden would, the shabbiness of her attire. Though simple, the gown she wore had once been a pretty garment made of fine soft wool in a blue several shades darker than its wearer's eyes. Now, though, much of the original colour had faded to a dull, watery grey while the gown's skirt was patched here and there with pieces of Cistercian white. The Countess's more elaborate gown, I had noticed, was in a similar sorry condition.

"Mistress Vernon, it is too much to expect the holy brothers to know about finery," I teased her. "After all, any man electing to spend his entire life dressed in a scratchy white robe is unlikely to notice a gown past its best. Why, I fancy you would have to stand before the abbot in your shift before he would see aught amiss."

As I had hoped, far from being offended by my saucy jest, the girl laughed and replied to me in a similar light-hearted vein.

"Alas that my vanity is so apparent!" she joked. "My lady would chide me for it if she heard, and rightly so for we have been shown naught but kindness here. Only, I am so heartily sick of this shameful gown that I have vowed to feed it to the flames the very instant another comes my way!"

I liked her spirit and told her as much. And then, because she was a beauty and I pitied her, I paid her an extravagant compliment that was so near to the truth as made no difference.

"Living at Middleham with my lord of Gloucester, every day I am privileged to see his Duchess and her ladies decked out in the costliest fabrics. Very fine they look, without a doubt, yet none delight my eyes so much as you in your tired blue gown."

Thus far in my conversation with the girl Tyrell had been content to sit back and attend to his wine cup but as my careless flattery reached his ears he widened his eyes and, under cover of the table, delivered a sharp kick to my shin. I winced and glanced at Eleanor to see if she had noticed but if she had she gave no sign of it. Instead, I saw that her shining blue eyes were looking upon me with something I could have interpreted as love, had I believed in the absurd notion of falling in love on such brief acquaintance. Cursing myself inwardly for failing to consider that a maiden starved so long of male attention was liable to lose her heart to any scoundrel with an agreeable face and easy manners, I resolved to be more guarded with my pleasantries.

Correctly interpreting my silence as a request for help, Tyrell chimed in with a good-natured compliment of his own but before Eleanor was able to respond the Countess rose from her stool and turned towards us.

"God be praised!" she proclaimed with fervour. "It is over! At last it is over."

Eleanor leapt to her feet and sped to her mistress's side with a deal more urgency than grace.

"Truly?" she asked, in that one word revealing to me how fathomless was her longing to escape the confines of sanctuary.

"Truly, Eleanor, truly. Gloucester writes that the King has given leave for me to live with him and my dear Anne at Middleham. And you are to come, too, my child. Be assured, there is a home for you, also."

"Oh, my lady, that is the best of news," Eleanor cried.

The two women stared at one another for a moment and then embraced as Tyrell and I looked tactfully away. Well, there was tact on my part but Tyrell, I suspected, turned from a reluctance to witness the women's tears. All the same, he gave them time to rejoice, waiting with patience until they had separated before clearing his throat and enquiring when they would be ready to leave.

"On the morrow, if it should be possible!" the jubilant Countess exclaimed. "Kind as the monks have been, I am not anxious to impose upon them one day longer than is necessary."

"My lady," Tyrell interrupted, alarm for his London jaunt writ large on his usually cheerful features, "I fear...."

Giddy with delight, the Countess stopped his words with a playful hand to his mouth. Her behaviour astounded me; in the many years I had known her I had never seen her anything other than composed and stately.

"Fret not, Sir James, I know that we cannot hope to depart on the morrow, not least because, having travelled far and fast, I daresay you and Francis need time to rest before setting out again. Besides, Eleanor and I have arrangements to make."

Like a gleeful girl she jangled the bag of angels that Dickon had sent for her use, catching Eleanor's eye as she did so.

"Gold, Eleanor," she laughed, "enough of it to buy handsome new cloaks for both of us! Alas, I am too impatient to wait while new gowns are made but we can choose the cloth and then, when we reach Middleham, ah then, Eleanor, we will set the tailors working 'til their arms ache! But for now, think how good it will be to have a fine new cloak, of velvet, perhaps, or broadcloth if you prefer! And there will be enough left over for all those other things we have lacked so long."

Here she smiled coyly, leading me to guess that the ladies' more intimate garments were in a more parlous condition even than their gowns.

"Oh, those wretched Southampton merchants who denied me credit! How fast they will rush to please me once they see I have angels to spend.

"But," she continued, speaking more soberly now as she turned her attention back to Tyrell and me, "we shall not dally long. A day or two should suffice, three at most."

The expression on Mistress Vernon's face left me little doubt that she too relished the prospect of new finery. All the same I sensed that something troubled her. She made to speak, then stopped and frowned as if struggling with some weighty concern. Finally, squaring her pretty shoulders, she addressed her mistress with breathless purpose.

"My lady, forgive me for daring to oppose you but you really must not travel so soon. It was only yesterday you rose from your sickbed! Nay, do not frown, I beg you! You must know that I am as anxious as you to be gone from this place but I would be failing in my duty if I did not mention your recent poor health to Sir James and Master Cranley. You were so ill, my lady, and remain frail even now. I truly believe it will be another seven days at least before you are well enough to travel."

So that explains it, I thought. I had attributed the Countess's altered looks to the shocking reversal of fortune she had experienced since I last saw her but now I understood there was more to it than that.

"For a sensible girl you fuss too much!" the older woman snapped, a touch of the Proud Nan I remembered of old creeping into her manner. Eleanor blenched a little but remained obdurate and Tyrell took advantage of their temporary discord.

"Well then, it is settled. If the abbot has no objection, Cranley and I will bide with him a day or so until our horses are rested. Then we will make for London where certain affairs require our attention, though I do not expect them to delay us overlong. So, my lady, rest while we are gone and eat well to build up your strength. It is a long, hard ride back to Middleham and I want you fresh and ready to depart soon after Prime on the third day of June."

The Countess grimaced at Tyrell's brusque instructions but acquiesced meekly enough, leading me to suspect that she was secretly glad to have these extra days in which to replenish her strength. Soon afterwards we bid the ladies farewell and rode back to the abbot's house for a night of well-earned comfort on his plump feather beds.

Returning to St Leonards the next morning, Tyrell and I invited the Countess and Mistress Vernon to ride with us within the abbey's Great Close on docile mounts cadged from Brother Martin. We hoped the pleasure jaunt would relieve the tedium of their existence and also that the gentle exercise would help prepare the Countess for the difficult journey ahead. She chose to ride alongside Tyrell, peppering him with questions about Edward's kingship and the state of the realm since Barnet, to which he replied with polite but evasive answers. Thus it fell to me to accompany Mistress Vernon who, I could not fail to notice, contrived to look desirable even with her magnificent hair tucked neatly inside a plain hood. Talking light-hearted nonsense as we rode, it was not long before I was struck by a significant change in her manner which I attributed to her imminent departure from Beaulieu. The awkward, flushing girl from yesterday had been replaced by a witty, confident young woman who swatted away my compliments with easy laughter and poked gentle fun at me.

"Do you never weary of flattery?" she asked at one point, her eyes lively with amusement. "Have you no other words to speak? Come, you must have, for I cannot believe you found favour with the Duke of Gloucester by complimenting him on his complexion!"

"And why not?" I riposted with feigned indignation. "My lord, I will have you know, has a very fine complexion, surpassed only by the nobility of his brow, the clarity of his eyes and the thick lustre of his hair."

I spoke with solemnity but Eleanor read my face and knew I jested.

"Ah, I see," she remarked, and fell silent for a moment. "And yet I also see that beneath your buffoonery you have great affection for him."

"As do all who truly know him," I replied, speaking seriously now. "He is the best of men and a friend like no other. My life I owe to his father, and all else I owe to him."

Somehow, I then found myself telling this surprising chit how I had been rescued by the Duke of York after my mother had abandoned me, and raised alongside his youngest children.

"So in boyhood I was another brother to Dickon – my lord of Gloucester, I should say – and though we are now men he still honours me with his friendship and trust. I know I am much blessed and never forget it."

What I told Eleanor was no secret but she seemed moved that I had shared something of myself with her and responded by speaking of the Derbyshire home she had lost.

"Like you," she began, "I never knew my mother for she died soon after I was born. I wish she could have lived, for her own sake and that of my father who by his own account adored her, yet I must speak the truth and say I never felt the loss of her. You see, I had the love of the fondest, most attentive father I could wish for and also of my brother, William, who was to me what your lord of Gloucester is to you. I knew such happiness then," she sighed, "and dreaded the day that I would have to marry and leave my dear home."

"Doubtless you were thronged with ardent swains," I ventured, in an attempt to lift the veil of sadness that had settled upon her as she spoke of her dead kin.

"Entirely thronged!" she agreed with a bright smile that indicated her readiness to put melancholy aside.

"And was there a favourite amongst this horde?" I continued. "One whose strength, valour and goodness would, in time, have reconciled you to leaving Butterton in order to become his wife?"

"Oh, there were many such," she teased, "so many that I found it quite impossible to choose between them. William, I know, was most desirous that I should wed his friend Ralph Abney, and the close proximity of his manor to ours gave the notion some merit. Alas, that was its only merit! Poor Ralph, I did like him but he was too dull and plodding to win my heart."

"Where is this dullard Abney now?" I enquired, wondering why this family friend had not come forward to aid Eleanor following the death of her male protectors, as any man of honour should have done. She did not answer at once and I feared I had been insensitive. Perhaps he, too, had perished at Barnet. I was about to apologise for my clumsiness when she spoke again.

"Ralph is in France. At least, I think that is where he is. Certainly it is where he told me he intended to go when last I saw him. He was one of the men assigned by my lord of Warwick to protect my lady, you see, and thus was spared the slaughter at Barnet. Afterwards, when we knew that all was lost, we urged Ralph to flee to safety. At first he was reluctant to go but we insisted. My lady believed that in time the King might pardon him for his part in the rebellion and then he would be able to return. I do not think he has done so yet."

I examined her face for any trace of regret that her suitor remained absent and was pleased to find none.

"You were wise to encourage his flight," I told her, "yet I'll wager he could return now with impunity. Edward has never been a vindictive king."

The thoughtless words were out before I could stop them. It was true that the King was often lenient, many times choosing to take a heavy fine in lieu of a traitor's head. But until very recently he had shown no such leniency towards Anne of Warwick and I expected her devoted attendant to remind me of it. Instead, she chuckled at my foolishness.

"My lady will be glad to know it," she remarked, lightly deflecting any unpleasantness.

By tacit agreement our speech moved forward to safer subjects and soon after we returned to St Leonards. That night as I reflected on the events of the day I realised I had found great pleasure in Mistress Vernon's company and was glad Tyrell had ordained we would ride again with the ladies on the morrow.

Since this was to be our last day before leaving for London the abbot had invited the Countess and Eleanor to dine with us after our ride. With two spirited, well-born women at the table, and the portly Prior Baldwin who had now recovered from his recent indisposition, the meal proved a lively affair. John Piers' finest Rhenish played its part in loosening tongues and inhibitions, though I took little of it as is my custom, save in times of distress. Even so I found myself flirting with a responsive Eleanor under the benign gaze of the Countess.

When all was done, I volunteered to find Brother Martin and instruct him to ready the horses. As I rose from the table, I was much surprised when the Countess announced that she would accompany me since great ladies seldom trouble themselves with errands. As soon as we were outside, her motive became clear.

"Francis, you must forgive me for speaking so directly on a matter of such sensitivity," she began, "but since you are leaving on the morrow I would settle this with you now. I have observed you with Eleanor and see that you like her. This is good, for I believe her to be half in love with you already."

I had no wish to hear this and made to interject but she silenced me with an imperious gesture I remembered of old.

"Let me finish," she commanded. "You shall have your say soon enough. Listen well, Francis. Eleanor is dear to me, near as dear if she were my own daughter, for during these past lonely years we have been everything to one another. So you can believe me when I say I want nothing but happiness for her."

She took a breath here but I knew better than to interrupt Anne of Warwick a second time.

"Eleanor deserves a good marriage to a decent man, with a litter of children to replace the family she lost at Barnet. And God knows, with her lovely looks and disposition she should have her pick of suitors. Instead, because of her father's obstinate loyalty to my late husband, she must find a husband where she can. No ambitious man will take her, tainted as she is by treason, and no poor man either for she has no other dowry but her beauty."

"My lady, why speak of this to me?" I asked although I already knew the answer.

"Because you could and should marry her, Francis. No, don't roll your eyes at me, you impudent puppy. Think of it. You have a good position at Middleham, and for reasons understood by none but him, my daughter's husband loves you like a brother. Yet as a bastard you cannot expect to rise high, and so cannot be harmed by the circumstances of Eleanor's family. Your illegitimacy also means you will never marry a gently bred girl with money. Speaking frankly, Francis, your marriage prospects are unhappy, since any girls who fancy you a catch are more suited to preparing my daughter's dinner than to sharing it."

I was angry now, for without knowing it the Countess had touched a tender spot. These were the very thoughts that had caused me to lose Margaret and I was in no mood to remember it. I cursed roundly, something I rarely did in the presence of a lady, but the filthy imprecation made no impact on the Countess. No doubt she had heard worse from the lips of her soldier husband.

"Use your wits, Francis! You and Eleanor are perfect for one another. And have no doubt, she is smitten with you. It was wrong of you to steal her heart if you have no use for it."

It was this last that stopped my anger and made me consider what she said. I knew that I had paid attention to this vulnerable girl for no better reason than that her unguarded admiration soothed my wounded pride. And I realised that what had started as an exercise in vanity had become something more serious. I could not deny that I enjoyed Eleanor's company, nor that I found her desirable. I did not love her yet, it was far too soon for that, and perhaps I never would. I believed my capacity in that regard had been stunted by my painful experience with Margaret. Yet love was rarely a consideration in marriage, so it might prove to be enough that I liked and desired Eleanor.

The Countess saw that I faltered and with the skill of a consummate negotiator drew back from her argument instead of pressing the issue.

"Well, consider what I have said, and give me your thoughts on the morrow before you leave. I do not ask you to quit Beaulieu a betrothed man but, if you decide the idea has merit, I will tell Eleanor that a match with you would have my blessing. She mentions your name so often, her strong attachment to you is plain for me to see. Why, I do believe that though she has known you but three days, she would follow you to the mouth of hell and count herself lucky."

That night sleep eluded me as I pondered this unexpected turn of events. With Tyrell's soft snores providing an accompaniment, I imagined a life at Middleham with Eleanor as my wife. Her lack of dowry meant nothing to me; though I had little wealth of my own, Dickon had told me often enough that he would be generous when I found a bride. He would approve of her, I knew, both on her own account and because she was loved by his wife's mother. The more I thought of it, the more I recognised the advantage to me in Anne of Warwick's suggestion. What a close knit group we would be, the King's brother, his wife, her mother and their two dearest companions. With this happy thought in mind I finally slipped into a brief but restful slumber.

Rising shortly before Lauds, Tyrell and I gave the abbot respectful thanks for his hospitality, collected Knewstubb and Brankin from the guesthouse and then rode out to St Leonards. Despite the earliness of the hour the ladies were dressed and waiting for us, Eleanor looking so eager and fresh that I found myself wanting to kiss her mouth until it bruised. Haste was needful with many miles to travel that day but Tyrell was reluctant to leave without issuing a caution to the Countess to remain within the confines of the Great Close during our absence.

"Even with the King's permission to leave, you are not safe without our protection," he reminded her. "Clarence will not abuse the rights of sanctuary but I doubt not that he has churls ready to pounce should you venture beyond Abbey land."

His words invoked the Countess's anger.

"But Eleanor and I are to go with Brother Christopher when he takes the wool to Southampton," she argued. "It is all arranged. While he attends to his business we will buy what we require for the journey. I will be quite safe, I do assure you, for Brother Christopher has promised to bring two sturdy lay brothers to guard me."

Though I could tell how desperately she wanted this spree, I had to concur with Tyrell's view that it was too dangerous. With his mother-in-law dead nothing would prevent Clarence from making a strong claim for her vast wealth, wealth she had been unable to touch since entering sanctuary. My friend Dickon did not believe his troublesome brother capable of murder but I did.

Still, the Countess was a noblewoman notorious for knowing her own mind. Forbidding her to go would get us nowhere whereas an appeal to her good nature just might. At any rate I deemed it worth the attempt.

"My lady, I beg you to consider this. If you go and any ill befalls you, Sir James and I will be fortunate to keep our heads."

She scoffed loudly, her face stormy with displeasure, but I could tell that she had seen the justice of my argument.

"You are a devious man, Francis Cranley, and I would have you know I see your trickery. Still, I concede the point, though I am grieved that you would deny me this small pleasure. Well, so be it. Eleanor shall go to Southampton without me, unless you can dredge up some petty objection to that."

"I can think of no objection at all," I replied easily, turning a bland face to her sarcasm. "Clarence has no cause to harm Mistress Vernon and since she has not been arraigned for treason she is at liberty to come and go as she pleases."

With the matter concluded to our satisfaction, we remounted our horses and said a brief farewell. Tyrell's impatience to be away left me no time for the private adieu I would have liked to have had with Eleanor. Instead, in full sight of all I placed one hand on my heart and, raising the other to my lips, blew a courtly kiss in her direction. Her response was to widen her eyes in mock alarm and then give me an impish smile before sinking into an elaborate curtsey. While Eleanor's eyes were downcast I glanced at the Countess, aware that she was awaiting my answer. Without pausing to consider the wisdom of binding myself to a girl I had only just met, I gave her a fleeting nod signifying my agreement to her scheme. I had arrived at Beaulieu broken-hearted and determined never to trust another woman; I left, not betrothed exactly, but ready to be so in due course.

Of the time Tyrell and I spent in London little needs to be said save that he enjoyed a merry carnal interlude with his mistress while I succeeded in finding a captain who was willing, for a price, to enquire after my mother. It was no easy thing for me to entrust a stranger with this mission but the fellow was vouched for by an acquaintance of Tyrell and that had to suffice. I asked him to seek out anyone with knowledge of a Frenchwoman who had once gone by the name of Fayette St. Honorine-du-Flers and had entered a Normandy convent approximately thirteen years ago. My expectations of success were small but, having vowed to make the enquiry, I felt obliged to try.

We slept two nights at Tyrell's house in Hosier Lane and then quit London. With hard riding we made it back to the Abbey late in the evening of the second day of June, intent on setting out for Middleham the following morn. I was more at ease with the world than I had been for months and knew that a large part of my increase in spirits stemmed from the prospect of setting eyes again on the girl I had decided to marry. This made it all the more shocking to learn on our arrival that Eleanor Vernon had vanished without trace.

Chapter Four

"Eleanor is gone! Vanished! Jesu alone knows what has become of her!"

It was the Countess herself who gave us these incomprehensible tidings. Since first light she had been watching for us at the gatehouse and now we had come, the strain of her vigil proved too much and she crumpled into my arms. Knowing Anne of Warwick as a noble-woman of strong character and no little courage, finding her in such an agitated state alarmed me greatly, as did the news that my prospective bride was missing.

With my own wits scattered by this shocking news it was as well that Tyrell maintained a clear head.

"Come, my lady," he said soothingly, "you shall tell us all but first, with your leave, I would like to make you more comfortable."

Responding to the kindness in his voice, she disentangled herself from me and suffered us to cajole her towards a place of greater privacy. Once we had her settled by the fire in the abbot's chamber I poured her a cup of restorative wine and waited in anxious silence while she fought for composure. Still thinking ahead of me, Tyrell summoned a hovering servant and bade him fetch John Piers the moment Vespers was done.

When at last the Countess was able to speak, her first utterance did nothing to clarify our understanding of the events that had unfolded during our short absence.

"Find her, Francis, you must find her, for Father John will not countenance a continuation of the search. He says she has gone of her own volition and thus there are no grounds for him to interfere, yet that is madness!"

I opened my mouth to speak but Tyrell quelled me with a look. In the usual way of things it would have galled me to yield to his direction but in this instance I knew he was right. The tale would be told more swiftly with him leading the questions for, having known him but a few days, the Countess would be moved by pride to control her emotions as she answered. With me, however, with whom she was more familiar, there was a greater chance that her tale would be delayed by tears.

"Now my lady, if you feel ready, tell us what has befallen Mistress Vernon," Tyrell coaxed.

She looked to me, saw my quick smile and approving nod, and began.

"Three days since, Eleanor travelled to Southampton in company with Brother Christopher and two of the conversi, their names I do not recollect. They made straight for the Abbey's wool house in Bugle Street where Brother Christopher had business. There Eleanor left them, having fixed a time to rejoin them once she had completed her errands. When she did not appear at the appointed hour the Brothers waited a while. Growing concerned for her welfare, they began to ask for her about the town but all to no avail. Some townspeople they spoke with recalled having seen her earlier in the day and a serving girl at the house of Nicholas Bonvylle, the town's most prosperous merchant, said she had attended to Eleanor when she called to make purchases. But none admitted seeing her after she left the merchant's house!"

"What did the monks do when Mistress Vernon could not be found?" Tyrell enquired in a gentle voice quite unlike his usual blunt manner of speaking.

"They returned to Beaulieu forthwith and acquainted the abbot of her disappearance. I do not blame *them*," she avowed, her tone making it plain there were some to whom she did apportion blame, "for what else were they to do? Summon help from the Castle? I think not. I was a soldier's wife long enough to know there is no commander in Christendom that would order his men out to search for a missing girl at the behest of an anxious monk."

I knew she spoke truly. Had he turned to the Castle for help in locating Eleanor without the abbot's written authority, portly Brother Christopher would have been laughed from the keep with a myriad ribald insults ringing in his ears. Perhaps it was as well, for I did not like to think what might have been the outcome had pretty Eleanor been discovered by a detachment of rowdy soldiers bent on sport.

From Tyrell's expression I knew he thought the same though he made no comment, choosing instead to put to the Countess a question that had been troubling me for some minutes.

"My lady, why does the abbot believe Mistress Vernon has left of her own accord?"

"Because he is wrongly convinced that she has run off with some boy from Netley, a novice monk who has also gone missing."

Netley, I had learned since first coming to Beaulieu, was one of the wealthy Abbey's daughter houses, situated near to the eastern shore of Southampton Water and no more than three miles from Southampton itself.

"Yet the notion that Eleanor has eloped with this novice is preposterous!" the Countess continued, her voice now ringing with angry indignation. "She has never so much as met the wretched boy, of that I am certain, and in any case we all know that her heart belongs to another."

Neither Tyrell nor I failed to catch the meaningful glance in my direction.

"And she would never abandon me without a word," she finished, her voice breaking as she looked up at me, her tired eyes imploring me to believe in the irreproachable virtue of her young friend. She need not have tried so hard; I knew from the first that Eleanor had not absconded with some dubious youth. Call it instinct, vanity or what you will, I was in no doubt that Eleanor Vernon had not of her own volition abandoned both her beloved mistress and the prospect of a union with me. But why did the abbot believe otherwise? Tyrell, I sensed, was anxious to continue with his questions and I was no less eager to have them answered but I hesitated all the same, understanding the Countess's need to hear some words of reassurance from me.

"It is the sheerest folly to think this of Eleanor!" I duly declared. "Only a knave or lack-wit would credit it!"

My hot words won a wan smile from the Countess and a rumble of polite agreement from Tyrell.

"Nevertheless, improbable as the notion seems, the abbot must have grounds for believing it," he ventured.

"So what are they, beyond the fact that the lad has absconded?"

"Naught but evil tittle-tattle and conjecture!" the Countess declared, her indignant tone signifying her wish to say no more.

"Even so….," Tyrell prompted, earning for his pains a look of haughty disdain.

"As you will. This calumny is founded on no firmer ground than the fact that Eleanor visited Netley the day of her vanishing. As the travelling party was readying to leave Beaulieu two days ago, the Infirmarian hailed Brother Christopher with a request to call in at Netley with some physicks and potions. He agreed readily as they would be passing close by en route to Southampton."

This surprised me. Although my knowledge of the area was slight I had been given to understand that Netley lay some short distance beyond Southampton.

The Countess read my enquiry and answered it.

"Rather than take the circuitous land route they went by boat across Southampton Water," she explained. "Thus they were almost at Netley when they reached the other side. When they arrived Brother Christopher took the basket of medicines to the infirmary while Eleanor remained on the cart with the conversi the whole while. He was gone no longer than it took him to unpack the supplies and return, yet this was long enough, apparently, for some scandalmonger to note that one of the novices was eyeing Eleanor with lascivious intent."

"This novice, did he speak to her? Or she to him?" Tyrell asked with interest.

"Neither said a word to the other, the conversi will vouch for that. They say Eleanor spent the entire time badgering them with questions about the best merchants in Southampton. They recalled it most specifically for they are simple men with no knowledge of the city beyond the wool house and thus were at a loss how to answer her."

This made me smile despite my anxiety for Eleanor, for I could picture her bewildering the rustic lay brothers with her eager questions, oblivious to their confusion in her quest for new finery. Tyrell, though, was less easily diverted and he pressed on with the matter in hand.

"The scandalmonger you speak of, did he observe Mistress Vernon exchanging looks with the youth, or paying him any attention whatsoever?"

"He did not."

"Then why in the name of the Blessed Virgin does Father John believe Eleanor's disappearance is linked to this boy's?" I exploded, my fury bursting forth like matter from an angry pustule.

No doubt gratified by my outburst, the Countess paused for a moment to sip her wine and in the ensuing interlude I detected movement behind me and then heard a voice which I recognised at once.

"I believe it, Master Cranley, because Mistress Vernon and Brother Peter were seen together at Southampton, boarding a ship making ready to sail."

I spun around to face the abbot, battling with no great success to keep my expression clear of disbelief and disappointment. Fresh anger flared in me and was swiftly extinguished as I observed that the amiable fellow had aged ten years in the few days I had been gone, and with good reason. At the time of her vanishing Eleanor had been under the Abbey's protection and so, by extension, under his. It would not look well should it turn out that she had come to harm.

The Countess and I began to speak at once, she to remonstrate with the abbot and I to interrogate. Tyrell waited some moments and then halted our hubbub with a noisy cough.

"Let my lord Abbot to speak," he ordered once he had our attention. "I am keen to hear what he has to say on this matter."

Edging past me into the chamber, John Piers eyed the noble widow with a wary expression composed of one part sympathy and three parts caution. Helping himself to a cup of wine, he located a spare stool since his own handsome chair was occupied by the Countess, and embarked on his narration.

"As my lady of Warwick will have informed you, Brother Christopher and two lay brothers, Brother Adam and Brother Hubert, returned to the Abbey after scouring Southampton in vain for Mistress Vernon. The Countess was much distressed, as were we all, but at that hour it was too late to do anything other than pray for the poor child's safety.

"Yesterday at first light I sent a contingent of Beaulieu men back to Southampton to continue the search. Leading them was Prior Baldwin who carried with him a letter from me to Maurice Berkeley, Keeper of Southampton Castle. At my urgent request, the Keeper put a detachment of his men at the Prior's disposal. A thorough search of the town was then conducted, alas to no avail.

"Returning to Beaulieu, Prior Baldwin's party stopped and enquired after Mistress Vernon at every hovel, forge and ale-house along the way, letting it be known that a generous reward would be given to any soul coming forward with information regarding her whereabouts. Still they gleaned no useful intelligence and returned here heart-sore and dispirited some time after Vespers. Notwith-standing his great weariness, Prior Baldwin joined us in the cloister to consider what might be done next.

"We had scarce begun when a pedlar, one Dick Chapman, arrived with news of a possible sighting of Mistress Vernon. This Chapman had happened upon a charcoal burner, one of the common folk Prior Baldwin's party had spoken with some hours earlier. From him Chapman learned that a young lady was sought by the Abbey. Hearing this he hurried here without delay, eager to share his knowledge with us. He had, he averred, seen a maiden in Southampton who from her appearance he now believed must be Mistress Vernon. It was at the West Quay he had seen her, boarding a ship called The Doucette, arm in arm with a youthful fellow the pedlar took to be her lover. This was the very day she disappeared.

"Of course we did not believe him, judging his tale a feeble fabrication concocted to exact reward. Yet as he took the refreshments we gave him out of Christian charity, a lay brother from Netley arrived with a hastily penned missive addressed to me from Father Marmad-uke, the Netley abbot. This letter informed me that one of his young novices, Peter of Keverne, had absconded from the Abbey."

"What has any of this to do with Eleanor?" I put in, anxiety roughening my manners.

"Allow me to continue, my friend, and you will see," the abbot replied, regarding me with a worrying hint of regret in his expression.

"At first none could say where Peter might have gone until Brother Walter, the Netley novice master, recalled the conspicuous interest the boy had taken in Mistress Vernon."

Then Brother Walter is the Countess's scandalmonger, I thought.

"Brother Walter is a pious man but perhaps a little over zealous on occasion. When he saw Peter staring at the young woman with, shall we say, a degree of interest improper in one so soon to take his vows, he felt compelled to punish the lad."

"Ah, beat the randy devil, did he?" Tyrell chuckled. "Should have saved himself the trouble. A boy with an itch for the ladies will never make a monk!"

The Countess made a noise of exasperated disgust but to my surprise the abbot nodded his agreement.

"I fear you are right, Sir James. Indeed, I must confess that Peter's novitiate has not been the happiest. In truth I have always harboured grave doubts that he is fitted for the religious life but even so I asked Father Marmaduke to take him in at Netley in order to save the boy's life."

Now he had snared the interest of us all.

"You will know that our Abbey is blessed with property that extends far beyond the environs of Beaulieu, even so far as the most westerly reaches of Cornwall. That is where Peter comes from. He is the unfortunate by-blow of a Cornish squire whose manor abuts our church at St. Keverne. These matters are always regrettable but the father, an honourable man by all accounts, did his duty by the lad and saw to his care and education.

"Yet despite the advantages of his upbringing, Peter's wild nature embroiled him in some sordid trouble with the local folk. I do not know the details but apparently they would have hanged him without the swift intervention of his father and our people at St. Keverne.

This was some twelve months since. They sent him to us, a safe distance from his Cornish foes, in the fervent hope that a life of prayer and abstention would vanquish the iniquity in his character."

Tyrell gave a loud, derisory snort here which the abbot chose not to acknowledge.

"At first Peter's behaviour was very bad indeed. He played truant on a daily basis, stole food from the Kitchener and openly sneered at Brother Walter's attempts to discipline him. And then, a few months since, it seemed that a small miracle had occurred. One morning Peter arose with his manner much improved. He attended to Brother Walter's instruction, put a curb on his insolence and in every way strove to make himself pleasant and useful. We were all completely taken in, rejoicing that the Lord had seen fit to turn the boy from sinfulness. In our folly we even made plans for Peter to take his vows next month. Now it seems that we were deliberately hoodwinked."

There was such sorrow in his tone that for a moment I forgot my concern for Eleanor as I scrambled to offer him some words of consolation. Not so the Countess, whose thoughts were not so easily deflected.

"We were speaking of Mistress Vernon, not some baseborn wretch of dubious character," she hissed.

"So we were," the abbot replied, putting aside his own feelings for the moment. "But though you do not care to hear it, there is good reason to believe the two are connected.

"When Brother Walter realised Peter was missing his first thought was to look for him here at Beaulieu, in case he had taken it into his head to come and prey on Mistress Vernon. A thorough search revealed he was not here, nor was he at St. Leonards, but when I quizzed the pedlar as to the appearance of the youth he had spied at the quayside, he described a well-made lad with sun-browned skin and curly black hair. Then I had to accept the worst, for though the pedlar knew nothing of our errant novice he had described the lad's appearance accurately in every degree."

It looked bad, no doubt about it, but still I could not believe that Eleanor had thrown herself away on this despicable youth and neither, it seemed, could Countess.

"Then the only rational explanation is that he has taken her by force," she offered.

I was inclined to agree and Tyrell looked set to do likewise until the abbot strangled that notion at birth, reminding us that the pedlar spoke of the couple wrapped around one another in the style of ardent lovers.

This proved too much for the Countess.

"How could Eleanor be his lover?" she spat. "Not only does it go against all that I know of her, it defies all logic. She never set eyes upon this Peter of Keverne until the day of her disappearance. Am I to believe that after no more than one fleeting glimpse of him, the sweet, virtuous girl I have known since childhood has become so infatuated as to lose all reason and abandon one who has been as a mother to her?"

I felt her pain and wished that I could find a means to ease it. Sadly, Tyrell's next words only increased it.

"My lady, you cannot be sure that this Peter was unknown to Mistress Vernon. Did you not tell me that during your recent sickness she was much alone and was wont to spend her days out walking by herself whilst you slept?"

"What of it? What does that signify?"

"Nothing my lady, save that Mistress Vernon could have encountered Brother Peter at such times without your knowledge."

The Countess widened her eyes, aghast to find Tyrell whom she had allowed herself to trust now siding, as it seemed, with the abbot. Sharing her disappointment, I hastened to her aid.

"But it is no small distance from the Grange to Netley, especially for a girl travelling on foot. Though Mistress Vernon is young and healthy she could not easily have walked there and back during her solitary ramblings. And how would she have crossed the Water? If by boat, then surely the boatman would have reported her journeying to the abbot as something out of the ordinary. Or perhaps you would have it that she swam across the Water?"

Tyrell's expression hardened.

"No, Cranley, that is not what I believe. But you will admit that the distance would not be so great an obstacle to a lusty youth intent on mischief. This Peter might have heard about the ladies at the Grange, and perhaps come out to spy on them during one of his truancies. Seeing Mistress Vernon in all her loveliness, I can readily credit that he would set out to make himself personable to her."

I glared at Tyrell, belligerence seething in my veins. At that moment only his friendship with Dickon prevented me from swinging my fist into his handsome face. Aware of my fury, and of the effort it cost me to control it, he spoke again, this time in a more conciliatory manner.

"I do not say that this is what occurred, Francis. It is no more than a supposition. I only lay it before you as a possibility that must be considered. For my part, if you will believe me, I am still inclined to agree with my lady of Warwick and you that the lass did not leave of her own accord."

Relief flooded me then, relief that I could still call Tyrell my friend and also that he shared my faith in Eleanor. The Countess also looked comforted but Father John was less pleased.

"You must believe what you will," he sniped, "but there is no doubt in my mind that what Sir James calls supposition is fact. Peter spied on Mistress Vernon, made himself known to her and turned her head. It is regrettable and I blame myself for bringing the boy here in the first place, but since she has gone of her own accord there is no more to be done. Besides, since The Doucette has already left port any further pursuit will have to continue in France."

Behind his words I sensed a deep unease in John Piers. He was a good man, I was certain of that, but Eleanor's vanishing, if involuntary, had the potential to create all manner of trouble for him. Therefore it was in his interests to give credence to the pedlar's tale but there was no reason why I should. As so often happened, Tyrell's thoughts marched in parallel with mine.

"Where is this Chapman now?" he asked the abbot. "I should like him brought here for questioning."

John Piers' face reddened and for the first time his demeanour conveyed embarrassment.

"Ah well, of course this is most unfortunate but I regret that he is no longer here. According to the gatekeeper he left at first light, taking his leave while we rested after Lauds. It is my fault; I should have thought to leave instructions that the man should be detained.

For my error I am truly sorry. But I hardly think it matters, since I heard his tale direct from his own lips and have recounted to you everything of substance that he said."

The Countess and I exchanged a look of dismayed incredulity. The only witness to Eleanor's supposed elopement had been allowed to slip away before we could question him.

"No matter," Tyrell said briskly. "Just tell me which way he was heading and I'll send my lads to fetch him back."

"Alas, it's not that easy," the increasingly discomforted abbot answered. "The gatekeeper did not notice which road the fellow took and none with whom he came into contact last night recall him speaking of his intended route. In fact, it seems he spoke very little which our good hosteller considered unusual given that pedlars are often inclined to loquaciousness. But given the quantity of ale that Chapman consumed, perhaps it is small surprise that he took to his cot early and slept the night through. In any case he must be far from here by now."

"Not so far as I soon mean to be from this den of duplicity and misery," the Countess snarled, rising from her chair and beckoning Tyrell and me with an imperious gesture.

"We leave now, for I will hear no more of these lies and excuses," she told us, icy hauteur dripping from her tongue as she exited the chamber. Aware of our duty, Tyrell and I followed, dumb and obedient, in her wake.

Chapter Five

Tyrell and I lodged that night at St. Leonards, reluctant to leave the Countess in her distress with no company but the taciturn conversi. Her show of anger had dissipated the moment we quit the abbot and as we made our way back to the Grange I realised that it had been a facade put up to cover her distress. At the Grange she made us a perfunctory offer of wine but since we could see that her fatigue was great, we urged her bed-wards and then settled ourselves as best we could upon the floor outside her sleeping chamber. Before she would agree to rest, however, she pressed us for assurances that we would continue the search for Eleanor on the morrow.

Such sleep as I managed was made fitful by dreams in which a coterie of women led by Margaret, Fat Nell – my spiteful childhood nurse – and the shade of my recently deceased sister taunted me for aspiring to marry a gentlewoman. When Eleanor herself joined in with their derisive laughter I awoke with a filthy curse on my lips and saw that it was daylight already. Scanning the chamber I noticed that Tyrell had risen and was in conversation with the lay brother whose task it was to supply the Countess with her meals. This considerate fellow, having watched our arrival the night before, had thought to bring sufficient pottage and ale for three. As he set the food down I heard Tyrell give him thanks and then request that our horses be readied, stating our intention to leave within the hour. Although he spoke lightly, there was an unusual urgency in his manner that made me wary. And wisely so, for when he saw I slept no longer he walked to the door and gestured for me to follow him outside, a finger to his lips indicating that I should not wake the Countess.

We stood in silence for a moment as we emptied our bladders against one side of the great barn, and then he began.

"I know you will disagree with what I am about to say so let me save us some time by stating that whatever argument you make, I have reached a decision from which I will not be moved. I agree that Mistress Vernon has most likely been abducted against her will, for reasons and by persons we do not know. Given freedom of choice I would like nothing better than to set off with you at once in pursuit of her, never resting until she is safe. Yet we do not have that freedom of choice."

I little relished what I was hearing and guessed I would find what was coming even less to my liking.

"We were sent to Beaulieu to conduct the Countess of Warwick back to Middleham. This we are still bound to do, regardless of the misfortune that has befallen her waiting woman.

"Francis, whatever I might have said last night I think Father John is wrong to credit the pedlar's tale. I put no faith in his account of Mistress Vernon scampering aboard a France-bound ship in the arms of her lusty swain. It is altogether too neat to be credible, yet I comprehend why it suits John Piers to accept it."

"Then we must show him his error by finding Eleanor!" I interrupted.

"We must," he agreed, "but not before we have completed our primary duty which is to take the Countess to safety. Francis, has it not occurred to you that the girl's disappearance might be linked in some way to Clarence?"

Honesty compelled me to confess that the idea had indeed crossed my mind.

"But to what purpose?" I asked, for I could see no obvious benefit to Clarence in seizing the impoverished Eleanor Vernon.

"Who can say? To barter her person for financial gain, maybe, or simply to torment the Countess whose continued existence is a thorn in his side. Or to trick us into delaying our departure while he lays a trap for us on the road back to Middleham. This is what I fear, Francis, and this is why we must leave at once, our concern for the girl notwithstanding."

Bitter reason told me he was right. My every instinct was to stay, to hunt the pedlar down and beat his worthless hide until he confessed that his account was a fabrication. And then I would ride to Southampton and tear out the guts of every building great and mean until I located Eleanor, or found someone who could tell me what had become of her. But I knew I could not, for my duty was to Dickon and his instructions were clear. The safety of the Countess was paramount.

It was my own choice to inform the Countess of our imminent departure while Tyrell rode back to the Abbey to take formal leave of the abbot and to collect Brankin and Knewstubb. She took the news as well as I had expected, which is to say not well at all, and thus we rode the first part of the journey home bathed in the freezing waters of her disapproval. From the outset it was clear that Tyrell bore the brunt of her anger and by the time we reached Winchester Proud Nan had unbent sufficiently to tell me that she exempted me from all blame, understanding that Tyrell's superior rank required me to obey his orders. This grated, but even so I was thankful to be spared her resentful glowers which were now visited on Tyrell alone. To Brankin and Knewstubb she said little but the few words she did speak were always gracious whereas with their master she did not trouble to disguise her animosity. Since I had not yet forgiven him for obliging me to face my duty I confess I enjoyed his discomfiture.

We journeyed in this manner for ten days, hindered from travelling faster by the delicate health of our noble charge. Though she scoffed at Tyrell's insistence on frequent rest stops, her increasingly pallid countenance convinced me that pride alone kept her upright on her obliging palfrey. Just outside Coventry we fell in for a time in with a party of Yorkist knights who were riding to join the King on his summer progress through the Midlands. They gave us grave tidings. A small force of armed men led by the Earl of Oxford had lately landed at Chich St. Osyth on the Essex coast with the treasonous intent of rousing the country in support of Lancaster. Mercifully, none had rallied to their cause and so the traitors had fled to their ships and sailed away, doubtless hoping to find a harbour more favourable to their treachery. I found the news of this aborted incursion unsettling. Something about it smacked of Clarence, the King's troublesome brother being as comfortable with duplicity as he was with his favourite whore. I was thankful that thus far on our journey we had come across no sign of him nor any of his followers, and the closer we grew to Middleham the less probable it became that he would move against us.

Even so, after learning about Oxford's coastal raid Tyrell and I increased our vigilance, speaking little as we rode and always keeping Brankin in the vanguard of our party with Knewstubb following in our wake. We knew we could rely on those handy lads to sniff out lurking assailants and raise the alarm in time for us to protect the Countess. As it turned out, we were assailed by nothing more deadly than horse flies the size of a newborn's thumb which plagued us with their bites until we all looked poxed. In truth we made a dismal company, a far cry from the jaunty souls who had set forth to remove the Countess from sanctuary less than four weeks since. Small wonder that when we were still several miles from Middleham and I spied the castle's towers standing proud above the lush green landscape, my heart lifted as it had not once since leaving Beaulieu.

We found Dickon, his Duchess and a few of her ladies waiting for us at the gatehouse, Brankin having ridden ahead to acquaint them of our imminent arrival. I was heartened to spy Matthew, my gawky servant, loitering a respectful distance from the ducal party and I met his gaze with a slight twitch of my mouth before returning my attention to the fine folk. Tears spilled as mother and daughter were reunited in a jumble of embraces and happy exclamations though I noticed a formal stiffness in the exchange between my noble friend and his belle-mère. This did not surprise me, for I knew Dickon still felt the pain of her husband's treachery whereas she, unaware of how often he had petitioned the King on her behalf, likely felt aggrieved that he had not secured her release before now. It did not matter. Anne's happiness would keep his spirits buoyed until such time as all hurts were healed.

When the first joy of reunion was over, Anne swept her mother away to become acquainted with her new grandson, little Edward of Middleham, and to see her refreshed before showing her to the apartment that had been readied for her. As they moved off I overheard Anne querying the whereabouts of her mother's attendant, having overlooked the girl's absence in her initial delight. Reluctant to eavesdrop as the sorry tale unfolded, I was glad when my lord of Gloucester suggested an immediate removal to his privy chamber. There, ably fortified by the wine brought us by a cheery page, we told him what we had learned about the Earl of Oxford's latest mischief.

"This aborted landing took place where?" he asked, his voice betraying little of the disquiet I knew he must be feeling.

"Chich St Osyth's, my lord. A windy place boasting little but a priory and some pigs. I know the village a little," Tyrell explained, "for it lies but forty miles south of Gipping. I have lodged at the priory a few times when journeying to and from London."

I was surprised to learn that Tyrell's home was not much more than a day's ride from Chich for he had made no mention of the fact when we had first learned about the raid. I guessed that he had been loath to mention the fact in front of the King's trusty knights since it was their ilk who were prone to whispering about Tyrell's unfortunate Lancastrian background. Though he might feign unconcern at such talk, he did not fool me or my lord of Gloucester.

"Oxford could have raised his banner in the very heart of Gipping and I would not have not questioned your loyalty," he told Tyrell, gripping his arm in a gesture of support. "And it pleases me greatly that not even the pigs of Chich rose to Oxford's call.

"Nevertheless, I would dearly like to know what damage, if any, the incursion has wrought in the region. If the people sense weakness in my brother's reign they may not stay true a second time. So, my good Tyrell, I feel it is high time you paid a visit to Gipping. I fear I have kept you from your bride for far too long."

Here he indulged in a wry smirk, fully aware that Tyrell chose to keep his distance from Gipping on account of his fearsome mother-in-law who had insisted on making her home there until her daughter, Tyrell's virgin wife, was ready for bedding. He had wed Anne, daughter of Sir John Arundell of Cornwall, some four years since but could not lie with her until the girl's monthly courses began. As yet this had not happened, or so the mother declared, though Tyrell reckoned the girl must be fifteen or sixteen by now and surely ripe for plucking. I knew the suspected deceit did not trouble him; the girl was said to be moderately pretty but he had no taste for wilting maidens, preferring his women lusty and willing like Joanna, his London strumpet.

Wisely choosing to ignore Dickon's sardonic remark, Tyrell gave his promise to leave for Gipping on the morrow, and why not? It was a mark of high favour to be entrusted with a second mission by the Duke so hard on the heels of completing the first. It might even be enough to start the gossips wondering if he had taken the place of that upstart musician, Cranley. On this score, though, the upstart himself was unconcerned, knowing that his place in his master's affections was unassailable.

Of more import to me at that moment was the worrying disappearance of Eleanor Vernon. I was poised to begin telling Dickon about it when the door of the privy chamber opened and the little Duchess bustled in. Rarely did she intrude on her husband's private discussions but on this occasion it was clear that concern for her mother's distress overrode her usual reticence.

"What is to be done about Mistress Vernon?" she asked without preamble. "My lord, please tell me we will not abandon the poor child to whatever fate has befallen her!"

A shudder of her slender shoulders told me she was recalling her own experiences in captivity. That awful time seemed so long ago now, almost as if it had happened in another lifetime, yet in truth it had been little more than two years. After Tewkesbury, when her Lancastrian husband had been slain and his forces routed, Anne had been taken to live with her sister Isabel, Clarence's wife. Dickon knew already that he wanted her for his wife but before matters could be arranged the King required him to lead a campaign against the Scots. In his absence Clarence, anxious to prevent his younger brother from gaining control of Anne's share of the vast Neville fortune, had snatched her from the safety of her sister's hearth and had her secreted as a dogsbody in a greasy London cook shop. Had he understood his younger brother's steadfast nature he would have known it was a desperate venture, doomed to failure from the start. I had been at my friend's side as he scoured the streets, grim-faced, in search of the woman he loved, and had been with him when at last he had unearthed her from her squalid confinement so I knew all that she had suffered. And now she was imagining Eleanor Vernon in similar straits.

Dickon saw her distress and moved at once to her side.

"My love, I know not of what or whom you speak but I promise you that no innocent will be abandoned if I can help it. Now, calm yourself, I beg you, and tell me what troubles you."

Reassured, the Duchess then sketched a brief report of the affair to which Tyrell and I added greater detail. When we were done, Dickon's face was sombre and his eyes had turned to flint.

"You are certain the girl did not leave of her own volition?" he asked, looking first at me and then at Tyrell.

"So certain I would stake my life on it," I replied at once, remembering Eleanor's face as I had bid her farewell the morning we left for London. I knew women well enough to know when one had lost her heart to me. A woman who looks that way does not run off with another.

"Tyrell? What say you?" Dickon demanded.

"I agree with Cranley," he answered without pause. "The maiden has been taken against her will."

"Then it is our duty to recover her."

Hearing this, his tender-hearted Duchess gave way to tears of relief. I, too, was visited by great emotion which I hid by feigning an interest in the inside of my wine cup, only looking up again when the danger had passed. Yet my gladness proved short-lived, for Dickon then astounded me by asserting that he could make no start without his brother's explicit sanction. His position was that the abbot of Beaulieu was too important to annoy without proper authority and, though Anne pleaded with him to change his mind, he remained obdurate on this point.

"I dare not risk offending John Piers without the King's permission," he explained. "Beaulieu lies too close to the Channel for comfort. If I make an enemy of the abbot there is a danger that he might give succour to our foes."

I thought of Oxford's fleet sailing up and down the south coast in search of a hospitable landing place and knew that my friend had a valid point. Having met the man, I doubted that John Piers would ever turn traitor but it was a risk that could not be taken. Even so, I did my best to dissuade Dickon from wasting valuable time.

"The abbot is wrong in his judgement over Eleanor Vernon but for all that he is a good man and true to your brother. He will not harbour our enemies, my lord, I would swear to it."

Tyrell chimed in with his agreement but we should both of us have saved our breath. Once my lord of Gloucester had decided on a course of action, there was no turning him from it. So we waited while the messenger James Metcalfe was despatched with an urgent letter for the King, still on progress throughout the Midlands. Nine days we were forced to wait, young Metcalfe being unable at first to locate Edward's whereabouts, and all the while he was away my heart chafed at the hopeless delay. In this I was not alone, for the Duchess saw how the waiting fretted her mother, inclining her already uncertain health to greater fragility. In consequence tempers frayed and those nearest us suffered; my servant

Matthew bore the brunt of my surliness with sturdy peasant fortitude but my lord of Gloucester, accustomed to naught but sweetness from his lady, floundered in the depths of her disapproval.

At length Metcalfe returned, bringing with him a royal warrant which authorised Gloucester to enquire into the matter referred to in the warrant as the strange matter of the Beaulieu vanishing. The warrant emphasised the King's utmost confidence in his youngest brother and approved in advance any actions he might deem necessary in order to track down Mistress Vernon. Furthermore, recognising that Gloucester was too occupied with important matters of state to conduct the investigation himself, the warrant authorised him to appoint a proxy to lead the enquiries in his stead. Since this individual would be acting in the King's name, every loyal subject was required to render him their fullest co-operation. It was everything Dickon had hoped for and in his eyes fully justified the delay. I remained unconvinced upon this point but was relieved that now at last I could begin to unravel the mystery, for it was to me that Dickon entrusted the matter, as I had always known he would.

Chapter Six

With Tyrell and his lads in Gipping, I returned to Beaulieu alone save for Matthew, my spit-boy turned body servant. Dickon urged me to bulk out our number with two or three of his men-at-arms but I declined his offer, declaring I had no need of them. In a previous scrap Matthew had proved himself well able to hold his own and in any case I would be protected by the King's warrant. Well, so I thought when we quit Middleham as dawn broke on the twenty-fourth day of June. Perhaps I should have known better but my new official status had gone to my head and rendered me uncharacteristically giddy.

Travelling at speed in the clement summer weather, I found myself once again at Beaulieu Abbey as the sun was setting on the first day of July. Father John was cordial in his welcome even though he could not quite conceal his surprise at my unexpected reappearance and, when he learned why I had come, his countenance faltered. Even so, my possession of the King's warrant ensured there was nothing he could do but vouchsafe me his full support. To his credit, it was with good grace that he pressed me to stay in his house, occupying once again the comfortable chamber I had previously shared with Tyrell. Matthew, however, was directed towards the guesthouse until I demurred, flexing my new authority with thinly concealed enjoyment. It would inconvenience me, I explained, to summon my servant from the guesthouse whenever I needed him. If my errands were to be run without delay, I must keep him at hand. The Abbot saw the sense of this and agreed readily enough. By the time these arrangements had been made, fatigue and aching limbs inclined me towards my bed. Bidding my host a good night, I was through the doorway when I remembered another request I had to make of him. A local guide would speed my mission, I said, and if he could be spared from his duties, Brother Martin would be my choice for I knew the Abbey's horse master to be shrewd and steady. Though I made it sound like a request, Father John recognised a demand when he heard one and acquiesced with no more than a hint of weary resignation.

During the long ride from Middleham I had given much thought as to where to begin my search for Eleanor. Southampton, the scene of her vanishing, was long overdue a visit but rather than head directly there, I chose to make a short detour to Netley Abbey in order to find out more about their missing novice. To that end, early the next day Matthew, Brother Martin and I rode the short distance from Beaulieu to the squalid village of Hythe from whence we were conveyed by the Abbey's boat across Southampton Water. Since his was the only boat authorised to carry folk across the Water, I enquired of the boorish boatman if he had ever given passage to Eleanor or to the novice, Peter of Keverne. Though he spoke rudely, his reply pleased me for he swore that he had never so much as set eyes on the boy, let alone taken him as a passenger. As for Eleanor, he had seen her once only, on the day she had travelled to Southampton with the Beaulieu contingent. I believed him, in part because Brother Martin assured me of his honesty but mostly because I judged him too stupid to lie so convincingly.

With the boatman's testimony, I was surer than ever that Eleanor had not become embroiled in a sordid liaison with the novice during the Countess's long illness. Admittedly it was still possible that the boy had taken the long land route to St. Leonards in order to spy on the fine ladies but even if he had, I found it entirely implausible that Eleanor should have formed an attachment to him. Thus, in gratitude for the good news he had unwittingly given me, I slipped the startled boatman a handful of groats and then bade Brother Martin lead the way to Netley.

I knew little of this abbey save that it was a daughterhouse of Beaulieu with no more than fifteen monks and perhaps twice as many lay brothers. On the basis of this alone, I had envisioned it as a mean establishment, roughly hewn from the surrounding woodland and maintained at a level of comfort well below that of the mother-house. Well, this preconceived notion was rapidly proven false; Netley was smaller than Beaulieu, it was true, yet it was anything but mean. This was made abundantly plain as I approached the abbey and took in the glorious sight unfolding before me. Dappled in sunlight, graceful stone buildings with arched windows soaring up to heaven sat in perfect tranquillity amongst richly verdant slopes. In general the wild Wensleydale country of my boyhood was more to my taste than the milksop landscape of the south yet even so, I had to acknowledge that I had rarely looked upon a more pleasing vista.

We were hailed as we rode through the open gateway by a number of conversi toiling amongst the beds of a neat kitchen garden. Recognising a Beaulieu lay brother amongst our party, one of them unbent with a hint of gladness from his labours and took charge of Matthew, leaving Brother Martin and me to make our way past the chapter house towards the abbot's lodging. There we were greeted by Father Marmaduke and, having apprised him of the purpose of our visit, were invited to wait in his private chamber while word was sent for the novice master to join us. As we waited I used the time to take stock of the Netley abbot. His physique, I saw, was considerably fleshier than Father John's though his countenance was more severe. Here was a man, I decided, who would demand from his subordinates stringent adherence to the frugal Cistercian dietary rules while denying himself nothing. The arrival of Brother Walter obliged me to revise this opinion at once since the corpulent novice master made two of Father Marmaduke.

The abbot saw me studying Brother Walter and interpreted my thoughts correctly.

"Though we are God's servants, Master Cranley, we are men also and are prone to the same weaknesses of the flesh as our secular fellows. Gluttony is a sin but I believe God forgives it more readily than He does carnality. By permitting my flock to indulge at table, I endeavour to turn their thoughts from lustful yearning."

Amused, I raised a sardonic eyebrow at this questionable justification for greed.

"Is your flock prone to more such thoughts than others in holy orders?" I enquired, barely troubling to conceal the scepticism in my voice.

"I do not know that it is," he replied, apparently unruffled by my lack of courtesy, "but with Southampton and all its temptations so near, I prefer not to take a chance with their souls. As you must know, eternal damnation awaits any monk who breaks his sacred oath of chastity.

"Now I regret I must leave you," he continued, "for I am needed in the sacristy but Brother Walter will be able to tell you all you need to know about the wretched Peter."

Unable to contain a wince as he mentioned the errant novice, the abbot rose from his chair and quit the chamber. The moment he was gone, Brother Walter exhaled loudly and folded his hands beneath his comfortable paunch.

"I'd not presume to contradict Father Marmaduke," he laughed, "but for my part I must say that I am motivated to overeat through greed alone. Impure thoughts have not troubled me these many years, nor in truth did they do so overmuch before I took holy orders. But food, now! Aye, there's my weakness. Master Cranley, I confess I am a trencherman through and through and if you ask me, though he does not like to own it, I fancy Father Marmaduke is one also!"

The novice master's jovial manner startled me for it was at odds with what I had heard of him at Beaulieu. There, Brother Walter had been described as a stern disciplinarian with a tendency to beat his pupils at the first excuse. Unwilling to mince my words I said as much to his face, causing poor Brother Martin no little mortification. Brother Walter, however, was not offended.

"Ha, so tongues have wagged about my heavy hand, have they? Well, I'll not deny it. I beat the lads whenever they transgress, or simply give me pause to think they might be about to. But I do it for their benefit. You may disbelieve me, Master Cranley, if you so choose. I should like your good opinion but I'll not earn it with a falsehood."

The frankness of his manner encouraged me to believe he spoke in earnest yet I struggled to make sense of his meaning.

"Help me understand why your beatings are for their own good. Are you purging the evil from them, is that it?"

He chuckled then, his fleshy face wobbling with amusement.

"No, my friend, I beat them to save them from worse punishment from our good Father Marmaduke. You heard him speak of his extreme abhorrence of licentious behaviour. Well, if I fail to chastise the boys for suspected impurity he takes the matter into his own hands and then their suffering is much greater.

"Look at me, Master Cranley; I am stout, aging and short of breath. My thrashings are of necessity brief for I have not the strength to prolong them. But Father Marmaduke is younger and has more vigour, and he is zealous in such work where I am not."

Convinced by the sincerity in his expression and tone that he spoke truly, I broached the matter that had brought me to Netley.

"Did you often have cause to chastise Peter of Keverne?"

For answer, the novice master raised his eyes heaven-ward and then fixed me with his shrewd gaze.

"Candidly, Master Cranley, I beat the unhappy wretch so often that my arm grew weary from the effort. Rarely can there have been an individual so unsuited to the religious life. He did not have a vocation and no amount of punishment was ever going to alter that fact. Any fool could see he despised our life of worship and quiet contemplation and was ever on the lookout for ways to enliven the tedium."

"Yet at Beaulieu I was told some improvement in the lad's behaviour had been noted shortly before he absconded. Is that not the case?"

The novice master sighed before answering.

"Your informant speaks the truth. For a few blessed weeks Peter obeyed all my instructions and hung about me like a motherless lamb. We all rejoiced at this new version of him yet even then I could tell his behaviour was caused by something other than religious fervour, though what I cannot say. In any case he reverted to his old ways soon enough. Why, I had cause to give him a mighty thrashing the very day before he made off."

At these words a prickle ran down my neck and across my shoulders; my senses told me I was about to learn something of import.

"This would be the day before Mistress Vernon called here with the Beaulieu contingent en route to Southampton?" I ventured, seeking clarification.

Brother Walter considered, frowned and then shook his head.

"No indeed, it was not. How could it have been, when it was the lascivious interest Peter took in Mistress Vernon that necessitated his beating? I myself saw him ogling her! No, it was the following day that he ran away, leaving me to worry that I had hurt the boy too badly after all."

For a moment I failed to comprehend the significance of this utterance but not so Brother Martin whose jaw had fallen slack with confusion.

"Your pardon, Brother Walter, but surely you are mistaken," he stammered. "Peter left Netley the self-same day as the poor young lady vanished."

Irritation flashed across the novice master's face, doubtless occasioned by his shock at a mere lay brother daring to challenge his version of events.

"It is you that is in error," he snapped. "I may be old but I retain my faculties. I last saw Peter at dinner on the first day of June. I recall that he was more than usually sullen but I attributed this to the beating I had administered before dinner. Afterwards we ate, and then retired for our customary rest. When we assembled later for Nones he was nowhere to be found. On Father Marmaduke's orders we conducted an immediate search of the abbey and outlying fields but he could not be found. Then I remembered his marked interest in Mistress Vernon and suggested that he might have gone to spy on her, so Father Marmaduke despatched a message to Beaulieu to warn Father John."

Finishing, he glared at Brother Martin whose face looked so ashen I feared for him.

"There has been the most dreadful misunderstanding," he gasped. "When your letter arrived it was assumed that Peter had scarpered the previous day. Father John believed you had spent a full day searching before despatching the messenger to us."

My head grew hot as I grasped the import of this revelation.

"So the pedlar's tale is shown to be a towering mountain of dung! I always knew he lied! He cannot have seen Mistress Vernon boarding a ship entwined in Peter's arms, for the day she disappeared the knave was still making trouble here at Netley."

Hearing the jubilation in my voice, the monks exchanged a knowing look.

"But, Master Cranley, the pedlar never actually claimed the youth he saw with Mistress Vernon was Peter," Brother Martin reminded me. "How could he claim that, when he had never met the boy? If you recall, he spoke only of a well-made lad with dark curls and there are many who could be described thus. We simply assumed it was Peter since it explained his disappearance."

"You mean Father John believed it," I snarled, "because it suited him to brand Mistress Vernon a whore rather than shoulder any culpability for her loss. Had he troubled to establish the date of Peter's departure from Netley, he would have known her innocent of eloping with the boy. Yet it was more convenient for him to believe the worst of her!"

There was an uncomfortable silence as Brother Martin struggled to find adequate words to defend his abbot's actions. At a loss to do so, he subsided and allowed Brother Walter to step in.

"Hasty words, Master Cranley, hasty words!" he murmured. "You must know Father John is the very best of men. I'll allow it was remiss of him not to establish the date of Peter's absconsion but it was an honest mistake, I am as certain of that as I am of my own name. And indeed I can readily see how the girl's unfortunate disappearance, followed so swiftly by news of Peter's, might have led him to suspect a connection which the pedlar's account only confirmed."

I glowered at him but held my peace as he continued.

"But consider this. All we now know is that the youth seen boarding the ship with Mistress Vernon was not

Peter. If anyone has been absolved of wrongdoing, it is our errant novice, not your young lady."

I sprang at him then, ready to make him a meal of his teeth, but Brother Martin guessed my intent and grabbed my arm before I could disgrace myself. Years of handling horses had given the lay brother muscles of iron so though he was my elder by ten years at least, he restrained me without too much effort. The worst of it was the look of pity I saw in Brother Walter's eyes. It was a look that said he knew I cared for Eleanor and was sorry for me because she had played me false.

Safe in the knowledge that Brother Martin held me firm, he ventured to speak again.

"Your anger is excusable, Master Cranley. But Father John is blameless in this matter. If you must have blood, find the wretch who seduced the girl."

I sagged, momentarily blindsided by the monk's stark conviction of Eleanor's guilt. Feeling the violence ebb from me, Brother Martin released his grip.

"I'll not think ill of Mistress Vernon," he declared stoutly, placing a comforting hand upon my shoulder. "She could no more do wrong than I could turn horse shit to gold!"

I was bolstered by this unlooked for support and felt my spirits rise further as the good fellow continued.

"One thing we took for a fact has already been shown a lie, so why not another? I for one am no longer ready to give credence to the pedlar's tale. My guess is that he concocted the entire story to gain a reward."

A sudden onrush of gratitude strengthened me sufficiently to gather together the shreds of my dignity and take my leave, accompanied by the stalwart horse master.

Chapter Seven

Retrieving Matthew and the horses, we quit Netley
without pausing to bid Father Marmaduke farewell. This ill-mannered behaviour was unworthy of one
acting in the King's name but I was far too agitated to
care. As we rode I gave Matthew the gist of Brother
Walter's revelation and then fell silent until we were at
the outer fringes of Southampton. During the interim
I had time enough to wonder why the novice master's
insinuating words had rattled me so, and came to the
sorry conclusion that perhaps I was less certain of Eleanor's blamelessness than I cared to pretend. I could not
doubt that she had liked me yet in the deepest recesses of
my mind a niggling uncertainty refused to be quelled.
What if she had used our flirtation to deflect attention
from the true object of her affections? Though Peter of
Keverne had not been her lover, there remained at least
the possibility that she had been entangled with another
whose identity was as yet unknown.

In the depths of my heart, however, I still believed that
whatever had happened to Eleanor had been none of her
doing and it heartened me that Brother Martin shared
my conviction. As for Matthew, though he had never met
her, he was prepared to take my word for it that Mistress
Vernon was a wholly virtuous young lady and he declared

himself willing to dedicate his life to her recovery. I frowned and accused him of buffoonery but found myself cheered all the same by his unthinking loyalty.

We entered Southampton through its imposing Bargate and set to work at once, pausing at every tavern, ale-house and pie shop we encountered in order to enquire after Dick Chapman, the pedlar whose dubious claim had curtailed the original search for Eleanor. I cherished a faint hope that we would find him here, though I knew such itinerants meandered far and wide in search of customers gullible enough to buy their shoddy tools and trashy gewgaws. It could be many months before he returned to Southampton. Even so, I persevered with our enquiries, sure that someone in the town must know the man and perhaps have an inkling of his likely whereabouts.

It proved thirsty work navigating the teeming streets in the fierce July sun. After a dozen or more fruitless enquiries we stopped for refreshment at The George, a tidy-looking tavern situated a short distance behind the castle in Simnel Street. Consigning our mounts to the care of an ancient ostler, we entered the tavern and found an empty table near the doorway. Taking in its spick and span interior and prosperous-looking clientele, I decided it was unlikely that the pedlar would have been an habitué of the place. Nevertheless, in the interests of thoroughness I did question the taverner, a burly, open-faced individual named Bernard Gover. As it turned out, it was well that I did.

"Aye, master, I know him," the amiable fellow told me as he placed three cups of passable Spanish wine upon our table. "Chapman's a regular, supping here oft-times when he comes to town."

I raised a questioning eyebrow, surprised that a disreputable pedlar would find a welcome in this superior establishment.

"Oh, he's a rascal, I know that well enough," Gover continued, "yet I'll take anyone's coin and thank them kindly so long as they mind their manners. Trouble is, Chapman seldom does. Take the last time he was here; I had to turf him out after he gobbled up food he could not pay for. Cheating swine, he only admitted he was penniless after he'd eaten his fill. When I complained he compounded the insult by offering to pay his debt with a pan so flimsy my spit could puncture it."

"What day was this, do you recall?" I questioned Gover, excited that I had at last stumbled upon news of my prey.

"Ah well, that's the nub of it," he replied with an unpromising frown. "Such incidents are not uncommon. Truth is they happen all the time, more's the pity. Fact is, it's a wonder I earn enough to keep my own belly filled."

"So you do not recall the exact day you evicted Chapman?" I persisted, so patently disappointed that Gover shook his head in amused exasperation.

"Why, that's just it, good master! I should not be able to, since one day is usually much like another in my line of work. Folk come in, drink their fill, maybe eat a bite and then they leave. But by happenstance I do recall that day, for it was the self-same one that the monks lost the poor young lady in their care. I daresay you've heard of her?"

Pausing, he shot me a sly look which told me he knew full well what lay behind my questioning but was willing to pretend otherwise if it suited my purpose.

"See," he continued, as I felt hope soar in my chest like a frightened sparrow, "with all the uproar in the town after the maiden had gone astray, it is a day I'll long remember."

"The last day of May?" I queried, anxious to be entirely clear upon this crucial point. "That was when you last saw Chapman?"

"No, master, that was the day I booted the tricky beggar out on his scrawny arse, excusing my language. The last day I saw him was two days later, when he fair swaggered back into my tavern with a bulging purse and an insolent manner. Paid me in full for his stolen dinner, he did, and then dropped me a few extra coins as well. Told me to buy something pretty for the missus, to make her face less sour, the bold fellow! I don't mind telling you, I was that angered by the offence offered to my poor wife, I was sore tempted to shove his coins down his gullet and watch him choke."

"Why did you not?" Matthew enquired, his interest piqued by the taverner's colourful story.

Gover grunted.

"Money is money. Only the rich can afford the luxury of squandering it on gestures. Me, I swallowed my ire and allowed Dick to buy me a drink. As I supped it, I encouraged him to tell how he came by his newfound wealth. He'd not say, mind, for though he's a slippery knave he's no fool. All he would say is that he has friends in high places."

"What did you take that to mean?" I asked with heightened interest.

The landlord shrugged his meaty shoulders.

"Didn't take it to mean anything," he answered. "Chapman was born with a falsehood on his tongue. If he has friends in high places, why then, I am the Bishop of Winchester! No, master, my guess is he that pinched the purse from some unwary traveller and then span a yarn of high-placed friends to satisfy the nosy."

I knew Gover's theory was plausible but nevertheless I discounted it since my mind was already galloping after another train of thought. On the last day of May, Chapman had possessed insufficient funds to pay for a meagre dinner; a mere two days later he had returned to The George with money enough to waste on petty insults. On the intervening day, as I well knew, he had been to Beaulieu to tell the abbot about his supposed sighting of Eleanor as she eloped to France with a lover. This was progress.

A new thought occurred to me.

"Why bother coming back to Southampton so soon?" I asked the affable taverner. "Surely once he'd left, the pedlar would not normally return for several months at least?"

Gover gave a short snicker.

"He didn't have no choice, given that his pack with all his merchandise in it was locked up at The Mermaid in Castle Lane. It's a decent inn, too good for the likes of him, with a better class of flea to bedevil the arses of the fancy folk that stay there!"

He scratched his own posterior as he spoke, a look of hauteur momentarily replacing his friendly expression. I was bewildered for an instant until I realised that he was aping the superior clientele of The Mermaid Inn. Fortunately, Matthew and Brother Martin understood the jest at once and chuckled appreciatively. It was all the encouragement Gover needed to continue.

"Dick had been lodging at The Mermaid for a few nights while he went about replenishing his goods. This time of year, he starts looking ahead to the colder months, so he ferrets around the markets and docks for thin scratchy blankets and poorly cured furs, stuff he can buy cheap and make a tidy profit on when he finds a poor sap to sell to. Like I say, The Mermaid is too fine an inn for his sort but Dick don't seem to realise that and whenever he's in funds he likes to treat himself to a soft bed. Seems fair enough, I suppose, given that he spends most nights lying flat on his back on the hard earth, staring up at the stars. But this time the stupid great lump got his reckoning wrong; he overspent on his stock and ended up without enough to pay for his board. Well, Old Stumpy – him that owns The Mermaid – he keeps a pretty inn but by temperament he's an evil bastard who don't stand for no tricks when it comes to payment. Gave Dick a good walloping, he did, and sent him on his way without his gear, telling him not to bother coming to collect it until he had the wherewithal to pay what he owed."

"Was this before or after he rooked you for his dinner?"

"After. Of course, he never let on to me about his ruckus at The Mermaid or I'd not have served him so much as a stale crumb for his dinner."

"I can understand him needing to collect his pack from The Mermaid," I pondered aloud, "but why did he bother to come back here?"

Gover shrugged once more.

"To taunt me, I suppose. To rub my nose in his good fortune and salve the memory of my boot up his arse. I daresay even pedlars have their pride."

The disdain on his face as he uttered these words told me that Gover thought such pride entirely misplaced.

I was inclined to agree but then at that moment I would have agreed with even the most outlandish sentiment the good taverner cared to voice. As far as I was concerned, his account of Chapman's character put paid to any suggestion that the wretch was a reliable witness. Moreover, I saw his return to Southampton in possession of unexplained riches as distinctly suspicious. Though I had no proof, it was abundantly clear to me that someone had paid Chapman to carry a spurious tale about Eleanor to Beaulieu in order to halt the search for her. Whoever that someone had been, they must have been possessed of deep pockets. According to Gover, the pedlar's purse had remained full even after his debts were settled. The thought made me uncomfortable. Examining why this should be, I realised it was because now, for the first time, I had to take seriously the notion that Clarence might be behind Eleanor's vanishing. He had sufficient wealth, that was certain, and a motive of sorts, in that seizing his detested mother-in-law's companion would be bound to cause her pain. Please God, let it not be so, I prayed fervently, knowing that though he was not habitually a violent man, George of Clarence would not scruple to inflict hurt in order to further his aims.

Overpaying Gover for the wine we had taken in gratitude for his co-operation, we retrieved our horses and made straight for the castle. There I presented my credentials to the Keeper, Maurice Berkeley. I knew that Berkeley was relatively new to the post, having been granted it by the King only a year since. A youngish, solidly built fellow with an air of dull respectability, Berkeley welcomed me with gratifying unctuousness and promised me his unstinting assistance as well as a comfortable bed at the castle for as long as I should need it. Thanking him, I told him I would accept his aid with thanks should it be required. The bed I turned down, explaining that I preferred to sleep outside the castle walls where I could keep a closer watch on the town and all its comings and goings. Although I did not tell him outright of my suspicions regarding Clarence, I dropped heavy hints about intrigue in high places and warned him I might have need of armed support at short notice. To his credit, Berkeley then reiterated with great earnestness his readiness to render me whatever aid I should need, whenever I should need it. I thanked him again, and thus we parted.

My next destination was The Mermaid Inn which stood in the shadow of the castle in the aptly named Castle Lane. Recalling Gover's description of the inn as a place of superior accommodation, I made my way there and arranged lodgings with the innkeeper, a malevolent looking character who went by the name of Old Stumpy. The reason for this peculiar nickname became apparent to me when I noticed the three fingers lacking from his left hand. Though flinty-eyed and gruff in manner, he had a clean and tidy appearance and his establishment more than lived up to Gover's recommendation. As well it should considering the price the old rogue demanded for bed and board. With these domestic matters settled to my satisfaction, I told Brother Martin it was time he returned to Beaulieu. Though I liked him, with Berkeley and his garrison at my disposal I could no longer justify keeping the horse master from his duties. At the last, as we were saying farewell, I enjoined him to perform one more favour for me. Recollecting with shame my truculent departure from Netley, I asked him to call there on his way back in order to proffer my apologies to Father Marmaduke. Ever obliging, the good soul readily agreed.

After Brother Martin had left, I felt restless and in urgent need of some activity. Leaving Matthew to idle a while in the comfort of our costly chamber, I quit the inn and strolled to St. Michael's Square where Nicholas Bonvylle had his house. According to my informants, Bonvylle was the foremost trader in Southampton, shipping wool and cloth overseas and importing luxury goods from distant lands. Discounting the pedlar's fabricated story, the last confirmed sighting of Eleanor had been at Bonvylle's house. It was for this reason that I planned to question his household on the morrow. For now, however, I thought it worth my while to take a look at his house and its proximity to the quayside.

Though daylight was fading, the fish market in St Michael's Square was still thronged with customers. I idled awhile outside the handsome church from which the square took its name, then meandered from stall to stall, feigning interest in the pungent end of day produce as I studied Bonvylle's house. Berkeley had told me where it stood but even without this prior knowledge I would have guessed that the square's most impressive residence belonged to the town's wealthiest inhabitant. Three storeys tall and with glazed windows framed by shutters which were open at present, the property gazed onto the square with a benign air that suggested a life of industry and plenty for its inhabitants. Skirting hastily past a barrow laden with fish that had lingered too long in the sun, I crossed the square and walked purposefully towards the house, veering right at the last into Wytegod's Lane. Running the length of Bonvylle's house and then twisting on down to the quayside, this narrow alleyway offered me a restricted view of the rear of the property. Studying it, I saw that here the windows, much smaller than those at the front, were blocked with stone; a defensive measure, I presumed, against attack from the sea. A high wall provided the house with privacy from the jumble of lesser buildings that were crowded together on the opposite side of the lane, their overhanging top storeys casting the alley into permanent shadow.

As I watched, an unobtrusive gate set into Bonvylle's wall opened and a lad dressed in smart crimson livery stepped out. Peering through the open gate, I had just enough time to make out a well-ordered garden before it closed again, plunging the lane back into gloom. Spying me, the servant gave me a curious stare before hurrying off in the direction of the quay. It was where I had intended to go but now I thought better of it, unwilling to follow the lad in case he should take fright. For all its proximity to a grand house, I sensed a lurking threat in the close atmosphere of this part of Wytegod's Lane. If I felt it, a callow boy would feel it too, and fear it. With no current wish to alarm anyone, I turned about and retraced my steps to St. Michael's Square, the raucous screech of gulls ringing in my ears as I walked.

Not ready yet to return to The Mermaid, I toyed with the notion of finding a tavern but then realised I must be but a short distance from the abbey's wool house. At the top of Wytegod's Lane, I turned sharp left past the entrance to the Bonvylle house and found myself in Bugle Street, a hotchpotch of humble dwellings interspersed with cookshops, apothecaries and the homes of moderately prosperous tradesmen. Noticing that there was less bustle here than I had found elsewhere in the town, the street cleaner and the air less noxious, I conjectured that

Bugle Street would be a pleasant enough place to live. As the street tapered down to the sea the houses fell away, leaving me a clear view of the abbey's store house, a vast stone edifice that dominated the quayside. Alongside it stood the harbour crane, a malevolent crouching beast of timber and winches that would not have looked out of place at a besiegement. I had known that Beaulieu was a rich abbey but I was filled with awe at the sight of its wool house and the machine needed to load its contents aboard the trading vessels. Perhaps belatedly, I understood that Father John was a figure of considerable power and importance.

Thoughts of Beaulieu's abbot inevitably brought Eleanor to mind. Closing my eyes, I pictured her parting company with Brother Christopher and the conversi before walking up Bugle Street, flushed with excitement at the prospect of shopping for new finery. I wondered if she had she been thinking of me at the time, and then chided myself for my vanity. Sick at heart, I went back the way I had come, pausing as I reached Nicholas Bonvylle's house. It was no more than a few minutes' walk from the wool house to here; small wonder, then, that the monks had allowed her to go unaccompanied. They would have been preoccupied with their wool delivery and in any case, as I had seen, Bugle Street was a safe enough place. There was no reason for them to suspect that their young guest would come to harm there.

Returning to The Mermaid, I roused Matthew from his leisure and set him to brushing and sweetening my clothes as best he could. Having seen their house and the smart suit of livery their errand boy wore, I surmised that the fine folk I planned to visit on the morrow were likely to judge me on my appearance, King's warrant notwithstanding. As Matthew laboured, I sat a while in silence, allowing all I had heard and seen since leaving Beaulieu that morning to sift slowly through my thoughts. In the stillness, a faint stirring of my blood whispered to me that I was edging ever closer towards knowing the truth about Eleanor Vernon.

Chapter Eight

Any sense that I was at last making headway into the mystery was suspended next morning when I attempted and failed to gain an audience with Master Bonvylle. The liveried manservant who answered my knock was politeness itself, inviting me into a waiting area that doubled as a store room on the ground floor of the house while he went upstairs in search of his master. I had brought along Matthew in a half-hearted attempt to resemble a man accustomed to wielding authority though in truth all it took was mention of the King's warrant to send the servant scuttling. As we waited, Matthew found himself a snug perch on top of one of the many oak chests that lined the walls of the chamber and sat, gazing up in admiration at the high vaulted ceiling. I remained standing, scuffing at the bare wooden floorboards with my boots as I imagined the mounds of figured satins, rich damasks and jewel-coloured silks that must be contained within those chests. Eleanor would have been wild with excitement to see them, I thought, and then shivered. Unbidden, a notion had come to me that her broken body might even now be lying inside one of them, concealed beneath the fineries she had coveted so dearly.

No sooner had I taken myself to task for such foolishness than the servant returned, a sheepish expression pasted onto his slippery features.

"Your pardon, sir, but my poor master regrets he cannot see you. He is sick a-bed," he squeaked, blanching as he saw how his words displeased me. "Mistress, too, else she would come in his place."

Though I had no cause to doubt him, I was too rattled by my recent vision of Eleanor decaying under a silken shroud to be refused so easily and with such apparent contempt.

"Too ill to obey the orders of the King?" I snapped. "Ah well, that's a pity. Now I must return to the castle and give the Keeper the dolorous news that your master sets himself above loyalty to the crown."

Dumbstruck, the fellow flapped his jaws a moment and then withdrew.

"Stay there, I pray you," he managed to call as he darted from the chamber. "Master means no offence and will manage to see you, I am certain."

Impressed by this display of my new authority, Matthew flashed me a smile of pure delight. I returned it, wondering if like me he was recalling a time not so long ago when the success of my endeavours had relied on my wits rather than a royal warrant. Nevertheless, when the lackey returned I bridled to see that it was again without his master, although this time he brought news that placated me somewhat.

"Begging your pardon, sir, but poor Master bids me say he only cannot see you on account of his excess purging. Something terrible it is, sir, and just the same with poor Mistress. They believe some putrid meat they ate is to blame for their suffering. But Master begs me assure you they are taking a physick left by the apothecary. If it works as the man promises, Master believes he will be recovered enough to speak with you on the morrow."

"Tell your master I shall return today, before sundown. That should allow time enough for this miraculous remedy to take effect. If it has not, I shall attend him in his sickbed and you may hold the slop bowl as we speak."

Frustrated by the delay, I left the Bonvylle house without further comment and strode down Wytegod's Lane towards the quayside, Matthew following at my heel like a faithful hound.

"What angers you?" he asked with his customary impertinence. "Do you think the merchant feigns sickness so as not to see you?"

A good question, I thought, though I declined to answer it. Perhaps there was no sickness in the Bonvylle house, yet if they had something to hide, why should they draw attention to it by refusing to see me?

"Go back," I instructed Matthew on a whim. "Get the name of the apothecary who attended the Bonvylles and then visit him. Find out if he confirms their story. Then come and find me at the quay."

At the bottom of Wytegod's Lane I turned left and made my way towards the West Quay. It was from here, I knew, that The Doucette had set sail on the day that Eleanor went missing. Today there were no vessels in evidence but the wharf was alive with activity as bales and crates were hefted from waiting wagons onto the quayside. It was clear that a ship was expected imminently. Glancing in the direction of the Town Quay I caught a glimpse of the massive crane I had seen at close quarters the day before. Today it was in action, swinging cargo onto what looked like a Genoese carrack. Beyond that, in the distance I glimpsed a few tall mastheads at what I knew must be the Watergate Quay.

Flipping a coin to one of the workers, I enquired after the port official and was pointed in the direction of a stocky man of middle years. He was sitting under a makeshift canopy at a table laden with ledgers and scrolls. Swarthy-skinned from spending his days in the open, he had grizzled hair and brown eyes framed by eyebrows so thick and bristly they threatened to overrun his forehead. Not a handsome face, I decided, but perhaps an honest one.

Approaching, I overheard him energetically berating a subordinate for an inventory error but he broke off as I drew near and greeted me with brusque courtesy.

"Master Cranley, if I'm not mistaken. I'm Andrew Coterel. Berkeley told me to expect you."

Rising from his three-legged chair, Coterel sketched me a slight bow and I replied in kind, equal to equal.

"You'll want to know about The Doucette," he continued with brisk efficiency. "French merchantman, fat little crayer. Slow in the water but holds more than seems possible for her size."

"A witness claims he saw Mistress Vernon and a companion boarding The Doucette the day she vanished. Can you verify that?"

"I cannot. Nor can any of my lads. Might've happened, but I doubt it. Would've been noticed. And remembered."

His words were balm to my frustrated temper but before I could rejoice I had another tack to follow.

"What of The Doucette's captain?"

"Know him a little," Coterel volunteered. "Not a bad sort. For a Frenchie. Sometimes share a jug with him when he's in town."

"Think he's the type to abduct a maiden?" I asked, unconsciously adopting Coterel's truncated manner of speaking.

As he considered his answer he frowned, drawing his extravagant brows together to form a monstrous hairy arch that framed his eyes.

"Unlikely. But possible. Yet to what end?"

That is a very good question, I thought but did not say.

"Does he have money troubles?" I ventured.

Coterel shook his head.

"Not that I know. Never ducks his turn to pay for our wine, I'll say that. For what it's worth, he has a daughter. She must be sixteen or seventeen years. His heart's delight, that's what she is."

Not following his train of thought, I spoke with impatience.

"What of it?"

"Just that I would not expect such a fond father to dirty his hands in anything that harmed a lass little older than his own girl," he explained gruffly, clearly uncomfortable to be required to speak a full sentence for once.

Now I comprehended what he was trying to tell me. Though he could not substantiate it with hard facts, Coterel was convinced the French captain had not connived in Eleanor's abduction.

"Could someone have brought Mistress Vernon aboard the ship without his knowledge?" I asked.

"Not a chance. Every scrap of space was loaded with goods. Would have been nowhere to hide the lass. Except in his cabin."

"Then in your opinion there's no truth in the tale that Mistress Vernon left Southampton by ship?" I persisted, fully expecting Coterel to concur.

His answer set my enquiry on its head.

"I'd not say that," he replied. "Just that she was not aboard The Doucette. But she might've left on the Hanseatic hulk. Don't remember its name."

I stared at Coterel, dazed incomprehension slowly giving way to a searing rush of clarity.

"There was another ship in port that day," I stated rather than asked, and the official nodded his agreement.

"But why has no one mentioned this to me until now?" I bellowed, furious disbelief overcoming my instinct to regard Coterel as an ally.

Happily, he seemed not to object to my ill-mannered raging.

"Can't speak for others. As for myself, you enquired about The Doucette. "

As he spoke the realisation dawned on me that he was right. I could hardly blame him for not mentioning a second ship when all my interest had been focused on the French merchantman. Someone had been very careful to make sure The Doucette was the sole target for any investigation into Eleanor's abduction – for abduction was, I was now convinced, the correct way to describe her sudden disappearance. Putting the facts together, I saw that the pedlar had been paid to take his malicious lies about Eleanor to Beaulieu so that the pious abbot would call off his search. Placing her on the departing Doucette ensured nobody would start sniffing around the other ship that had been in port that day. So who had bribed the pedlar, and why had they been so keen to deflect interest in the Hanseatic vessel? For the first question I had no answer other than a vague suspicion of Clarence but for the second, I had an uneasy feeling that the answer was all too apparent.

The thought of Eleanor in the hands of foreign ruffians turned my blood to ice. Coterel must have sensed my discomposure for without comment he summoned an assistant to take his place at the table and then suggested in a friendly manner that we take a cup of wine together. Grateful for his quiet perception, I agreed and went with him from the quay, remembering at the last to leave word for Matthew to find me at The George.

Over a jug of surprisingly acceptable Gascon, Coterel told me the little he knew about the Hanseatic vessel. Although not unheard of, it was rare, he said, for ships from such parts to call at Southampton and when they did they put in to the Watergate Quay, some distance from his own sphere of influence at the West Quay. When I asked him to take me to the official responsible for the Watergate he became sombre. It transpired that the man, a friend of Coterel's called Robert Gower, had been discovered floating in the harbour the day after the ship left port. At the time his death had been regarded as accidental, Gower having become renowned for excessive drinking since the death of his wife in childbed. Now both Coterel and I smelt foul play in the drowning, particularly since Gower's ledgers were nowhere to be found. Not only had someone taken pains to prevent the man from speaking of anything he might have seen, they had also removed the record of the Hanseatic ship's sojourn in Southampton.

From talk he had overhead about the town, Coterel believed the hulk had been Danzig-bound but that was all he could tell me. That and the fact that it had left port on the first day of June, a full day after The Doucette. I nearly wept when he said this, knowing that Eleanor might have been discovered if only John Piers had extended the search for her by twenty-four hours.

My spirits at low ebb, I was eyeing the wine jug with avid intent when Coterel saved me from over-indulgence with a casual suggestion.

"Your best bet is Nicholas Bonvylle. Ask him about the Danzig ship. He knows everything that happens in this place. More than likely, he will have bought its cargo."

Seeing that his words had heartened me, he made his excuses, anxious to return to his post before the arrival of the anticipated vessel. Giving him heartfelt thanks for his help, I watched him go with strange reluctance. I did not wish to be alone with my thoughts. Luckily, before I became too maudlin Matthew appeared with news of his own. An apothecary in Bugle Street confirmed that he had supplied the Bonvylles with a remedy for sickness that very morning. Glad to have my suspicions about the merchant allayed, I allowed Matthew to drain the dregs from the wine jug before taking him to the castle for a decent dinner at Berkeley's table.

After sleeping off the wine at The Mermaid, we returned to the Bonvylles' house earlier than arranged. This was deliberate, for the merchant's indisposition had irritated me and, pettily, I hoped to pay him back by arriving before he was ready. This small-mindedness backfired on me when the manservant responded to my knock with alacrity. Leaving Matthew to wait in the store room, he ushered me upstairs to the family's private quarters without delay.

Entering a spacious hall bedecked with painted wall hangings, I was greeted by a handsome woman who, by my reckoning, was only just the right side of child-bearing age. Tall and lean with grey eyes, thin lips and prominent cheek bones, she was saved from a shrewish appearance by the softness of her complexion and the sweetness of her smile.

Introducing herself as Agnes Bonvylle, she despatched the manservant to fetch her husband and then beckoned me to the far end of the hall where a linen-draped table was laden with costly pewter and silverware. As she poured me some unwanted refreshment I was able to admire her gown of green figured damask and the jewelled collar around her narrow throat. Though it was a finer ensemble than some I had seen worn by the Duchess Anne and her ladies at Middleham, I was not overly surprised that she dressed above her rank. Merchants of substance often flaunted their success in such ways, deeming any fines they received for breaking the sumptuary laws a small price to pay for proclaiming their wealth to the world.

I was about to compliment her on the comfort of her living arrangements when her husband arrived, a flabby bear of a man with prematurely greyed hair and paunchy cheeks. Studying his face for signs of sickness, I conceded that it had an unhealthy sheen and dark circles were evident beneath his friendly blue eyes. As for his wife, I detected no such signs on her face but then women, I knew, had their own ways of disguising these things. Not that any I knew would ever admit to it.

"Master Cranley," Bonvylle boomed, clasping a flaccid arm about my shoulders as though greeting a dear old friend. "A thousand apologies for not seeing you this morning. I know Thomas explained the situation. Thanks be to God that our apothecary knows how to settle a stomach unsettled by tainted meat. Though how we came to be served it, I cannot imagine. In this house our servants are given lavish funds to buy the best provender available, is that not so, Agnes, my dear? If I discover our cook has been cheating us by buying cheap, I'll whip the devil from here to Portsmouth!"

It struck me that this threat was belied by the geniality of his tone. If the cook had poisoned his employers by serving them meat sourced from an unreliable quarter, Bonvylle would be justified in punishing him with the utmost severity, yet he spoke as though the matter were a joke. Seeing my perplexity, his wife intervened.

"Nicholas is a fond master, Master Cranley" she explained. "Most of our servants have been with us for years and are part of our family. Indeed some came with me when Nicholas and I were wed and thus I have known them from girlhood. We know their worth and value them accordingly. The meat was an honest mistake, we are in no doubt as to that. So my husband jokes when he speaks of whippings!"

Husband and wife exchanged a smile so full of amused fondness that I felt a pang for my own solitary condition. Yet if Eleanor could be found, might I not one day share such moments with her?

With this thought in mind, I launched without preamble into the purpose of my visit. Though both Bonvylles recollected Eleanor's visit, they told me they had not seen her themselves, having been occupied already with another visitor, a customer of great wealth and stature who demanded their full attention.

"It has long since troubled me that we were unable to attend to Mistress Vernon ourselves," Agnes Bonvylle confided. "Had we done so, I would have made sure to send one of our people with her when she left us, for her protection. But alas, she called here at the most inopportune moment when there was none other than poor Jane to see to her needs."

"Why poor Jane?" I queried, and Mistress Bonvylle answered with a smile that was no less sweet for its sadness.

"She blames herself for not giving Mistress Vernon an escort back to the monks. Though quiet enough at present, Southampton can be a rough place, Master Cranley, especially down by the docks. It is unsafe for a gently bred lady to go there unchaperoned and Jane knows it. I have tried my best to tell her she is not at fault but she is no fool. I fear it is a heavy burden for one so young."

Further questioning revealed that Jane was distant kin to Nicholas Bonvylle. She seemed to occupy that most uncomfortable position in any household, being neither servant nor yet quite family. An orphan, she had come to live with the childless couple when she was ten but had never managed to make the leap from penniless connection to substitute daughter.

"We do our best for her, of course we do," Bonvylle was at pains to stress, "but though it grieves me to say it, I find I cannot feel for another man's child as I would for my own. Yet she shares my blood and for that reason we do our duty by her."

I felt a fleeting pity for this wretched Jane since her situation in life was not that far removed from my own. Even so, I knew that many orphan girls would swap places with her in an instant, life as an unloved cousin in a prosperous household being infinitely preferable to having to beg or whore to earn one's bread.

I was poised to request an interview with the girl when Agnes Bonvylle pre-empted me.

"You will need to speak with Jane, of course. I shall see that you do so in privacy as soon as she returns."

"Returns?" I repeated foolishly. "From where?"

"Our house in the country. I will be going there next month for a few weeks, as I do every summer. Last year I found it badly aired and generally in a lamentable state so this time I sent Jane on ahead to supervise the work. Guessing you would wish to question her, we despatched a messenger to bring her home immediately. She has not far to come, we expect her on the morrow."

The delay was a nuisance but in truth I did not feel inclined to grumble. In spite of their recent indisposition the Bonvylles had been open and accommodating with me, to the extent that I was now sorry for my former surliness and was glad that their man Thomas had borne the brunt of it. Agnes Bonvylle's admission that she thought often about Eleanor and regretted that she had been unable to attend to her on that fateful day struck me as sincere. I confess that it warmed me, as did the deep marital affection that neither Bonvylle made any effort to disguise. Though I was inclined to like them, I knew that if I stayed longer in their company I would begin to begrudge them their felicity. A felicity I might have known with Margaret had I not been such a worthless fool, a self-righteous voice whispered inside my head before I banished it to hell.

Declining an invitation to sup with the Bonvylles on the spurious grounds that I was engaged elsewhere, I collected Matthew and headed back to The Mermaid where I planned to drink my cares away. Instead I found myself confronted by the innkeeper in a more than usually sour temper.

"Bed and board is all your money gets you. Anything else will cost you more."

I knew not what the old villain meant by this and told him as much in a few sharp words.

"Taking messages. Passing them along. I am busy enough without all that carry on. You want the message, you pay me extra."

He rubbed together the thumb and forefinger of his good hand in a gauche attempt to drive home his meaning. We shall see about that, I thought, angered by his mercenary ways.

"What message has been left for me?" I demanded, drawing my rondel dagger and resting its tip against his scraggy windpipe. "Tell me, and we can yet be friends."

This gentle persuasion was enough to coax from him the news that I was wanted at Netley. Peter of Keverne had been found.

Chapter Nine

Peter had not been Eleanor's lover, I was certain of that, but I could not ignore the coincidence of his disappearance so soon after hers. It might be that he had been involved, either directly or indirectly. If not, perhaps he had seen something pertaining to her abduction while he was doing whatever it was that had taken him from Netley for so long. I knew, therefore, that I must question the novice without delay.

Leaving Matthew to settle with the unpleasant innkeeper and gather together our belongings, I hastened to the castle to inform Berkeley that I was quitting Southampton for the moment but would return presently. It had never been my habit to explain my comings and goings to anyone save my lord of Gloucester but since I was in Southampton on the King's business I felt the courtesy was required of me. Besides, it behoved me to keep Berkeley friendly in case I needed a favour from him. These pleasantries concluded, I made for The Mermaid's stables where Matthew was waiting with the horses.

As we journeyed back to Netley I gave Matthew a summary of my interview with the Bonvylles.

"To be thorough I must return and question the girl when she has returned," I concluded, "but I doubt she can shed any more light on the affair than her employers have done."

Matthew sucked his teeth and said nothing. I knew this trick of his. It signalled that he had something to say and was waiting for me to prompt him. As usual, I refused to oblige him. As usual, after a short delay he chose to speak anyway.

"Mark my words, the lass is dead already. Your merchant fellow is hiding something and has done away with her to keep it hid. That's why you couldn't see her."

His fanciful words did not surprise me; indeed, I had expected something of the sort. My servant was a good lad but he had the fault of always thinking the worst of those in possession of money or power.

"You know what your trouble is?" I chided him. "You never trust the fine folk. What you need to remember is that you are an ignorant churl who doesn't know what he's talking about."

"Well, I trust you, master," he told me, wilfully turning a deaf ear to the second part of my speech. "But then, I wouldn't call you proper fine folk."

He beamed at me as though he had paid me an extravagant compliment and I found myself laughing at his innocent impudence.

"Then if you trust me, lad, trust my judgement of the Bonvylles. My instincts are rarely awry in these matters. The wife leads her husband by the nose, of that I have little doubt, but that does him no disservice since she is as clever as she is amiable."

Matthew looked as though he would speak again but now, having had my fill of his audacity I asserted my authority and checked him with a sharp word.

"I'm sure you know best," he said with poorly feigned meekness, and there of necessity the discussion ended for we had reached the abbey.

At the gatehouse we were met by a sombre Brother Walter who hurried us without a word to the abbot's lodging.

"You are good to come, Master Cranley," Father Marmaduke greeted me as we entered his private hall. "This is a sorry business indeed."

"Where is Peter?" I enquired without preamble since I was chafing to speak with the young scoundrel.

Brother Walter pulled a strange face.

"In one of our storerooms. We thought it best to hide him there for now."

To keep the reprobate from polluting his fellow novices with tales of his antics, I surmised silently.

"How does he account for his absence?" I asked as we skirted the chapter house and made our way to the cellarium. "What does he have to say for himself?"

Both men stopped and stared at me as if my wits had taken wing. After a moment the novice master dropped his jaw as though comprehending something of great surprise, leaving the abbot to explain.

"He says nothing, Master Cranley, for he is dead."

Now it was my turn to gape like a fish on a slab. The message Old Stumpy had relayed to me was that Peter of Keverne had been found, whereas the message that had been left for me was that the lad had been found murdered. The old devil had omitted to give me that important detail and I had no doubt that he had done it deliberately, out of malice. Well, he would pay for that in due course but first there was work to be done.

The corpse lay on a pallet on the floor, wrapped in a length of old sacking which, the abbot told me, was how he had been found. From the doorway I was assailed by a distinctive stench that told me this was no recent death. Edging forwards with my nose and mouth covered by a cloth thoughtfully provided by Brother Walter, I pulled away the sacking and examined what remained of the once handsome young novice.

Though I have a strong stomach I confess even I was disturbed by the sight. The corpse was greenish-black and seeping foul fluids like a fruit left to moulder in the sun. As I peered closer I discerned here and there gobbets of decayed flesh gaping open where sharp teeth had torn at them, exposing the pale bone and viscera beneath.

Following my lead the abbot looked too, groaning aloud as he saw what I saw.

"What unholy fiend did this?" he croaked, clutching at Brother Walter's stout arm for support.

"Animals, Father, only animals. But rest easy, your novice was not bitten to death, either by man or by beast. These wounds were inflicted after his death."

"God be praised," the ashen-faced abbot breathed before turning his head from the terrible sight.

"My guess is that his body was disturbed by something on the scent of a meal," I ventured. "A fox, perhaps."

"He was discovered by dogs," Brother Walter informed me. "Brother Wulfric keeps a few for catching rabbits. He was out with them this morning when the dogs found poor Peter in a shallow grave."

"Yet some of these marks are not fresh," I commented, peering more closely at the wounds despite the stench. "I'd say the hounds had uncovered the corpse before today and were returning to feast anew before they were called off."

The novice master signalled his agreement.

"Aye, that's likely. Wulfric says the torso was already part exposed when he caught up with the dogs."

"But how then was he killed?"

I did not reply at once to the abbot's question for I was studying the remains for signs of violence inflicted by man rather than beast. While it was possible that Peter had died of natural causes, the hasty nature of his burial indicated otherwise. Scanning the corpse face up, I saw no obvious cause of death so I summoned Matthew and together we turned it, revealing a sticky mass of splintered bone where the back of the skull had once been.

"Head staved in from behind," I remarked. "Terrible injury. The lad never stood a chance. Whoever did this used considerable force. Where was he found?"

Father Marmaduke slumped to his knees, his face buried in his hands.

"It's my fault," he moaned, "all my fault. I never should have given the fellow leave to stay."

"What man?" I snapped, brought to impatience by the abbot's histrionics. "Peter?

"Not Peter, no," Brother Walter replied, crouching as low as his portly frame would allow in order to comfort his superior. "Father Marmaduke speaks of Gilbert Aldis. Peter was found buried behind his cottage."

"Where is this Aldis now? And why should he not have been given leave to stay?"

Roused by the irritation in my voice, the abbot raised his eyes to my face.

"Ten years ago Aldis came to us with a sick wife and two small children. A carpenter by trade, he had been dismissed from the Southampton Craft Guild for laying violent hands on a fellow member. But Aldis swore his innocence, claiming he'd only struck the man to protect his wife from the man's lascivious advances. His hand rested upon our most sacred relic as he swore so I had no choice but to believe him. In any case the whole family was in a piteous state, the children cold and hungry and their mother near to death. I let them stay with us while we cared for her in the infirmary.

"Despite our prayers God did not spare her. Aldis was then left with children to feed and no means to support them. What was I to do? Turn them away and let those innocents starve? Perhaps I should have done, yet I could not think it was what God wanted. We had a cottage standing empty, halfway between here and the ferry. All it needed was a little effort to make it habitable. Out of Christian charity I told Aldis he could live there and pay for his rent by performing occasional repairs around the abbey."

There was a shiftiness in the abbot's manner as he spoke which I interpreted with ease. For all his talk of charity, he knew he had secured a fine bargain when he had acquired the services of a skilled carpenter in exchange for a dilapidated hovel.

"But how did he feed his family?" I wondered out loud.

The abbot answered with defensive swiftness.

"He was not with us every day. When we had no work for him he was at liberty to look for it elsewhere. I believe he managed very well in that regard."

Thinking about it, I could find little fault with the arrangement which had been of benefit to both parties. A single thought occurred to me.

"Did you verify his story in Southampton?"

"We did."

Brother Walter spoke now, the abbot having lapsed into taciturnity.

"With no witness to the assault it was the word of one man against the other. They did not say as much but we understood that the Guild sided with the other fellow for no other reason than that he had influential kin. But whatever the truth of the matter, Aldis never gave us reason to regret helping him."

"Until now," Matthew put in helpfully.

Hiding a grin, I asked something that had been nagging at me since learning that Peter of Keverne was dead.

"Why did you send for me? I cannot question a corpse about Mistress Vernon's disappearance, so what do you want of me?"

"We need you to bring the carpenter to justice. We want you to fetch him from his cottage and bring him here to answer for his action."

I snorted, disliking the notion that I was to be at the beck and call of these irksome monks. My duty was to locate the whereabouts of Mistress Vernon. That was why I had come south and I did not see that embroiling myself in this separate matter would bring me closer to achieving that aim.

"I cannot. I am making good progress in Southampton," I exaggerated, "and must return before the trail goes cold once more."

"Reconsider, I beg you," Brother Walter wheedled. "We need your assistance in this matter. Prayer is our business, not violence, and you have seen the damage Aldis wrought to Peter."

"Take staves and ropes," I advised him, unmoved by his pleading. "And your strongest lay brothers. You have more than enough to overpower him."

"Mayhap we do, though some at least would be injured in the attempt. Come now, surely you cannot refuse our request, Master Cranley? You are entrusted by our beloved King to bear his warrant, surely a sign that he holds you in high regard. Would not that regard falter if he knew you had spurned our plea for help?"

Aware that the wily old fox was threatening me, I chuckled to myself, knowing as he did not that I had no standing whatsoever with the King. Any authority I currently possessed was of a temporary nature and was entirely due to my friendship with his favourite brother. Nevertheless, I realised that if Netley made a complaint about me to the crown it would reflect badly on Dickon.

Accepting defeat, I agreed to fetch Aldis but first I wished to clarify something.

"You are certain, then, that the carpenter is responsible for Peter's death?"

"Not certain, no. But Peter was buried behind his house, and the man has a history of assault. That is cause enough to suspect him," the abbot reasoned.

I agreed. Aldis very likely was the killer but even so, if I was to bring him in I wanted to know that he would be treated fairly.

"Just don't let him hang until you are fully satisfied," I enjoined the abbot and, rather to my surprise, he signalled his agreement.

"That is fair. Aldis may not be the culprit. He has a son, after all, and a daughter, too, come to that."

Here the novice master interjected.

"The son is long gone, I believe. He left to ply his trade as an itinerant carpenter, so Aldis told me."

"Well, whoever dealt that blow possessed great strength," I volunteered, gesturing towards Peter's smashed skull. "I'd be surprised if a girl could do it. What is the daughter like? Is she a hefty wench?"

Brother Walter shot a look at Father Marmaduke and shrugged his pudgy shoulders.

"I cannot say," he mumbled, a little resentfully, I thought. "I have not seen her for some years. None of us have"

Father Marmaduke closed his eyes in exaggerated exasperation and then slowly reopened them.

"While she was still small she was welcome here," he explained carefully. "She came sometimes with her father, playing in the dirt until she was needed to hand him some tool or other. It brought me joy to see her growing strong and healthy, for she had been such a pathetic scrap with no more than a wisp of life about her when the family first arrived. In truth I believe she became a favourite of us all, for she was a good and quiet child, always ready with a pleasing smile. But when she reached womanhood I told Aldis to keep her away and he agreed. He had little choice, for I made it plain that it was agree or leave Netley."

Recalling the Abbot's obsession with impropriety – real or imaginary – I had no problem comprehending why he had banned the girl from the abbey. And I knew he had probably acted wisely, since monks are only men, after all, and vows of chastity are easily broken when temptation beckons. Yet it must have been hard for the girl to be petted by the monks one day and rejected by them the next.

Taking Brother Wulfric to show us the way, Matthew and I left the abbey and rode the short distance to the carpenter's modest dwelling. At a nod from me, Matthew stole around the house and took up position at the rear whilst I strode forward ready to hammer at the door. Before I could do so, however, the door was flung wide revealing a girl, heavily with child, standing red-eyed on the threshold. Her first words caught me off balance.

"Have you caught him?"

There was dread in her voice but a hint of bitterness, too.

"Your father? No, we have not caught him. We thought to find him here."

The girl's face crumpled at these words and she opened her arms wide in a gesture of despair.

"He's gone," she told me, "but you must look for yourself if you don't believe me."

I followed her into the cottage, stifling the surge of pity that threatened to overwhelm me as I took in the sparse furnishings. There was a stool, a cooking pot by the unlit fire, a bench that doubled as a table and, in the far corner, a lumpy pallet on the floor. Though it was no worse than many such hovels I had seen, the emptiness seemed to exacerbate the girl's solitude to an unbearable degree.

"He took all we had of value," she remarked with a sniffle, lowering herself gingerly onto the stool. "Even my cup and blanket. Said it was my fault he had to run, so I was not to argue. As if I would! I know what happens to them that does."

So my prey had fled. It did not surprise me; he had likely observed Brother Wulfric removing Peter's corpse and guessed what next to expect.

Seating myself at the bench, I fixed the girl with a searching gaze. In other circumstances she might have been pretty but now, with her big belly and tired eyes she did not make an enticing sight.

"What is your name?" I asked gently.

The question seemed to startle her and it was a moment before she mumbled a reply.

"Alys, sir."

"Well, Alys Aldis, you must not fear me but you must tell me the truth. Did your father kill the man known as Peter of Keverne?"

She nodded meekly.

"He did, sir."

"And did he do so to avenge your rape by this Peter?"

Colour blazed in her cheeks.

"That's a lie!" she snarled, leaping to her feet with as much agility as her bulky frame would allow. "Peter never raped me!"

Taken aback, I did not at once believe her. From the first moment I had seen Alys's swollen belly I had been convinced I knew what had happened here. The lusty novice had spied the girl and raped her. From shame she had kept it from her father for as long as she could but eventually he had seen she was with child and had forced her to name the wretch responsible. And then he had taken his mallet and killed the lad. It all made sense, all except the fact that Alys was denying it.

"Then tell me what did happen," I urged her, rising and guiding her to sit beside me on the bench. "Speak the truth and no harm will come to you."

"So it's the truth you want, is it? Well then, here it is. Peter loved me. He never wanted to be a monk and never was a soul less fit to be one. He was made to love and laugh and savour life, not wither away with those old men inside a living tomb."

From what I had heard about Peter of Keverne, that part at least rang true.

"I met him one day when he had slipped away to dodge a beating. Always beating him, they were. I was wandering alone down by the Water and when I saw him I knew I had never seen such beauty before. Father was working at the Abbey so I brought Peter back here and we talked."

I must have looked sceptical because she gave an angry toss of her head.

"Doubt me if you will, sir, but that is all we did. He didn't so much as kiss me that first time. We became lovers later, aye, but when that time came I gave myself to him willingly for I loved him. That first day all I gave him was a crust of bread and a drink of water. And then I listened as he spoke about his life before coming to Netley."

A dreamy look came into her eyes.

"A fine gentleman's son he was, did you know that? He came from a life of ease and plenty and promised me that when we were wed we would return to it together. But first he had to get a letter to his father, to explain that he was innocent of the crime that had led to him being sent to Netley. Bad folk had falsely accused him, you see, but he knew his father would believe him once he read his letter."

I could tell that she had faith in every word of this nonsense.

"Why could he not send this letter?" I asked and she gave a scornful laugh.

"The monks, of course! They forbade him to write. But at last he somehow found a way to pen a letter. That was one thing, but then he needed to cajole someone to take it for him. Time was running out, for Father was looking at me strange. I joked that I was getting fat though eating too much but he was not fooled.

"The very last time I saw Peter he wept and told me he had missed a chance just the day before. A fancy lady had come on a cart from the other abbey, the big one, with some monks. She looked kind, he said, so he thought to beg her to take it for him but he never got the chance. Brother Walter was watching him too closely. So the lady left and then it was too late."

My heart leapt, for I knew the lady on the cart must have been Eleanor. Brother Walter had been right to think Peter took unusual interest in her but wrong to attribute it to lust. This troubled me as it made me realise that now I might have to reconsider the opinion I had formed of the novice.

As I continued with my questions, new sympathy for the pregnant girl encouraged me to speak with greater gentleness.

"Why was that the last time you saw him, Alys?"

Before answering, she lowered her head and under cover of her long hair wiped away some tears.

"Father watched him leave me," she said. "He had snuck home early to spy on me and was waiting behind the cottage. That bastard! He never gave poor Peter a chance to speak. Just felled him with his mallet as he walked by. Then calm as you like began to dig his grave."

The tears fell harder now.

"When I heard the sound of digging I knew what had happened. Hadn't I heard that sound before? I came screaming from the cottage and saw my poor love lying broken in the dirt."

"Why did he need to kill him?" I wondered aloud. "Surely he could have spoken with the pair of you first, to discover your plans?"

Alys gawped at me, the incredulity plain on her tear-streaked face.

"You don't know Father. When the rage takes him there's no stopping him. Besides, he feared Father Marmaduke would blame him for raising me a whore. Told me my wickedness would have cost him his place at the abbey if he hadn't dealt with Peter his own way. That's why he says it's all my fault."

She started to sob, shattered by the cruelty of these words, but then regained a measure of composure.

"But it is *his* fault," she spat. "I loved Peter and he loved me. If Father had not interfered, we would have found a way to wed. Now Peter is slain, Father is fled and how I am to survive alone with my baby I do not know!"

Overcome with despair, she hurled herself onto the lumpy pallet with such violence that I feared for the safety of her unborn child. I rose to see that she was unharmed but then froze as something she had said reverberated in my mind.

"When did you hear digging before?"

I was forced to repeat the question twice before she replied from her prone position.

"What does it matter?"

Hearing her misery, I knelt beside her and took her roughened hand.

"You know why it matters. Peter is not the first loved one your father has murdered, is he?"

She stared into my eyes and shook her head mutely.

"He killed your brother, didn't he? And then put it about that he had left home."

"They were always arguing," Alys sighed. "Gil tried to leave many times but Father always found a way to make him stay. But this time his persuasion ran out, and so he made him stay by killing him. He's buried deeper than Peter, and in a box Father had time to make. I think that's why those dogs didn't find him first."

It was a sordid business with no real connection to my search for Eleanor yet simple humanity made me feel for the girl. With her Father on the run and her brother and lover both dead, she had no one to protect her or her child. It was sad but there was nothing I could do for her save give her a few coins and some advice which, if she took it, was worth a deal more than the money.

"Listen to me, Alys," I said, tugging at her hair to force her to look at me. "I have to return to Netley now to tell them your father has fled. I must also tell them about your brother. People from the abbey will come for his remains. Very likely they will also organise a manhunt for your father. If he is found he will certainly hang, as he deserves.

"Now heed me, for this is important. You must never tell the monks that Peter was your lover; that you lay with him willingly. You must tell them that he took you by force. If they think that, I believe they will help you for they will feel some responsibility for the actions of their novice. By God, I myself will demand that they take care of you! But allow them to know the truth and they will turn their backs on you. Then you will starve, you and the babe, also. I know the abbot, as do you, so you know I speak the truth. Put away your tears. Peter is dead but his child will live if you are wise."

Leaving her then to her misery, I went back to Netley and made my report to the abbot.

Chapter Ten

At Netley there was consternation when I returned with the news that another body lay mouldering in a grave behind the carpenter's house.

"His own son!" Father Marmaduke had gasped as we supped together in his private chamber. "Such a heinous sin. It seems we have been harbouring a monster all these years. Well, now that monster must be found and prevented from sinning again. Master Cranley, will you help us?"

Having been prepared for this question, I had my answer ready.

"Gladly," I agreed cheerfully. "When I return to Southampton on the morrow I will make it my priority to inform Keeper Berkeley of this troubling matter. He will waste no time in despatching men to aid you in the search for Aldis, I promise you."

The abbot's face registered disappointment.

"I had hoped that you would stay and conduct the manhunt yourself," he grumbled.

"And so I would right gladly," I lied, "if only my duty to the King's wishes did not take precedence."

Mention of the King stifled further protests, as I had known it would, leaving Father Marmaduke no choice but to accept my offer to act as his messenger with a fair attempt at good grace.

Now, having extricated myself from a prolonged stay at Netley, I faced the task of persuading the abbot to shoulder responsibility for his novice's unborn child.

"It is a tawdry affair," the pious abbot had opined with a moue of distaste when I told him that Peter had impregnated the Aldis girl.

"No, it is much worse than that!" I barked with artificial outrage. "Your degenerate novice forced himself upon a girl against her wishes and now her life is ruined."

"Oh, as to that, can we be sure the wretched girl was innocent?" he asked, much as I expected he would.

"Without a doubt we can. For the father would have slain her, too, had he thought her culpable. The fact that he did not is all the evidence I need that your novice raped her."

I fixed the abbot with a fierce stare, willing him to accept my dubious reasoning. Seeing that he hesitated, I decided to exert a little pressure.

"Well, it is no affair of mine, after all. You must do as your conscience ordains. I am sure John Piers will support any decision you reach. He will confirm as much, I feel certain, when I visit Beaulieu before heading home to Middleham when my enquiries are complete."

This less than subtle threat to complain to the Netley abbot's superior achieved all I had been hoping for. After some half-hearted wrangling, Father Marmaduke agreed to let Alys remain rent-free in the cottage and to grant her a tiny stipend on which to raise the child. Thus I was able to put her from my mind, or I would have been had I managed to blank out the conviction that however unreliable and unruly a character Peter of Keverne had been, to Alys his intentions had been true. His thwarted attempt to pass the letter to Eleanor told me as much, and though their ill-fated love was none of my concern, it cast a pall over my spirits as I rode back to Southampton early next morning.

My first action on arrival was to report to the castle where I found Berkeley breaking his fast with fresh baked manchet and fish from the harbour. Gladly accepting his invitation to join him, having quit the abbey on an empty stomach, I apprised him of the Netley murders and passed on Father Marmaduke's request for men to hunt the fugitive. Then, recalling the score I had to settle with Old Stumpy, I told him about the innkeeper's attempt to extort money from me and how, when the attempt failed, he had exacted a petty revenge by withholding the most crucial part of the message. Berkeley did not need to be reminded that I was in his town on the King's business. Within minutes of finishing his repast he was leading an armed contingent the short distance from the castle to The Mermaid, Matthew and I strolling leisurely in their wake.

I have rarely shied away from doing my own dirty work but on this occasion I was content to wait outside as Berkeley barged inside the inn and made his displeasure known. Even so, Matthew and I were able to hear with perfect clarity every crash and thud of the ensuing ruckus. Only after the castle party had left did we venture inside to survey their handiwork. The place was a disorderly mess but I saw at once that the damage was superficial, Berkeley having followed my suggestion to give the crooked innkeeper a fright without entirely destroying his establishment. In fact the Keeper had judged his work nicely. A few tables had been upended and a jug or two smashed against the walls but nothing of real value had been harmed. The worst violence had been reserved for Old Stumpy himself; already the innkeeper's face was swollen and bloody and before long it would be turning a fetching purple hue. Watching him as he nursed a tender jaw, perhaps I should have known remorse but I confess I did not. All I felt was satisfaction that the knave would know better than to trifle with me again.

Taking again the chamber that we had previously occupied, I removed my boots and stretched out upon the bed for a short spell while Matthew fetched hot water. When he returned, I washed the summer dust from my face and hands and instructed him to do likewise before despatching him to the Bonvylle house to convey my wish to interview their young kinswoman later that day. Since I was now heading for The George where I planned to mull over my progress with a beaker of something palatable in my grasp, I told Matthew to return to me there when his message was delivered.

Bernard Gover hailed me with a friendly greeting as I entered his tavern and hurried over to my table with the news that Andrew Coterel had been asking after me. Having remembered something that might be of interest, the West Quay official had come looking for me at The George while I was at Netley, so Gover informed me. When he could not find me, he had left word for me to call on him as soon as convenient. Gladdened by the news, I thanked Gover, observing that the obliging taverner could teach Old Stumpy a great deal. Eager as I was to hear what Coterel had recalled, I lingered long enough to take a cup of costly Spanish white on the basis that the fellow's co-operation merited the recompense.

As I savoured the wine, anticipating a pleasant conversation with the likeable Coterel, I was jolted by a sudden recollection. The last time I had spoken with him, Coterel had suggested I should seek information from Nicholas Bonvylle about the mysterious Hanseatic vessel. Cursing softly, I realised I had neglected to do this; I had been so entirely charmed by the Bonvylles' domestic arrangements that I had forgotten to raise this important question. Well, it was no matter, I decided. The omission would be easily rectified when I revisited their house to speak with Jane Bonvylle.

Nevertheless, my foolish oversight had soured the wine. Throwing down some coins, I quit the tavern and went in search of Coterel, resolved to keep my wits about me from now on. It was as I was ambling down Wytegod's Lane that a sensation at the back of my neck gave me the uneasy feeling that I was being followed. Though the sun was high in the sky, there was precious little daylight in the narrow lane and amongst its deep shadows there were places enough for an assailant to lurk. Spinning around, I saw no one as I scanned the lane but my ears picked up a slight rustling that stopped almost the moment I became aware of it. Rats, I decided, even though the prickling at my neck continued. Picking up my speed, I was glad to burst into the clamorous safety of the West Quay.

Coterel's canopy was in its usual place but to my frustration there was no sign of the man himself. Enquiring after him, I was informed that the master had gone to his house in Bugle Street for dinner. Since this was a short distance away, rather than wait for his return I decided to call upon him there. It proved to be a fateful decision. As I retraced my steps up Wytegod's Lane a figure emerged from the shadows and in short order I found myself on the wrong end of a rondel dagger not dissimilar to my own. Though slender, the long blade looked keen and was aimed too close to my heart for me to feel sanguine. Its owner's first words did little to reassure me.

"What have you done with Eleanor?" he demanded, speaking in a shaky though determined voice that stirred a distant memory within me. "Answer, or I skewer you here and now!"

Retreating a pace, less from fear than from surprise at the ludicrous nature of this threat, I stepped into a sudden shaft of sunlight that had penetrated the lane's gloom, enabling me to make out my assailant.

"I know you!" I cried. "You're the twitchy weasel that fled from Tyrell in Winchester."

Perhaps the insult was unwise, for the dagger's tip pierced the fabric of my doublet and rested a whisper's breadth from my flesh. Ignoring it, I fixed the man with my sincerest gaze.

"Put down your weapon," I ordered. "You have no quarrel with me if you seek Mistress Vernon."

Far from soothing him, mention of Eleanor's name galvanised the stranger into action. Withdrawing his dagger – which I interpreted as an indication that he had no intention of killing me before discovering what I knew – he sprang at me with his free arm thrust forward to grab my throat. His actions were too slow and too easy to predict. Side-stepping him with ease, I thrust out a leg and tripped him so that he fell, sprawling, at my feet. Now it was my turn to rest a dagger against his skin.

"Need some help there, master?" came a cheery voice. Glancing up, I saw Matthew approaching from the top of the lane, having learnt of my likely whereabouts from Gover at The George. Together we pulled the stranger to his feet and between us manhandled him to the castle where I found Berkeley and informed him that I had a suspect to question. His countenance alight, he urged me to make use of one his men, a specialist in extracting information from unwilling informants. Hurriedly I declined the offer, explaining that I preferred to do such work myself. Accepting this as one of my foibles, the Keeper made over a small cell for my use and then made himself scarce.

At first my captor would not speak. Studying him across a rough hewn table I saw a man with an honest face that was currently cloaked in hostility. In all other respects his features were unremarkable. He had pride, I could tell, but at present it lay in tatters, brought low by the ignominy of his defeat in Wytegod's Lane. Whatever his faults, this was a man of honour. Strangely, I felt moved to pity him. Making a rapid judgment I despatched Matthew to bring food and drink and when it arrived, I sat with my prisoner and ate with him. As I had hoped, the companionable nature of this action thawed him sufficiently to answer my questions.

"William Vernon was my boyhood friend," he said when I enquired about his interest in Eleanor, "and I plan to wed his sister when I find her. If it happens that she is still alive. And if she will have me."

He glowered at me then, so I refilled his wine cup and proffered it to him.

"Stop scowling and drink up," I instructed, pouring another cup for myself. I needed the wine for steadiness, for in my head I was hearing again Eleanor's words as we had ridden together at Beaulieu. She had spoken of her brother who had died fighting for Warwick at Barnet, and of a hopeless suitor who fled to France in the battle's aftermath. The recollection of how teasing and merry she had been that day weighed heavy on my spirits.

"You are Ralph Abney," I said, noting with satisfaction the fellow's confusion at my knowledge. "You were with the Countess of Warwick when she learned of her husband's fate at Barnet. She sent you away to avoid capture and a traitor's death."

"She did," he agreed, "but I would never have gone had it not also been Eleanor's wish. Her interest in my welfare gave me a reason to live."

Poor dullard, I thought, guessing that any hope Eleanor had given him had been unintentional. Or else she had said whatever was needful to make him flee. Yet now he had returned.

"Has the King pardoned you?" I asked abruptly.

Abney's face fell.

"Not yet. I came back from France intent on seeking his pardon but first I had to see Eleanor. It was reckless, I admit, but I do not care. I have dreamed of asking her to be my wife every day for three years and could wait no longer. My ship put in at Folkestone. I was making my way from there to Beaulieu when I encountered you and your friends at Winchester. I thought travelling in company would make me less conspicuous, yet had I known Tyrell was one of your party I should never have spoken."

"Why does Tyrell frighten you?" I enquired, remembering Abney's ungainly flight when he learned that Sir James rode with us.

"He does not frighten me!" Abney retorted with hot indignation. "But he knows me, and would have known there is a price on my head. There is a long-standing feud between his family and mine, a dispute caused by a dowry that was not paid three generations back or some such folly. In truth I believe no one recalls the real reason for the quarrel but that matters little. In my family it has long been lore that Tyrells are not to be trusted."

"So you fled lest Sir James turn you in," I mused. "A pity, for I believe you wrong him. Had you told him of your intention to petition the King for a pardon, I daresay he would have left you at liberty."

In reality I was nowhere near as certain about this as I maintained but, liking Tyrell as I did, I hoped I was right. Abney snorted, clearly unconvinced by my words.

"Once I knew you and Tyrell were Beaulieu bound, I realised I must alter my plans so I changed direction and made for my estate in Derbyshire. It is the King's now, of course," he added with a frown, "but Abneys have lived and died there for centuries and there are folk in the vicinity that remain loyal to me. I lay low with good friends while they borrowed gold on my behalf, for if I know anything about King Edward it is that a pardon will cost me."

Loyal as I was to Edward, I could not refute this allegation. There was no denying that money spoke at his court.

"Raising the gold took time but at last it was done. My friends despatched an intermediary to make my case before the King, leaving me with nothing to do but wait for news. The enforced idleness did not suit me. Though my friends counselled against it, I thought I would attempt to see Eleanor once more. I knew I ran a risk before my pardon was assured but I could wait no longer."

His face darkened as he recounted the rest of his story.

"At Beaulieu I learned that she had vanished into nowhere just days after the arrival of you and Tyrell. The monks told me the two of you were in London when it happened but I doubted it, knowing that where Tyrells tread, foul play must follow. And the gossip was that you, Cranley, had shown a marked fancy for Eleanor, giving me reason to suspect you, also."

"Believing Tyrell untrustworthy, you made the same judgement about me," I finished for him. "You think we feigned our visit to London in order to snatch Eleanor for some malign purpose of our own?"

I had been speaking lightly when I began but my anger mounted as I appreciated the enormity of Abney's wrongheaded conviction.

"You think I ravished her, is that it?" I demanded, kicking away my stool and grabbing Abney by the throat. "And what then? Did I murder her and fling her body in Southampton Water? Is this what you believe?"

Relaxing my grip, I pushed him away in disgust and he stumbled to the floor.

"I did believe that, aye," he declared with undaunted spirit, "but swear it is not so and I will believe you, for despite your rough handling of me I think you are a decent man."

Unexpectedly I laughed, amused to hear an accusation of rough handling from a person who but an hour earlier had threatened to stab me through the heart.

"Here," I said, producing the King's warrant that authorised my search for Eleanor. "Read this and then say if you mistrust me still."

When he had done reading he put the warrant down and glanced up at me.

"Your pardon, Cranley. I see I have been mistaken. Earlier, when I saw you riding into Southampton with your servant, my blood churned as I imagined all kinds of evil. I thought you were returning here to ensure no trace of your crime remained. Or, assuming that she yet lives, that you had come to sport some more with my poor Eleanor."

I sighed, saddened and exasperated in equal measure that the Abneys' quarrel with the Tyrells should be so bitter as to make this fool condemn without cause any associate of Sir James. However, realising that that his mind was unsettled by grief I was inclined to forgive him, not least because his grief was sure to increase in the event that Eleanor was safely recovered. She would choose me over him, of that I had no doubt.

Discarding these thoughts for the moment, I told Abney that I did not intend to disclose his true identity to Berkeley.

"With his wife's voracious family to please, the King needs every penny he can get," I quipped, "so why should I deny him the ransom raised by your pardon? When we are done here you are free to go, though I urge you to stay out of trouble until you are safe."

Grinning, Abney thanked me and begged my forgiveness once more for thinking ill of me. In this new spirit of friendliness, I decided to share with him everything I had discovered thus far about the events leading up to Eleanor's disappearance, concluding with my fruitless interviews with the Bonvylles.

"I doubt there is more to learn from that quarter but I will speak with their girl all the same," I trailed away, noting that Abney had stiffened when he heard the Bonvylle name.

"Bonvylle, you say? The merchant Nicholas Bonvylle?"

"Aye, the very same. What of it?"

"Perhaps nothing. But I'll wager there is something you do not know about him."

Turning his head rapidly about the confined space, he leaned in close to me.

"Can we be overheard?" he whispered.

I shook my head.

"I think not. In any case, Berkeley runs the castle and he is trustworthy."

"I do not doubt it," Abney replied, still barely audible, "but I have heard enough about Bonvylle to make me careful. He is a powerful man, Cranley, with enough wealth to place spies wherever he wants them. Even here in the castle. It were better I tell you what I know in silence."

Like a mummer in a play, he pressed his thumb and forefinger together and waggled them up and down through the air in an attempt, I guessed, to mimic writing. The effect was comical but nevertheless I was intrigued enough to give him what he wanted. Summoning Matthew, I bade him locate Berkeley's scribe and pester him for writing materials.

As we waited for him to return we engaged in harmless discourse, mostly mocking the new horned headdress which was winning favour with certain ladies whose vanity when it came to fashion apparently exceeded their sense of the ridiculous. Sharing laughter with Abney, I realised I little cared that he had sided with the traitor Warwick and was, moreover, a rival for Eleanor's hand. All I saw in him at that moment was a likeable fellow, a trifle dull-witted but agreeable nonetheless, a companion with whom it was no hardship to while away a morning. I would never have guessed that he was about to give me the means to unlocking this baffling mystery.

When Matthew returned laden with inkpot, paper and quill, Abney set to work, scratching away in a clumsy hand until a short sentence appeared on the parchment. He passed it to me, I read it, and my first faint glimmer of understanding dawned.

Chapter Eleven

Telling Berkeley that I had found my captive guilty of nothing more reprehensible than inebriation, I removed Abney from the castle before the Keeper could discover he had a traitor in his midst. With Matthew at my shoulder we pushed through the crowded streets to The George where I consigned Abney to Bernard Gover's sake-keeping before sallying forth once more in search of Andrew Coterel. This time as I walked down Wytegod's Lane I made sure to have one hand on my dagger and my sturdy servant at my back in case an assailant more adroit than Eleanor's forlorn suitor should be lurking there.

I was pleased to find Coterel back at his post, supervising the unloading of a newly arrived vessel, a fat little cog laden with wines from Bordeaux and fine Arras tapestries. Hard pressed to keep an eye on this costly cargo, he nevertheless broke off from his ledgers when he saw me, beckoning me forward with an ink-smudged hand.

"Been pondering something," he began without preamble, raising his voice to be heard above the quayside clamour. "Your lass, Mistress Vernon. What became of her purchases?"

I made no answer, pole-axed by the realisation that it had never occurred to me to ask this question. The shameful truth was that I had not given any thought at all to the goods Eleanor had come to Southampton to purchase, not even when I had been questioning the Bonvylles. Appalled at the omission, I berated myself for being a senseless lump.

Misinterpreting my silence, Coterel hastened to clarify his meaning.

"She had much to purchase, you said. Two new cloaks, stuff for gowns. Other womanly necessities. Too heavy to carry herself, hey? Bonvylle must have helped her. Sent a strong lad with her to the Abbey wool house."

"But he did not," I breathed, grateful to Coterel for his clear thinking but still furious at my own abject failings.

"According to the Bonvylles, Jane – the impoverished cousin who lives with them – attended to Mistress Vernon. They say Jane blames herself for not sending a chaperon with Eleanor when she left. That's how we can be certain she was unaccompanied when she left them."

"Well then. Perhaps the goods were delivered later. On a cart," Coterel offered.

"If that were the case, Brother Christopher would have mentioned it when he returned to Beaulieu," I insisted, "yet he did not."

Convinced that Coterel had lighted upon something important, I was eager to pursue where it led. Having planted the thought in my mind, however, my co-operative friend now seemed anxious for me not to raise my hopes unduly.

"Could mean nothing, Cranley. Maybe the lass bought little. Managed to carry it herself. It is possible, you know."

But Coterel was wrong about that. I knew, as he could not, that Eleanor had been craving finery for too long to resist buying up every last length of velvet, damask, broadcloth and taffeta that Dickon's angels would afford.

Lost in anguished reverie, I was brought back by a cough from Coterel.

"Well, thought it worth a mention," he said, eyeing his ledgers with longing.

Taking his hint, I thanked him and retreated to my chamber in The Mermaid to contemplate the implications of the missing goods. Turning it every which way, I could not escape the conclusion that Eleanor had made no purchases that fateful day. Had she done so, the goods would have been delivered to the wool house. And since I knew beyond doubt that she had visited the Bonvylles, it followed that something must have befallen her while she was with them. Could she have been poisoned by refreshments, I wondered, recalling the spoiled meat that had apparently laid the Bonvylles low. If so, then it was their cook I should be questioning. I shuddered at the thought, recalling a previous encounter with a malevolent cook that had ended in calamity. Yet even as this notion played across my mind I knew there was a more sinister force behind Eleanor's disappearance than a dangerous servant. With Abney's revelation pounding in my head, it was becoming plain to me that she had stumbled across a conspiracy with the potential to unleash mayhem across the land.

When I wearied of my solitary reflections I went looking for Matthew. I found him sitting companionably among a group of fellow guests in the inn's public area which had been set straight and now showed no sign of

Berkeley's visit. Responding to my summons, he followed me back to our chamber whereupon I began to share my thoughts with him the moment our door was shut. He listened carefully as I explained my suspicions, stopping me only once to clarify a small point. As ever, I was impressed by the ability of this former spit-boy to follow my train of thought. Peasant-bred, he had but recently begun to learn his letters and still had far to go in that regard. His speech, though, had already improved, having lost the better part of his uncouth Lincolnshire dialect. He was still sometimes mistaken for a simpleton, it was true, but only by those too dull to mark the agile mind that was masked by the bovine cast of his features.

New to the role, as my body servant Matthew was at best adequate but as a confidant he made a surprisingly acceptable substitute for one of higher birth. When I had finished speaking he considered carefully before agreeing with my conclusion that the Bonvylles must be complicit in Mistress Vernon's disappearance. Then he helped me devise a course of action. That it stood a fair chance of failure and might lead us into jeopardy appeared not to worry him. Neither did it worry me; on the contrary, the thought afforded me a measure of grim satisfaction, so bleak was my humour when I allowed myself to consider what might have befallen Eleanor.

At the hour appointed for my meeting with the Bonvylle wench, Matthew and I left The Mermaid and strode briskly through the thronged streets to the merchant's house. We were admitted again by Thomas, the manservant we had met before, and led upstairs to the well-appointed hall. Awaiting us there was a young woman, standing on her own at the far end of the hall with her back to the pewter-laden table. Without waiting for further instruction Thomas withdrew, leaving her ostensibly alone with us. I understood. Agnes Bonvylle wanted me to believe that she was honouring her promise to give me a private meeting with Jane but I was not to be deceived a second time. When I had questioned them I had allowed the Bonvylles' marital harmony and easy charm to dupe me into believing their every word; now I was wise to their guile and knew that everything I said and did in this chamber would be under secret scrutiny. It mattered not, for I was prepared.

Jane Bonvylle was plump, plain and extremely nervous. After bobbing an unsteady curtsey she launched into a rapid account of Eleanor's visit, echoing the version already given me by her mistress. As she spoke, her colourless eyes wide with fright, I battled the impulse to quiz her about Eleanor's purchases. Much as I wanted to know what had become of them, Matthew and I had agreed I should not alert the eavesdroppers to my concerns in that regard.

She finished her tale with a well-rehearsed little homily about how much she regretted her folly in letting Mistress Vernon venture back into the unsafe streets unaccompanied. Despite their insincerity her words gratified me in as much as they afforded me the opening I had been wanting. Taking her work-roughened hand in mine, I told her with great gentleness that I exonerated her from all blame in Eleanor's disappearance.

"In any case, knowing the young lady's high spirits, I believe she would have declined the offer of a chaperon," I concluded with a sad smile. "So, I beg you, trouble yourself no more on the subject."

"Aye," Matthew interjected with an approving leer. "A comely lass like you should never frown."

As his gratuitous compliment hit home her pudgy face shone with pleasure. It was superseded by relief moments later when she realised the ordeal she had so transparently been dreading was over. With downcast eyes she dipped into yet another curtsey but this time when she glanced up there was a new expression in her face, something akin to shame or regret. Good, I thought, so there is at least some hope for our plan.

"I will show you out, sir," she said, leading us from the hall and down the staircase, failing to notice as Matthew sprang in front of me so that he was walking directly behind her, according to our strategy. When she was three steps from the bottom he stumbled against her, causing her to fall and land in a soft heap of tawny flannel at the foot of the stairs. At once all contrition, he leapt to her assistance, putting an arm about her thick waist as he raised her carefully to her feet.

"There now, no harm done," he said when he saw she could stand without aid. Then, instead of releasing her he edged closer and delivered a smacking kiss to her lips before moving his mouth to her ear.

"The game is up, mistress," he whispered. "We know treachery is afoot. If you'd save yourself, meet us in the yard behind The George when darkness falls."

Not waiting for an answer, we pulled the door open and left the dumbstruck girl panting and dishevelled on the threshold.

With the first stage of our scheme accomplished, there was nothing to be done now but wait for darkness. On our way back to The Mermaid I purchased spiced pasties which we devoured in our chamber before attempting to snatch some rest. Matthew was soon snoring but sleep eluded me as I fretted as to whether the wench would come. Having met her now, I thought it likely that she would for she seemed a poor, fearful creature. Such people often possess a strong instinct for self-preservation and this was what I was gambling on. But if I had misjudged her, there was a danger she would raise the alarm with her kinsmen and if that were to happen, we might encounter more than we bargained for at our rendezvous. For a few seconds I toyed with the notion of borrowing support from Berkeley but decided against it. My theory at this stage was too wild and half-formed to present to him and though I knew he would oblige me anyhow, I had no desire to be diminished in his eyes should I be proven wrong.

Darkness found us lounging against a convenient ledge in the backyard of The George, the landlord having consented gladly when I sought permission to use his premises for my clandestine assignation. I had expected as much, guessing he would relish the chance to be of service to me – and by extension the King – if only in this small way. As for Abney, he had been eager to join our vigil but I bade him remain indoors with Gover, explaining that Jane Bonvylle was expecting to encounter two men and might take flight if she saw a third. This feeble excuse satisfied him, reaffirming my impression that poor Ralph Abney was not possessed of the sharpest wits. It never occurred to him that my true motive for keeping him away was a lack of faith in his general competence.

Thoughts of competence brought Matthew to mind. The lad never ceased to astonish me with his unlikely talents.

"I hope she liked your kiss," I threw at him as we waited. "It might be all that saves our skins tonight."

"Oh, she liked it well enough," he boasted, before adding a little sheepishly, "and I liked it, too. Wouldn't mind doing it again."

I guffawed loudly, remembering the girl's homely features.

"Is that your notion of beauty?" I sneered, attempting to rile my servant for no better reason than to pass the time.

Refusing to take my bait, he answered me with his customary good humour.

"See, looks don't bother me so much," he said without heat, "not so long as what's beneath is tasty. Think of the medlar, master. It looks proper ugly but bite it and there's no fruit tastes sweeter, not to my mind."

We lapsed into silence and I thought about his words. I knew there was wisdom in them but even so, I understood my vanity well enough to realise I could never enjoy the caresses of an ill-favoured maiden. Well, not without a wedding and a fat dowry to enhance her appeal, and perhaps not even then.

We had not long to wait before Matthew's tasty medlar appeared, bearing aloft a lantern to light her way. As she approached I saw that she was snivelling and looked as jumpy as a hare at bay. Matthew saw, too, and came forward to calm her.

"Good lass," he murmured, taking her lantern and passing it to me before enfolding her in his arms.

I thought him rash, for we could not yet be certain that she had come alone; Bonvylle might have some armed thugs waiting for a signal from the girl. Nevertheless, I held my tongue, watching with admiration as he soothed her with sweet blandishments. When at last her tears abated he released her from his embrace and told her to heed carefully what I was about to say.

"I know you lied about Mistress Vernon," I told her sternly. "And I know she came to some misfortune at your kinsman's house. Tell me what happened, and why, and I will see you come to no harm. Lie to me and I will take pleasure in watching you end your days with a rope about your neck."

She whimpered at my harsh words and tried to retreat into Matthew's arms but he was having none of it and folded them against her.

"Come on, girl," he coaxed. "Speak up! Tell Master Cranley what you know and all will be well."

"They'll kill me," she squeaked, flapping her hands in a futile gesture of distress.

"Your affectionate employers? They'll not have the chance," I reassured her, before seizing her arms and pulling her to me so that her unexpectedly sweet breath was in my nostrils.

"But be very sure of this," I said with cruel composure. "You are in greater peril than you know and your one hope of survival lies in telling me the truth."

At that point it was all a bluff, of course, since the worst I could prove about Bonvylle was that his wife dressed above her rank. But proving was one thing and suspecting quite another. I suspected him of involvement in a plot that had brought misfortune to Eleanor Vernon and I needed this timorous serving girl to confirm my story. The best way to achieve that was to make her believe her life was in peril.

It was fortunate that I made a better assessment of Jane Bonvylle's character than I had of her employers'.

Threatened with her own demise, she buckled like an ill-made shield and blurted forth the truth.

"Like I said before, it was me showed Mistress Vernon into the house that day," she sobbed. "Master and Mistress were in their inner chamber, shut up tight with a guest who'd come into the house before the sun was risen.

"He was a very particular client, they told me; a man of some importance who preferred to keep his affairs to himself and in consequence would deal with none but Master and Mistress. John Ford, they called him, just plain John Ford from London, though any dunderhead could tell he was nobly born, both from his high and mighty air and the bully boys he left on guard outside the house. Kept to the shadows, they did, watching the house all the while. Thought themselves so clever with their concealment but I marked them soon enough."

Though I was beyond eager for her to speak again of Eleanor, I knew that the identity of the Bonvylles' secretive visitor was key to the whole affair so, curbing my impatience, I pressed her about him.

"You say this John Ford was closeted with your employers. How then do you know he had a high and mighty air?"

"I was summoned to bring him water for washing, and a change of clothes on account of his own being fair caked in mud and salt. Well, I could see he was leaner than Master so I brought him a servant's hose and jerkin, that being all I could lay hands on that would fit him well. I thought I had done right but when he saw the humble raiment he refused to don it. Mistress pinched me, then bade me fetch something from the Master's coffer after all, even though it hung loose on the gentleman."

"What did he look like, Jane?" I asked her softly. "Would you know him again?"

"Oh yes, sir," she blushed. "Like a lord he looked, handsome and splendid with his fine physique and thick dark hair. Bearded, he was, mind, and I don't so much fancy a bearded fellow" – here she shot a sly look at the beardless Matthew – "but that was only on account of him not having had leisure to shave, so he told my mistress."

So it is him, I thought, oh sweet Christ, it is! It was what I had been expecting, and the name John Ford had supported my expectation but still there had been at least a shadow of doubt. As the girl's description put paid to that a sharp fear for Eleanor leapt within me.

"Tell me what happened to Mistress Vernon," I demanded, unable to delay any longer.

"I tried to send her away when she came a-calling, I swear I did. I knew she ought not be there with John Ford in the house also, so I told her to try another place for her cloaks and cloth. But she would not have it! Bonvylles was the best, she had been told. Poor maiden, she misunderstood why I was reluctant to attend her, thinking it was because I doubted she had money. So she showed me her purse and demanded I take her to Master or Mistress."

Her words dried up and in my annoyance I almost boxed her ears.

"What did you do then?" Matthew intervened.

"I took her to them since she was so insistent. Blessed Jesu! I never thought she would come to harm! She had been pressing me so hard it angered me, I do admit, but all the same I never meant her evil."

Repressing the impulse to slap the spineless creature, I took a breath and spoke with measured nonchalance.

"So you showed Mistress Vernon into the Bonvylles' private sanctum. What then?"

She hung her head.

"I know not! Not for sure."

Enraged at her evasion, I thundered at her not to trifle with me and she shrank from my fury.

"I speak truly, sir," she whimpered. "But I did loiter a while by the open door and so was able to hear the great gasp the young lady gave when she entered the chamber. And then the stranger spoke to her."

"What did he say?"

"He called out her name. 'Mistress Vernon', I heard him say to her, surprised like. 'I did not think to meet with you this day.'"

Though the words sounded harmless enough, my chest heaved as I considered who it was that had uttered them.

"And what then?"

"I know not!"

I gave a menacing growl and she backed away in terror.

"Truly, sir, I beg you not to harm me! I cannot tell you what I did not witness. My mistress observed me and bade me be gone, saying no good ever came to those that listen in doorways. I did not need a further warning. As I left I heard the door of the chamber close and I never saw Mistress Vernon after that. I fled to my chamber at the top of the house and there I stayed, striving to close my ears to all the strange comings and goings.

"By and by Mistress Bonvylle came and bade me pack my belongings. Soon afterwards I was taken to Master's house in the country and there I have remained until two days gone, when one of Master's lackeys brought me here to answer your questions. My orders were to tell you it was I alone that had attended Mistress Vernon and then seen her out. And I was never to mention the visitor John Ford on pain of losing my tongue."

My throat choked with the frustration of being so close and yet not close enough. If I was to believe the girl's story – and I did – I still had no way of knowing whether Eleanor was at this moment dead or alive. Nevertheless, as a realist, I saw more cause to despair than to hope, despite my usual inclination to clutch on to hope until the very last.

To avoid contemplating the unthinkable I sprang a further question on the girl.

"To your knowledge, was this the first time John Ford visited your master's house?"

She considered before giving her reply.

"I cannot say. But perhaps no, for I have been sent to the country a handful of times before, and without sensible cause so far as I could tell. It is possible that he came on one or more of those occasions."

"And what of this malady your master and mistress were suffering from when I first called on them? Was it feigned?"

Wiping her nose on her sleeve, the tearful wench twisted her face into a smug grimace.

"Aye, of course. Master, they were taken unawares when you arrived, and much shaken to realise the King's warrant obliged them to speak with you. In their panic their one thought was to make you wait while they considered how best to proceed."

Sounding less terrified now, she leaned in close to me.

"Speaking plain, sir, I believe they had imagined no soul would care enough about poor Mistress Vernon to go to the bother of searching for her. Your arrival proved them wrong and it shook them. But once they had recovered from their fright they realised you had no grounds to suspect them of wrongdoing. So they saw they had nothing to fear in meeting with you, or in allowing you to question me so long as they were listening."

Matthew nudged me.

"That can't be right about the sickness being false," he objected. "The apothecary I spoke with confirmed their story."

Again the girl grimaced.

"Many folk in this town are in the pay of Master Bonvylle."

Abney had said something similar to me, I recalled.

"You saying that bugger lied to me?" my servant protested, outraged that he had allowed himself to be hoodwinked, whereas I was more concerned with practicalities.

"But surely there was not time enough for Bonvylle to get a message to the apothecary before Matthew arrived at his door?"

"Maybe not," the girl agreed, "but it makes no odds. When a stranger turned up poking his nose into Master's affairs, he knew it was in his interest to go along with Master's story."

That Southampton was rife with corruption did not surprise me. Most places were the same; it was how the world worked. Even so, it worried me that Bonvylle seemed to have half the town in his silken pocket. Thinking this, it occurred to me that Jane might have been observed leaving the house for her assignation with Matthew and me. If she had, her life really could be in danger.

"How did you slip away tonight?" I asked, wondering how best to protect her should the Bonvylles suspect her of blabbing to me.

Without warning she smiled, happy to flaunt her ingenuity.

"Master and Mistress never think of me until they need me. Unless they summon me, they will not notice I am gone. I slipped out through the side gate in Wytegod's Lane. Jack the errand boy let me out. As I passed by I whispered to him that I had a lusty lad to meet. Jack is as gossipy as an old grandmother so that tale is known now by all, I do not doubt. That is as I planned it. If I am discovered when I return, Mistress will call me a wanton trollop and beat me but 'twill be no worse than that."

She departed soon afterwards, basking in Matthew's beaming approval of her unexpected courage. As I watched her dumpy figure retreating, I trusted she would heed my reminder to speak to no one about our meeting, as much for her own sake as for ours.

Chapter Twelve

With my suspicions of the Bonvylles confirmed by the girl's testimony, I went directly to the castle and revealed to Berkeley all that I had discovered. I began by informing him that Nicholas Bonvylle's wife was the sister of John de Vere, Earl of Oxford, one of the King's most dangerous enemies and the man responsible for the recent attempted uprising in Essex.

"How came you by this knowledge?" the confounded Keeper asked, unable to conceal the humiliation he felt at being unaware of this significant detail.

Mindful not to reveal Ralph Abney's part in the story, yet keen to soothe Berkeley's wounded pride, I lied and told him that Jane Bonvylle had been my informant.

"But it is inconceivable!" he protested. "An Earl's sister married to a common merchant. However was such a misalliance countenanced?"

"Not so inconceivable," I replied, "since Agnes Bonvylle is not true born; she is the daughter of the old Earl's mistress. He cared enough to acknowledge the brat and have her raised with his legitimate issue at Hedingham Castle. When she was of age he gave her in marriage to Bonvylle, a young man of ambition and wealth who was content to overlook her bastardy in order to forge links with a great house."

"Where was the benefit for Oxford?" Berkeley demanded, obstinately focusing on the fact of the marriage rather than its current implication.

I shrugged, accepting that I must satisfy his curiosity on this point before getting to the meat of the matter.

"Initially, perhaps, the only benefit was in finding a respectable home for his by-blow. But as Bonvylle's importance in Southampton has grown, his value as an ally has increased. Think of all the ships he sends across the seas; what secret messages do they convey, or passengers, come to that?"

As Berkeley absorbed my words I saw Agnes Bonvylle standing in her husband's opulent hall, magnificent in her inappropriate finery. And I remembered the ostentatious crimson livery worn by her servants, which now struck me as markedly similar to the Earl of Oxford's own livery, lacking only a blue boar at the collar to be an exact replica. This was a woman who never forgot her noble blood, I was certain, nor permitted her husband to forget it, either.

"She has been sending aid to her half-brother, is that it?" the Keeper ventured fretfully, evidently vexed that such an unfortunate circumstance should have been occurring under his nose.

Though a large part of me was awash with grief for Eleanor, I still managed to feel sympathy for the man and was sorry that I had worse news to deliver.

"It's more serious than that, Berkeley. I have cause to believe they gave him succour after his aborted landing at Chich St. Osyth. When the populace failed to rise in his support, he fled to his ship and made for the south coast. He was sheltering with the Bonvylles the day Mistress Vernon visited their house. I fear it was her undoing."

It was nearly my undoing also, for my treacherous voice gave way and my eyes became moist. Observing my distress, Berkeley poured some wine for me and waited until I had recovered my equilibrium before continuing with his questions.

"You think he did away with her," he stated bluntly. "But why? For what reason?"

"She knew him," I all but shouted. "Her father was a close ally of Warwick. Before his death at Barnet, Warwick had been working for the Lancastrian cause which Oxford supports. God's blood! Eleanor was one of the Countess of Warwick's favourite attendants. She and Oxford would have met on many occasions. There is no doubt that she would have recognised him the moment she saw him."

"Yes, I see that," Berkeley said quietly, "but why would he do away with her? Given that her father fought and died for Lancaster at Barnet, what had he to fear from the girl?"

"You misunderstand," I said shortly, attempting to rein in my temper. "William Vernon did not fight for Lancaster, he fought for Warwick. He was the Kingmaker's man to his core, and followed where he led. But now both are dead, leaving their womenfolk to fend for themselves. With her daughters married to sons of York, naturally Oxford would expect the Countess's sympathies to lie with that house. And where the mistress goes, her loyal attendant would be sure to follow."

Berkeley furrowed his brow, endeavouring for my sake to find a flaw in my reasoning. Finding none, he tried a different tack.

"Though he be a traitor, Oxford is known as an honourable man. I cannot believe him capable of murdering Mistress Vernon in order to silence her."

Acknowledging Oxford's reputation for honour, I knew a moment's joy as I considered that Eleanor might not have been slain after all. Then I remembered Robert Gower, the Watergate official found drowned the day after the unknown Hanseatic vessel left port. Not only did this tell me that Oxford was indeed prepared to kill in cold blood to disguise his movements, it also reminded me that the Danzig ship was somehow embroiled in this affair. My best guess was that Oxford had been negotiating with a member of the Hansa League, using his sister's house for the meetings. Possibly he had met with this foreigner by prearrangement on the last day of May, yet that did not fit with his landing at Chich St. Osyth a scant few days before. Had that endeavour prospered, he would have been too preoccupied raising rebellion across Edward's kingdom to manage the rendezvous with the foreign trader. It was a conundrum that I could not as yet fathom and so I returned to my fears regarding Eleanor.

"Have no doubt, he is capable of murder," I growled, before outlining to Berkeley my conviction that Oxford had been responsible for Gower's death.

Agreeing now that the prospect looked bleak for my sweetheart, the Keeper avowed his intention to drag the Bonvylles from their house to make them answer for their treachery. It was with the deepest regret that I dissuaded him from this course of action, advising him instead to keep constant, secret watch on the house in case Oxford should return.

"Have everyone followed who leaves the house," I continued, "and find a way to intercept the Bonvylles' every letter. That way you should be ready if de Vere comes again. And Berkeley, when he comes, be as rough as you please when you seize him but be sure not to kill him. The King will want him alive for questioning. Pray God he chooses me for the task for I have a score to settle."

Giving me his word to follow my instructions to the letter, Berkeley asked what I intended to do next.

"I am for home," I answered. "I shall call at Beaulieu first, to give the abbot the grave tidings that Mistress Vernon is likely dead, and then I shall return to Middleham and hope most fervently, saving your feelings, never to visit this festering stink-hole of a town ever again."

I took my leave then, before emotion could unman me once more. Ahead of me lay the unwelcome task of telling Abney what had happened to the girl he loved. That could wait, I decided, until we were far from Southampton. I had concluded that the only thing I could do now for Eleanor was ensure that her childhood friend and unwanted suitor lived long enough to gain his pardon. To that end I intended to escort him back to his Derbyshire connections before returning to Middleham. He would learn about Eleanor's fate at a time and place of my choosing; certainly it would not be here in Southampton where the reckless fool could and probably would betray what we knew in his anguish.

At The George I paid Gover handsomely for his support and thanked him for keeping Abney safe. Then the three of us, Matthew, Abney and I, returned to The Mermaid where I instructed Old Stumpy to have our horses ready at first light, so anxious was I to be gone from Southampton. At this Abney woke up enough to quiz me about our abrupt departure, demanding to know why we were leaving without finding Eleanor. To quieten him I told him I had learned that there were answers to be had at Beaulieu and he was satisfied with this vague and improbable assurance.

Just as I was beginning to contemplate sleep, the realisation dawned on me that if we were to depart as early as I intended, I would have no chance to bid Andrew Coterel farewell. Unwilling to show discourtesy to a man I liked so much and in other circumstances would gladly call my friend, I made the impulsive decision to call at his house despite the lateness of the hour. When I told them what I was about, Matthew and Abney insisted on accompanying me. Like an over-anxious nursemaid, Matthew said he misliked the thought of me wandering alone at night in a strange southern town whereas Abney, having been confined for many hours at The George, felt inclined to stretch his legs.

Had we taken a different route to Bugle Street everything would have been different. I would have said my farewell to Coterel, perhaps shared some wine with him, and then staggered back to The Mermaid to snatch an hour or two of sleep before putting Southampton and everything it stood for behind me forever. Instead, some whim compelled me to cut down Butcher's Row into St Michael's Square. We had crossed the square, strolled past the Bonvylles' house which I pointedly ignored, and made it a small distance into Bugle Street when the loud rasping of a door opening caused me to turn around. There, by the light of a raised lantern, I saw John de Vere being admitted into his half-sister's house.

Unable to believe my good fortune, I commanded Matthew to summon help from Berkeley and to make haste in doing so. As he scampered noiselessly back towards the castle I pulled Abney into the shadow of a cookshop and in a whisper told him what I had just witnessed, of necessity keeping from him its significance regarding Eleanor.

"We must keep watch until Berkeley brings men," I hissed at him. Regrettably, Abney was slow to pick up on my desire for stillness.

"I am not staying," he said without lowering his voice. "I have no argument with Oxford, and in any case if he is apprehended by Berkeley in my presence, he may reveal my identity. Do you think I should risk that?"

Realising there was something in what he said, for all that my blood seethed when he spoke of having no argument with Oxford, I told him to return to The Mermaid and wait for me there.

"But go quietly, for the love of God," I entreated him.

Alas, the damage was already done. Alerted to our presence by Abney's overloud voice, a trio of armed men emerged from the darkness and surrounded us. Far too late, I recollected Jane Bonvylle speaking of John Ford's bully boys who kept watch over the house when he visited. She had keener eyes than I, for I had not noticed them until their swords were pointing at my belly.

"You will come with us," their leader said without heat. I could make out little of his features but his bulk was imposing and there was menace in his calm.

Laying rough hands upon Abney and me, the ruffians hustled us with kicks and curses towards the merchant's house where, at a whistled signal, the door was opened just long enough for us to be dragged inside. The moment it closed, our wrists were bound with strong rope and Abney's mouth was gagged to stop the torrent of imprecations that had been issuing from it since the moment of our apprehension. Next, rather than forcing us up the staircase as I had expected, we were manoeuvred into the store room where Matthew and I had been left to wait the first time we had visited the house. Charging his two companions to guard us closely, the leader then disappeared for what seemed to me an inordinate period of time though in truth it can have been no more than a few minutes. When he returned he brought with him the individual I held responsible for Eleanor's fate.

"You bastard," I yelled, springing at Oxford with a ferocity fuelled by outrage and impotence. Though my hands were bound, my captors had not reckoned on me wielding my own head as a weapon but wield it I did, smashing it into my foe's forehead with an impact that sent waves of pain and nausea spiralling down from my skull to my innards. That I had injured myself as much as Oxford did not matter to me, in fact I positively relished the hurt so great was my need to inflict suffering on this man. Seeing him sprawling on his back with blood flowing from his temple, I felt a small joy kindle within me. If Matthew did not return in time I might well be about to die but at least I had the satisfaction of having drawn blood.

I had little time to savour my triumph for Oxford's brutish lackeys were soon upon me, driving me to my knees as they rained blow after blow onto my head, neck and shoulders. Through my blood-smeared gaze I saw Abney struggle forward in an attempt to block my attackers even though, with his trussed wrists, he was unable to defend himself. This courageous act was rewarded with a contemptuous kick that propelled him face down onto the hard stone floor beside me and there he remained, stunned but conscious.

Still the onslaught upon me continued. It did not matter. I was beyond pain now and readying myself for the coup de grace when Oxford spoke.

"Enough now!" he ordered, rising gingerly from his prone position with one hand clutched to his brow.

At his order the buffeting ceased although one charmer took it upon himself to hawk phlegm into my face. I flinched in disgust, feeling the foulness on my skin as I had not felt the beating. Unable to wipe it away, I marked the culprit well, imagining how I would reward his discourtesy should I ever be in a position to do so.

Lost in these thoughts, I was startled back to the moment when a fresh linen kerchief was pressed to my cheek.

"We are not animals," Oxford remarked as he cleared the filthy matter from my face.

My reply was an ironic laugh and a nod towards where poor Abney lay groaning nearby. The nod was a bad idea for it seared my aching head and made the blood from my cuts flow faster but Oxford took my point. Seating himself on the stool hastily pulled forward by his senior cut-throat, he chuckled softly.

"What did you expect when you attacked me? That my loyal men would stand by and leave you unpunished? But I had called enough," he continued, the silk in his voice hardening to granite, "and so that last act was unpardonable. The fellow will be punished for it, take my word."

"We live in a topsy-turvy world when murderers punish their dogs for following their example," I croaked, delayed pain bringing waves of weakness to every part of my body.

Oxford raised his elegant eyebrows at this remark but made no direct reply. Instead, he leaned forward and pushed my chin up to examine my face more closely.

"Do I know you?" he asked. "It seems I do, yet I cannot place you. Of a certainty you know who I am."

Oh yes, I thought, this again. The grander the noble, the less likely they were to remember me, though many would have encountered me in Dickon's retinue since I was a boy. Admittedly Oxford and I had not moved in the same circles of late due to his treasonous tendencies but even so, he would have seen me often enough in the past to have some inkling as to my identity. As he himself stated with such infuriating complacency, I certainly knew him; if so, why not did he not know me? My name I did not expect him to remember but my face and the fact that I served my lord of Gloucester, surely the great Earl had wits enough to manage that? Yet, considering that my invisibility had proved to my advantage on occasion, perhaps I should have felt thankful for my apparent anonymity rather than insulted by it.

"Well?" he prompted me impatiently. "Will you give me your name?"

"I am Francis Cranley," I said with as much pride as I could muster from my kneeling position, "loyal servant of the most noble Duke of Gloucester."

Oxford's eyes gleamed with recognition.

"That's it! You're Gloucester's faithful hound. My pardon, I should have recognised you but your face is less pleasing than I recall."

Indicating my swollen eyes and bleeding brow he smirked a little, enjoying his paltry jest.

"Find a looking glass before throwing insults my way," I shot back, shaking my head in a gesture of false sympathy.

Again, the movement hurt but the riposte was worth the pain when I saw his countenance fall. My barb had met its mark. Oxford was famously a peacock about his appearance and with reason, given that he was as handsome as he was disloyal to the King. It amused me to think that as he moved towards my destruction, one minute part of his mind would be worrying about the damage I had done to his pretty face. I was glad he could not know how greatly I exaggerated; my assault, to my enormous regret, having worked insufficient injury to result in permanent disfigurement.

"You are a long way from your master," Oxford continued once his spasm of vanity had subsided. "Oblige my curiosity by telling me what brings you here."

As he spoke the burliest of his henchmen, the one who had seemed in command of my captors, made a threatening move towards me. He was intent, I had no doubt, on using force to compel me to speak. Fortunately, Oxford noticed the movement and waved the man away.

"Back, Jigger, back!" he commanded. "How will I hear what Master Cranley has to say if you render him senseless?"

Brawny Jigger stepped back a pace but remained a handy fist's distance from my face.

I did not answer at once and as he waited, Oxford studied me with every appearance of compassion. This angered me more than the beating, for what business had he to feel pity for me when he had shown none to Eleanor? Stoked by my fury, I made an incautious reply.

"I am here on the King's business, you worthless pile of excrement!"

Oxford widened his eyes at my rudeness but made no other reply. Jigger, however, took greater affront and proceeded to pummel me about the ribs.

"Keep a civil tongue for your own sake," his master clucked. "As you see, Jigger is less tolerant of discourtesy than I."

"You sicken me," I spat when I had breath again to speak, "prating of discourtesy when you have the blood of an innocent girl on your hands."

Jigger moved again but Oxford forestalled him, his features registering surprise.

"On what basis do you accuse me of this crime? I have the blood of many on my hands, I'll not deny it, deaths that were justified and for which I make no apology. But I have slain no girl, helpless or otherwise, and if I find that any of my men have committed such an act in my name they will pay with their own lives, I assure you."

I had not expected a denial. The deceit incensed me so greatly, my bound fingers burned with the desire to throttle him.

"You claim you act on Edward's behalf," he went on, refusing with foolish ostentation to give the King his rightful title. "Well then, what is the nature of your mission?"

Two separate thoughts ran through my mind at that moment. Firstly, it was apparent that the Bonvylles had not yet had time to tell Oxford about my presence in Southampton and my search for Eleanor. Secondly, where in the name of Christ was Matthew? If he did not arrive soon with a contingent from the castle, Abney and I were done for. Then a third thought burst through the others: the realisation that Oxford was afraid. Though he did his utmost to conceal it, I read fear in his eyes; fear that his movements were being followed and that his enemies were closing in on him. I would have liked to prolong that fear but the need to know about Eleanor overrode all other considerations.

"I am charged with discovering the whereabouts of Eleanor Vernon. I know she discovered you by purest chance in this den of traitors, and was silenced by you in consequence. Do you still deny it?"

Rarely have I seen a man so shaken as when I accused Oxford of Eleanor's murder, yet before he would speak of her he demanded I reveal to him what I knew of his movements.

"Tell me all you know and I will put your mind at rest about pretty Mistress Vernon," he said with a knowing leer that made me heave.

"Very well," I agreed. "For some months you have been using this house to make contact with those willing to further your rebellion against the King. When the people of Essex failed to rise for you, you fled here, to your sister and her husband, both of whom are embroiled in your treachery. Mistress Vernon had the misfortune to visit the house that same day. She recognised you and paid for it with her life."

"You are wrong, you know," Oxford murmured. "Oh, not about my argument with the man you call King, or my fervent wish to see his head rotting on a spike on London Bridge. And you are right about Agnes and Nicholas, a man whose usefulness to me far outweighs the undesirability of his mercantile status. Both have served my interests well and will reap their reward when the rightful king is crowned."

Rolling my eyes at his fervour, I ventured a bawdy jibe at the expense of this alleged king, a pasty youth of dubious lineage currently enjoying the meagre hospitality of Francis of Brittany.

"I should make you suffer for that," Oxford rumbled, "but since your life is soon to end I shall show you greater magnanimity than you probably merit. Well, Cranley, you have done well to piece together so much but you are less clever than you fancy. You have made errors, my friend, and not just the one that finds you in your present unfortunate predicament."

"How so?" I asked, anxious to prolong our conversation as long as possible, for surely Berkeley would be battering down the door of this house very soon. Then a chilling notion came to me. Abney and I had been observed easily enough by Oxford's brutes. What if Matthew had also been seen, and had been apprehended on his way to the castle. If that were the case, no help would be coming after all.

Through this cloud of doubt I became aware that Oxford was speaking again. With grave effort I wrenched my concentration back to his words.

"You have the right of it about Mistress Vernon in one regard only. She did come to the house when I was here. Considerable efforts were made to keep her from me but she was too strong-willed to be gainsaid. A maidservant admitted her to my chamber, a foolish chit who could not know the harm she did since to her I was plain John Ford of London. Alas, not so Mistress Vernon. She recognised me at once."

"What did you do to her?" I cried, desperate to hear that she had been spared undue suffering.

As Oxford shook his head in sadness my stomach lurched anew.

"I am no woman-slayer, Cranley. But I could not permit her to return to the monks. You must see that, for though she promised to tell no one about finding me here, I could not afford to take that chance. It was something I dared not risk. Not for the sake of my own safety, you understand, since I have other havens and plenty more friends to call upon. But my sister would have been exposed as an enemy of Edward and that I could not countenance. Thus the girl had to be silenced."

I closed my eyes, unwilling to let Oxford witness my wretchedness.

"How did you do it?" I mumbled, aware that until I knew the manner of her death I would imagine every conceivable horror until my wits became addled.

"She was put on a ship bound for the Baltic."

My eyes snapped open as my brain absorbed his words.

"I see no harm in you knowing. You will be dead soon, and I can see you had some liking for the maiden. Well, you can die easy on her account, Cranley, for I spoke true when I said I am no woman-slayer.

"The day before my arrival, Agnes had met with a ship's master from Danzig at my request. I had authorised her to negotiate the purchase of four new vessels for my use, with the Danzig captain acting intermediary for the town's ship builders. When their business was concluded, the foreigner left Agnes and rejoined his ship with the intention of leaving Southampton on the next tide. When I appeared in the early hours of the following morning, my sister could not have been more surprised or disappointed. At that very moment, you see, she had envisaged me blazing across Essex at the head of a burgeoning army. Alas, as you know, that enterprise failed, making it necessary for me to make good my escape. In due course I left my crew and found my way here with a few trusted men, thinking it a safe place to catch my breath and plan my next move. That's when your headstrong Mistress Vernon burst in, leaving me with the problem of how to stop her from tattling."

Understanding dawned on me at last.

"You put her aboard the Danzig ship! Oh sweet Jesus, poor Eleanor!"

When I had begun this search, the very worst I had imagined I would discover was that Eleanor Vernon was dead. Now I knew I had been wrong, for was death not preferable to life as a captive ship's whore, there to be used over and again without mercy by any sailor with an itch to scratch?

I groaned aloud, adding my voice to the increasingly frantic noises emanating from Abney's prone figure. Poor Abney! I had been so completely swathed in my own concerns that I had not considered how he must be suffering as he heard Oxford speak. Now I rebuked myself, remembering that in his eyes Eleanor was his bride to be. The recollection made me groan again.

"Compose yourself, man!" Oxford urged me. "The ship's master gave me his word that the girl would be untouched and I trust him. He was reluctant to take her in the first place but I gave him no option, threatening to buy my vessels elsewhere if he refused. Even then he would have said no had not Jigger added his own persuasive voice. But when he did agree, I gave him a handsome bribe to ensure the maiden came to no harm on his ship, and in due course to see her put safely ashore far from England.

"Unfortunately, the Watergate clerk caught sight of Mistress Vernon as she was brought aboard the vessel. Though I am not the cold-hearted bastard you take me for, Cranley, you must see that I could not risk him talking if anyone came looking for the girl. So I told Jigger to deal with him. He's a good man, Jigger, and reliable. He even arranged for some ne'er-do-well to carry a story to the monks at Beaulieu. Some folderol about the girl running off with a lover to France, so that any search party would start out on the wrong track."

It was enough. Almost certain now that Matthew had been captured or even slain, I no longer entertained any great hope that Abney and I would escape with our lives. Well then, it was something to know that wherever she was, Eleanor still drew breath.

"You have my thanks," I said to Oxford, acknowledging his civility in this matter, "though I call shame on you for speaking so glibly of murder and abduction."

He had the grace to look shamefaced for a second or two, and then he was all brisk business once more.

"Come, Jigger, time enough has been wasted. My sister will be wondering what I am about. Take these two to the quayside and finish them quickly.

"Understand that I take no pleasure in this," he concluded, casting a last apologetic glance in my direction before striding to the door, "but if I am to protect the Bonvylles I cannot let you live."

Chapter Thirteen

Oxford was halfway through the door when I stayed him with a last ditch bid to stave off death.

"Killing us will not save your sister or her husband. Their part in your conspiracy is already known to Berkeley."

As Oxford paused, I pressed on in a tangle of half-considered words.

"He is coming for them and when he seizes them their lives will be forfeit, unless I can persuade him to clemency. I cannot do that if I am dead, nor will I if Abney is slain."

Walking back into the chamber Oxford crouched down opposite me so that his eyes looked directly into mine.

"You are bluffing," he said with an attempt at nonchalance which was foiled by the waver in his voice. "If Berkeley suspected anything he would be here already."

New hope surged within me but I checked it, aware that my life and Abney's depended on my insouciance.

"Believe that if you must," I shrugged, for all the world as though we were discussing a matter of small importance.

As his men shuffled their feet in angry consternation, Oxford stared at me, searching my face for the truth.

"As you will," he snapped at last. "I think you lie, yet if I am mistaken I will pay a heavy price for my error. Jigger, I must leave at once. Make my apologies to Mistress Bonvylle and her husband and then come after me. You will know where to find me"

As the Earl strode to the door his henchman called after him with a note of disappointment in his voice.

"What of these two, my lord?"

"Finish them at the quayside and then make haste to join me."

As he quit the chamber I felt my hope wither inside me. My scheme had failed; in fact all I had managed to do was drive Oxford to safety. You fool, Cranley, I thought bitterly, yet what else could I have done?

"Mind this scum while I speak with the lady," Jigger ordered his fellows, exiting the chamber and making his way with heavy tramping footsteps up the staircase.

In his absence I occupied my thoughts with schemes for freeing myself from this perilous predicament. Everything came down to the dagger secreted in my boot, which Oxford's men had overlooked in their zeal to bring Abney and me before their master. I reckoned that by slumping forward a little and twisting my bound wrists to one side, I might be able to tease the dagger out with my fingers. The flaw in this scheme was the avid interest with which my captors watched my every breath; should I make a sudden lunge for the dagger they would be on me before I so much as made contact with my boot leather.

Even so, I concluded that dying in an attempt to get free was preferable to submitting willingly to my fate.

That decided, I was about to begin the manoeuvre when Jigger returned to the chamber, Agnes and Nicholas Bonvylle trailing in his wake. Although annoyed with myself for delaying too long, I was nevertheless gratified to see that Jigger's communication had put a sizeable dent in their composure.

"Get them out, get them out!" Mistress Bonvylle shrieked, gesturing towards Abney and me as though we were plague-infested rats. "Remove them this instant!"

"Be calm, my love," her husband said soothingly, though from the perspiration on his brow I could see that he, too, was alarmed by this turn of events. "Jigger will do what is necessary, we have nothing to fear."

"But he must not do it in this house," she rejoined. "Only when they are gone from here will we be safe, for then there will be nothing to condemn us."

"Let that thought comfort you as they tie you to the stake, Mistress Bonvylle," I shot at her, fear infusing my words with malice. "Your noble blood will not save you from a traitor's death; there is too little of it for that."

Seized by terror, she staggered, calling upon her paunchy spouse to silence me. His response was to punch me in the face with all the force of a dish of wet pottage hitting the ground. The manic laughter that rose in my chest at this display of ineptitude shrivelled and died as Jigger approached me.

"That's enough from you," he sneered, putting his boot into my back and pitching me forward so that, like Abney, I now lay with my lips kissing the dirty wooden floorboards.

After that there was no more time for thought as rough hands grabbed my shoulders and hauled me to my feet. The instant before a dusty sack was thrown over my head, I saw Abney likewise brought upright and, I presumed but did not see, crowned with hessian. Then, like unwieldy bundles, we were prodded and shoved through the doorway, into the entrance hall and out into the open air.

Now, I thought, surely now Matthew will burst from the darkness, leading Berkeley and his soldiers to our rescue. Straining my ears for encouraging sounds, all I heard were Abney's muffled groans as we were driven like cattle down Wytegod's Lane, stumbling and helpless in our blindness. When the saltiness of the air told me we had reached the quayside, I readied myself for death. Though my preference was for a dagger to the heart, I remembered Robert Gower's fate and knew that drowning was to be my lot.

"God be with you, Ralph," I cried out as loudly as I could, trying to make my voice heard through the muffling sack. Still gagged, Abney was unable to reply but I prayed that he had heard me and been comforted.

I was bracing myself for the end when help at last materialised. The first I knew of it was a thud and a cry as the hands that had been gripping me fell away. I was free for but a moment before another of my captors stepped in front of me and seized my shoulders. Before he had time to do more, I raised my knee and drove it with vigour into what I judged to be his most vulnerable parts. The resulting anguished curse told me I had judged correctly, and that Jigger had been on the receiving end of my thrust. As he recovered himself, my unknown rescuer leapt forward and cut free my bonds. There followed a confusion of sounds; scuffling, laboured breathing, angry swearing and above it all a hideous gurgling that reminded me of something I had heard before. All this occurred in the scant few seconds it took my rescuer to rip the sack from my head.

"Tyrell!" I roared, recognising his features by the light of Jigger's discarded lantern even as my mind struggled to accept his presence.

Before he could reply my battle instincts took over. Tyrell had despatched one of the bully boys and my well-placed knee had temporarily incapacitated Jigger. That meant one other remained. Slipping my dagger from my boot I turned to assist Abney who, in the chaos, had been left to fall, helpless, upon the ground. Now, when I saw the third ruffian crouching beside his prone form, I launched my dagger and knew a feral happiness when it struck the villain in the face. He lurched, screaming, into the soft mulch of the quayside.

My triumph turned to ashes when I brought the lantern close to Abney and pulled away the sack that covered his face. I thought I had saved him but I had been too late. A sword blow had struck his neck with such ferocity that it had all but severed his head. Blood was everywhere, drenching his jerkin, pooling about the gaping wound that used to be his throat and saturating the gag that remained in his lifeless mouth. Wracked with grief, I remembered the gurgling sound and knew where I had heard it before. Tewkesbury, where many brave men had been slain in like manner.

To ease my sorrow I threw myself upon Abney's murderer and despatched him. Pulling my dagger from his cheek, I plunged it deep into his eye socket so that it pierced the wretch's brain. That meant of my three erstwhile captors, Jigger alone, now held fast by Tyrell, remained alive to receive my vengeance. Stopping only to wipe the gore from my dagger, I advanced on the miserable dog, intent on finishing him off. In my rage my one thought was to slay him. It was what he deserved yet as I drew near, I read the grim satisfaction in his eyes and understood. Much as I craved the gratification of slaying him, it was my duty to take him alive for then he could be tortured and made to betray his master. He knew that, hence his preference for a quick death now.

Returning my dagger to its place of concealment, I smiled at Jigger, relishing his realisation that I had come to my senses.

"I am eager to know how you come to be here," I said lightly to Tyrell, "but my curiosity must wait. For now, what matters most is that we see this traitor safely delivered to his fate. Since I feel unable to move at speed" – here I indicated my knocked about body – "I suggest you fetch help from the castle while I stand guard over our prize."

Tyrell gave me a grave look.

"Be careful," was all he said.

I knew what he meant by those two words. My friend was counselling me not to give way to my desire for blood. I chose to interpret it as a warning to ensure our prisoner did not escape. Answering him with a curt nod, I began to bind Jigger's wrists behind his back and gestured for Tyrell to tackle his legs. When we had done, the hefty brute was leaning backwards on his haunches with his arms trussed securely to his ankles. It was an agonising position but it would not kill him.

Satisfied with this measure of vengeance, I again bade Tyrell go for help and this time he heeded me. As he sprinted away I found the sack that had been used to cover my face and laid it tenderly over Abney's hideous wound. I was content for my foes to lie like felled beasts for all to stare at but not this decent man.

Tyrell had not been gone long when I heard sounds of uproar issuing from the vicinity of Wytegod's Lane. Assured of Jigger's inability to escape, I grabbed the lantern and ran as fast as my throbbing limbs would carry me towards the source of the commotion. Stopping at the top of the lane to catch my breath, my eyes beheld the pleasurable sight of Berkeley's men ransacking Agnes Bonvylle's house. Raising the lantern to get a better view of the spectacle, I spotted a familiar figure loitering by the doorway.

"You poxy churl! I told you to make haste!" I bellowed, charging forward with the intention of boxing my errant servant's ears. I was forestalled by my treacherous legs which gave way in time for Matthew to catch me against his broad peasant chest.

"Easy now, master!" he huffed, giving me a steadying grip before releasing me to lean against a wall.

Berkeley chose that moment to appear from inside the house, accompanied by half a dozen men struggling with the burden of a prostrate Nicholas Bonvylle. Behind them trooped four more, these ones restraining none too gently a weeping and shrieking Agnes Bonvylle.

"Jesu, Cranley! What devil mangled you?" Berkeley asked as he took in my injuries.

"I'll wager the other fellow looks worse," Matthew chirped loyally, allowing me to forget for a moment that I was annoyed with him for his dangerous tardiness.

Berkeley grinned at the jest and then, with a casual viciousness I had not expected from him, lashed out with his fist as Agnes Bonvylle was led past him.

"I told her once before to cease her noise," he remarked conversationally as two of his soldiers bent to pluck her from the ground. "Now the bitch will know to heed me."

"Nicholas!" Mistress Bonvylle cried out, moaning in pain as she was lifted. "Where is Nicholas?"

Again, Berkeley showed his cruelty.

"He is dead, Mistress," he chortled, "and rotting in hell already, I do not doubt."

For a few seconds I did not know what to say. My brush with death hung heavy upon me, as did my sorrow at Abney's grisly demise, yet I could not exult as Berkeley so clearly did in the Bonvylles' downfall. Though they were my enemies, they served their cause as faithfully as I served mine. For that reason if for no other, I felt they were deserving of some compassion. Then I thought of Jigger and knew myself a hypocrite; he too served a cause but I had shown him no compassion when I bound him.

"You'll find one of Oxford's creatures at the quayside," I told Berkeley. "Two others, also, though they be dead. Jigger, the one that lives, will have much to tell you. And there is one other slain, a brave man who knew nothing of all this. He died assisting me."

"Come, Master, let me help you back to the castle," Matthew interposed, sensing I was close to collapse.

Standing beside me, he eased one of my arms about his neck and we began a slow shuffle forward. Moments later another figure stepped up to me and helped Matthew shoulder my weight.

"We will go faster with two of us carrying you," Tyrell said, and my gladness at his proximity went some way to easing my troubled mind.

I slept a few hours at the castle and, when I awoke, summoned Matthew to wash me and tend to my wounds. As he rubbed a salve with a peculiar, savoury smell into the livid bruises I remembered what a woman skilled in healing had once taught me about bruises. Then as now, my body had been covered in them and she had used leopard's bane to ease their pain. When I asked Matthew for it he gave an amused shake of his head.

"The soldiers here are hard buggers, master. They don't have much truck with wise women's remedies. Leopard's bane! Fat chance of finding that here! This here pig grease was the best I could scrounge for you. Back in the Plaincourt kitchen it was what we used to soothe burns and scalds. I don't know but I reckoned it might work with other hurts."

Resigning myself to stinking like a spit-boy's braies, I thanked Matthew for his tender care and then had him support me as far as Berkeley's hall. There I subsided onto a cushioned bench and waited while Matthew went in search of Tyrell. When he arrived, with Berkeley and Matthew following close behind, I was finally able to make sense of all that had happened that night.

I had many questions to pose but foremost amongst them was how the devil Tyrell came to be in Southampton at the very moment I needed him. The answer reminded me of how men's fates can be determined by merest chance. While attending to affairs at his manor of Gipping, which lay little more than thirty miles from Oxford's ancestral home of Hedingham Castle, he had overheard snatches of gossip connecting the Earl with a prominent Southampton citizen by name of Bonvylle. With the mystery of Eleanor's disappearance fresh in his mind, Tyrell had recognised the name as belonging to the merchant she had visited the day of her vanishing. Guessing that he had stumbled across something pertinent to my search, he left Gipping at the earliest opportunity and rode with all speed to Beaulieu where he thought to find me. On discovering that I was in Southampton, he followed me there, leaving my old comrades Brankin and Knewstubb to sleep off the exertions of their long ride at the abbey guesthouse.

"If I'd known the fix you were in I'd have brought them with me," he added ruefully.

"But what brought you to the quayside in time to save my hide?" I questioned my friend.

"Blind chance," he answered. "When I reached Southampton I sought you at the castle, thinking you would be lodging there."

"I explained to Sir James that I had pressed you to stay but instead you elected to seek accommodation in the town," Berkeley interjected, eager to divert any blame that might be directed at him.

"That is so," Tyrell agreed, "and furthermore good Berkeley did me the courtesy of showing me the way to your inn himself."

"I felt it incumbent upon me to do so, Sir James, given your rank and importance."

Tyrell made no reply to this but smiled thinly at the Keeper's toadying pomposity. In the brief silence that ensued, Matthew saw his opportunity to butt into the conversation.

"That was when I arrived with your message, master! Fair rushed here, I did, but the Keeper was nowhere to be found and his men refused to tell me his whereabouts. On account of it being none of my buggering business, so they said."

Berkeley flushed and tried to interrupt but Matthew breezed on as though he had not noticed.

"Knowing the urgency of the matter, all I could do was kick my heels and wait for the Keeper's return."

"I fared little better at The Mermaid," Tyrell put in. "You were gone when Berkeley and I arrived and the evil-countenanced innkeeper declared no knowledge of your whereabouts, even with my sword at his throat. My first thought was to sit it out and wait for you. Not wishing to keep him from his affairs, I thanked our friend the Keeper for his assistance and bade him return to the castle. It was only after he had gone that, wearying of the innkeeper's baleful scrutiny, I decided to take a stroll to St. Michael's Square. I was curious to see what sort of home the money grubber had made for his highborn bride. Lucky for you, I was surveying Bonvylle's house from the church doorway when I saw you and your companion being dragged towards the quay."

"How could you know it was me?"

"I did not. All I saw was two figures with sacks upon their heads. Some instinct told me one of them might be you but I had no certainty. However, the sight of bound men being propelled towards the sea was enough to pique my interest so I followed at a distance."

"And thus were there to save my life," I finished, gratitude welling inside me. "For which you have my deepest thanks."

Tyrell seemed about to say something when Berkeley blustered into speech.

"I had your man brought to me the very moment I returned to the castle and learned he was waiting," he said. "When he had delivered his message I acted with great speed, bringing a detachment of guards to apprehend the traitor Oxford. You must be sure to tell the King that, Cranley. Alas, he had already fled but Bonvylle and his wife were there. They feigned outrage when my men stormed the house, demanding to know by what right I invaded the home of honest citizens. I told them serious allegations had been made against them and ordered my men to bring them to the castle."

Pausing to draw breath, Berkeley gave a malicious grin as he recounted what came next.

"The woman's composure broke at this, and she cried out for her servants to come to her aid but they could not for we already had them fast. Then she called upon her husband to help her. In response, he drew his sword and endeavoured to keep my men occupied so that his vixen wife might flee. Foolish fellow! A feeble swordsman, he was as easily vanquished as an infant."

In spite of myself I was moved by the thought of flabby Nicholas Bonvylle battling hardened men at arms so that his wife might escape.

"Mistress Bonvylle did not make it as far as the stairs before she was apprehended," Berkeley continued. "As for the husband, I would have preferred to take him alive but since we have the woman his death is of small account."

"You will question her?" Tyrell asked, his tone laden with significance.

Berkeley understood his meaning. The King would not approve of the use of extreme measures to extract information from Agnes Bonvylle. In his opinion it was beneath a man's dignity to torture a woman.

"Questioned, yes, but that is all," the Keeper assured us hurriedly. "And if she refuses to answer, it does not signify since Oxford's henchman will surely oblige. He will have much to tell us about the Earl's plans, I have no doubt."

Tyrell and I exchanged a look, knowing full well the horrors that awaited Jigger. He would break, that was certain. I tried to feel sorry for the man. Tried, and failed.

"Your priority must be to discover Oxford's present whereabouts," I offered. "Jigger knows where he is, he was commanded to go there as soon as he had... once he had finished at the quay," I concluded weakly, unable to speak so soon of what I had escaped by the narrowest margin.

"Too late," Berkeley admitted with a frown. "We prised the location from the churl while you were sleeping. The rendezvous was Bonvylle's house in the country. The men I sent to apprehend him have just returned. Oxford's flown already."

Tyrell swore angrily while I turned my head away to hide my discontent. The Earl's escape was a grievous blow. I had wanted the pleasure of bringing him before the King to pay for his crimes and now this was denied me.

Seeing our displeasure, Berkeley attempted to cheer us.

"The man Jigger knows his other hideouts," he insisted. "We'll squeeze his secrets from him and leave Oxford with nowhere to run."

I knew this was folly. Oxford had friends all over the country, not to mention the dozen or more vessels at his command that had been bedevilling the Channel these last few months. He had only to make it back to one of these ships to slip through our fingers for good.

Making his excuses, Berkeley left us to prepare his report for the King of the previous night's occurrences.

When he had gone, weariness assailed me and I closed my eyes, re-opening them with reluctance when I heard Tyrell speak my name.

"That other poor soul, your companion that was slain. Who was he?" he asked. "In the darkness I could not see his face but I feared he might be your servant boy until I saw him with Berkeley at the merchant's house."

There was sorrow in Tyrell's voice, sorrow that he had not been able to save my companion's life. I wondered if he would he feel the same regret once he knew the man's identity.

"His name was Ralph Abney," I said dully. "Like me, he was searching for Eleanor."

"Abney?" Tyrell repeated. "I am unfamiliar with that name."

This was not the reaction I had anticipated. Staring at Tyrell, searching his face for dissemblance, I saw that he was in earnest.

"You surprise me," I admitted. "Abney spoke of a bitter, longstanding quarrel between your family and his."

To my consternation Tyrell threw back his head and laughed.

"Ha, not another one! Jesu save me from my disputatious family!"

When he saw that I did not share his amusement he straightened his face and spoke in a more sober manner.

"Half the realm bears a grudge against me and my kin, Francis. We Tyrells make enemies as easily as other men break wind. If I were to remember the names of all with whom we have quarrelled, there would be space in my head for little else. In consequence I have found it makes life easier if I judge a man by his actions instead of by his name."

I shook my head sadly.

"Poor Abney did not know that. His mistrust of your family had been acquired at his mother's breast. He assumed it would be the same for you, that any bearing the name of Abney would be your foe. That's why he fled from you at Winchester."

Tyrell remained bemused.

"So that was him? Whatever did he expect me to do? Skewer him on sight, was that it?"

Against my will I smiled a little at my friend's indignation.

"No, James, not that. But Ralph Abney was Warwick's trusted man; he was among those assigned by the Earl to protect his wife. The others deserted her when word filtered through of the defeat at Barnet, but Abney remained to the last. He would have defended her with his life had not the Countess persuaded him to escape to France."

"So he was he seeking a pardon when he encountered us," Tyrell guessed. "Why, then, was he making for Beaulieu?"

"He hoped to wed Eleanor," I explained, "and was too impatient to wait for the pardon before trying for her hand."

"So your lass had another suitor!" Tyrell grinned. "I am not surprised, a pretty maiden like her."

Unwilling to dwell overlong on Eleanor's physical attributes, I hurried on with my explanation.

"Abney thought you would know his part in Warwick's treachery and bring him to justice before he could gain his pardon."

That caught Tyrell's attention.

"That was why he bolted?"

"It was," I assented before lapsing into a gloomy silence which Tyrell shared, apparently lost in thought.

Eventually, he spoke again.

"Believe me, Francis, I would not have betrayed the man. Even if I had known who he was, I would have left him to make his peace with the King."

"I know that," I told him.

And it was true; perhaps once I had harboured vague doubts about Sir James Tyrell but now I knew him for a man of loyalty and honour and, therefore, a fitting friend for my lord of Gloucester. I could take comfort from that thought but first I must grieve a little for dull, decent Ralph Abney. I prayed that God knew him for a good man and would have mercy on his unshriven soul.

Chapter Fourteen

At Berkeley and Tyrell's insistence I remained at the castle while my injuries mended. Finding the enforced idleness not to my taste, after the first day I took to walking every afternoon to The George. This was partly to test the limits of my endurance but mostly so that I might enjoy a cup or two of Bernard Gover's palatable wine in company with Tyrell and Matthew. On the third day after my fateful encounter with Oxford, I despatched Matthew with an invitation for Andrew Coterel to join our table. I was gratified when he appeared before me minutes later. As he took the empty place between Tyrell and me, I sensed the West Quay official's curiosity. It was understandable that he would want to separate the truth of what had occurred at the Bonvylles' house from the lurid tales that were flying about the town so I decided to make things easy for him.

"What do the common folk say about this affair?" I enquired.

"That Mistress Bonvylle made a cuckold of her husband. With a noble lover, no less. The lover slew Master Bonvylle. So say the fishwives of St. Michael's Square."

He exhaled gustily, indicating his low opinion of this tittle-tattle.

"And what do you say?" Tyrell enquired, studying Coterel's swarthy face with interest.

"I say nothing. Not to the gossipmongers. Now, what I think. Ah well, that's different. I'd say friend Cranley here sniffed out a secret. Linking the Bonvylles to that mysterious Hanseatic ship. And to Mistress Vernon."

We had decided to say nothing about the Bonvylles' association with Oxford until Berkeley received word from the King. There was a possibility that the King or his advisers would think it advantageous to keep the matter secret, in case further rebels could be flushed out. I thought it unlikely but we all agreed that the decision was the King's to make. Nevertheless, I trusted Coterel and wanted him to know why his friend, Robert Gower, had died. Berkeley voiced no objection to me telling him but Tyrell had asked to meet the man first, to judge his trustworthiness.

Now, with a curt nod, he signalled his approval so I leaned forward and began in a low voice.

"You are close to the truth but one of your links is missing. The Earl of Oxford completes the chain."

Coterel's eyes widened, shooting his monstrous eyebrows towards his scalp.

"You need not know the details," I continued, "and you must not speak of this. But your friend Gower was slain at Oxford's command, to keep him from revealing what he knew of Mistress Vernon's disappearance."

Andrew Coterel compressed his lips.

"You can count on my discretion. But I hope the villain is brought to account."

"As do we all," Tyrell intoned, raising his cup in a silent toast to Oxford's downfall.

†††

With rest and Matthew's tender care my strength was returning fast enough for me to think about leaving. I was glad, since lazing about the castle left me with too much time for fretful thought. Eleanor still weighed heavy on my mind. Though I had uncovered some of what had become of her, until I found her I knew that my task was only half complete. The Countess would certainly expect me to go after Eleanor and that was my own inclination, also. First, though, I knew I must return to Middleham, to speak with Dickon about the Bonvylle affair and take his advice about Eleanor. On a practical level, I was aware that without his help I would get nowhere, my personal wealth being insufficient to finance such an undertaking. However, my desire to be back at Middleham went deeper than that. I missed companionable evening strolls with my noble friend, the sweet smiles of his wife and the chatter of her ladies; I longed for the comforts of my own chamber – my bed with its richly embroidered hangings, the chest of fine clothes that stood at its foot and, perhaps most of all, I longed for my precious lute. In short, feeble as it sounds, I missed my home. Haring across the sea in pursuit of my prospective bride could take me away for months, maybe longer. Accepting this as unavoidable, I concluded that Eleanor's recovery could wait until I had seen the green hills of Wensleydale once more.

When I announced that I was ready to leave South-ampton, Tyrell declared his intention to accompany me back to Middleham, convinced that I was as yet too infirm to withstand an outlaw attack.

"I did not save your skin to have you lose it immediately to some stinking brigand," he told me candidly.

I demurred, insisting that the Duke wanted him in Gipping and besides, Matthew was handy enough in a fight. Tyrell would have none of it.

"It is not Matthew's strength I doubt. Brankin tells me the lad's gift for scrapping is held in high esteem at Middleham. It's you I fear is weaker than baby piss, Francis, so resign yourself to acceptance. Gipping can wait. I am coming with you, as I am certain our good Duke would wish."

With that decided, we began our preparations for the journey, settling our debts about the town and bidding adieu to those we had come to regard as friends. Then, on the eve of our departure, Berkeley came to me with a gleeful smirk enlivening his usually stolid features.

"Jigger has broken," he told me with more than a hint of unseemly relish. "Held out longer than I expected, I'll grant him that, but my man knows his work. He swore the scum would be willing to give up his own mother in the end and he has been true to his word."

"And?" I asked quickly, hoping to deflect the Keeper from giving me a loving description of the persuasive methods employed by his torturer.

"We have a list of names of individuals sympathetic to the Earl and his cause. Small fry, mostly, but useful for the King to know about, all the same. As for Oxford himself, Jigger says he will be back at sea already and I daresay he speaks the truth."

"Did he tell you nothing of import?" I asked, disappointed with the trivial nature of the intelligence obtained.

"Indeed he did, Master Cranley! Oxford is planning another adventure. He is mustering men and supplies ready for a new invasion. Cornwall is his preferred landing site. Once he has a toe-hold there, he aims to set the county alight in rebellion against our most gracious King."

Triumph, indignation and excitement battled for dominance over Berkeley's face.

"You have done well," I told him. "But you must write to the King at once. Cornwall must be put on full alert."

Gratified by my praise, Berkeley hurried away to prepare his report, leaving me alone to savour his news. I had been somewhat dejected of late, frustrated by my lack of success in recovering Eleanor. Now I could return to Middleham knowing that my journey south had achieved something of value. Thanks to my enquiries, we knew Oxford's plans and would be ready for him.

Departing Southampton on the twelfth day of July, we made a short detour to Beaulieu to collect Tyrell's stalwart retainers, Brankin and Knewstubb. As they readied themselves for the road, I requested and was granted a private audience with John Piers, during which I apprised him of Eleanor's abduction, revealing the Bonvylles' complicity in the affair but not Oxford's. As I had anticipated, the abbot registered dismay that he had been tricked into abandoning his search for her too soon and begged to know how he might make amends. Seizing the opportunity, I told him of my desire to look for her overseas, should sufficient funds be made available to me. To my satisfaction he took the hint, promising to make a generous contribution to my expenses when the time came.

"What has happened to the Bonvylles?" he enquired as I was about to make my farewell.

"The husband is dead, slain by one of Berkeley's officers. The woman is held captive at the castle, awaiting the King's will."

A flicker of interest in the abbot's gaze betrayed his surprise at the King's involvement in the affair. I smiled, letting him know that my slip had been deliberate. It was enough to tell him that the Bonvylles had been embroiled in a sinister matter of great import, for why else would the King be interested in them? John Piers understood that I had given him this insight in recompense for his promise of financial aid. A favour given, a favour received: even in the cloisters, it is how the world turns.

"Their assets have been seized for the King," I continued. "He will make a tidy sum when he sells the house and business."

Ah, Edward, I thought, that at least will please you. Judging by snippets of information gleaned from Tyrell, I guessed that the King was in dire need of cheer. His wretched brother Clarence had been making mischief again, blustering noisily about his discontent at Edward's preference for his younger brother. Fleetingly, I wondered if Clarence might be connected in some way with Oxford's plotting. They had been allies before Barnet, after all.

John Piers cut across my thoughts.

"Will the woman be executed, do you think?"

"I think not," I answered after a moment's consideration. "Though she is guilty of heinous crimes, there are reasons to show her clemency."

Kept alive, Agnes Bonvylle could prove a useful bargaining counter in future negotiations with Oxford and his kin. Edward would realise that.

"My guess is that she will be confined somewhere for the rest of her life."

I realised that the prospect gladdened me. Although I abhorred what she had done, I could not think of her death with equanimity. All her servants, I knew, had been questioned and then allowed to go free when it became clear they knew nothing of significance. Though they were lucky to escape with their lives, I wondered what would become of them now they had lost their home and their employment.

That very question had caused Matthew to come to me before we left Southampton with a request I had not anticipated.

"Master, can Jane Bonvylle come with us to Middleham?" he had asked without preamble.

Seeing that I was taken aback, he had made a case for the pitiful wench.

"She is all alone in the world now, master. No kin, no home, and no friends, neither."

I shrugged, unclear how the girl's uncertain future was my concern. Matthew provided clarification.

"Without Jane we'd not have known what happened to Mistress Vernon," he argued. "And she took a chance coming to talk to us. If she'd been caught, she'd have been killed for sure."

Reluctantly, I agreed that he had a point.

"But I cannot bring strays home every time the Duke sends me forth on business," I insisted. "You were one thing, I knew I could find a use for you, but that simpering ninny? What use will she be to me?"

"She says she's a fair hand with laundry," Matthew offered helpfully, "and likewise knows a good deal about plain sewing. I guessed you would be against taking her so I made her tell me her special skills. A laundress and a needlewoman! Such a one will always be useful, master, don't you agree?"

In the face of his persistence I had relented, maintaining weakly that this was the last time he was to prevail upon me in such a way. The lad's delight at my surrender gave me pause and I put it to him that he was soft on the lass. In reply he had chortled mightily and denied the charge, maintaining that he felt nothing for her but pity. Satisfied, I had ended our discussion by reminding him that Jane's tenure at Middleham depended on my lord of Gloucester giving her leave to stay.

†††

We had reached Kenilworth when the fine weather broke and thereafter heavy rainfall impeded our progress, turning the road into a thick, miry sludge. Nevertheless, spirits were generally high in our party though for widely differing reasons. Since he had petitioned me to bring her with us, I made Matthew share his mount with the Bonvylle wench. He soon made it plain that far from viewing this as a hardship, he enjoyed riding with her considerable girth nestled tight against him, and the girl seemed to find no fault in the arrangement. As for Tyrell, it was his habit to remain in good cheer in most circumstances and his stout-hearted lads followed his lead. That left only me; I confess that in the early stages of the journey my mood had been subdued but as we travelled further north my glumness lifted. When we finally reached Middleham eight days after leaving Southampton, I felt as giddy as a child on May Day morn.

My gladness was diminished when I caught sight of the Countess's sorrowful expression as we entered the Great Hall and made our obeisances to the Duke and his family. When I had agreed to remain at Southampton while my strength returned, I had wheedled Berkeley into sending a messenger to Middleham. While I had known that the King would waste no time in informing Gloucester of Oxford's plotting, I feared that with a new uprising looming, the fate of one insignificant maiden would not be uppermost in his mind. For that reason, I had scribbled a few hasty lines of my own for Dickon and bade Berkeley's man deliver them with all speed. One look at Anne of Warwick's face was all I needed to know that my letter had been received and its contents shared with her.

When my lord of Gloucester saw that I had brought home another stray he narrowed his eyes and accused me of contriving to set up a rival household of my own within his castle walls. I was unconcerned for I knew he spoke in jest and when I explained to him Jane's role in exposing Oxford's plot, he gave her his thanks and, more crucially, his permission to stay. With the matter settled, a steward was summoned to lead the wench to her new quarters. As she left, Matthew watched her passage with a bright smile of reassurance upon his face. Dickon noticed, as he was wont to notice so many trivial details, and amusement flashed in his eyes.

"Your servant has a sweetheart, Cranley," he teased, causing poor Matthew to blush as crimson as Nicholas Bonvylle's fancy livery. Flustered, he shook his head in urgent denial while the rest of us smirked complacently. It was the Duchess who rescued him from his embarrassment. Casting a sympathetic gaze over our bespattered clothing and drooping weariness, she stepped forward and suggested, with a sharp look at her husband, that it was high time Tyrell and I were given leave to withdraw. Gloucester agreed at once, although underlying his assent I could sense an eagerness to speak more of the danger facing his brother's realm. To please him, I dissembled about my fatigue but begged leave to change my attire for something less pungent. When Tyrell followed my lead, the Duke beamed his satisfaction.

"Go, then, and make yourselves presentable, but rejoin me within the quarter hour," he instructed, effecting not to notice his wife's small sniff of disapproval.

Washed and respectable once more in a clean doublet and jerkin, I returned to the Great Hall hard on Tyrell's heels. Gloucester was gone but the Duchess, her mother and a few attendants remained, sitting with their needlework under the windows of the east wall. Skirting the little group for fear of the disappointment I was sure to see in the Countess's expression, I quizzed a hovering page about my lord's whereabouts and learned that he was awaiting us in his privy chamber.

His first words after we were admitted to his presence were to thank Tyrell for saving my life in Southampton.

"Praise God you were there, else I would be lacking a friend," he remarked lightly enough, though the depth of his sincerity was plain.

"Now I believe there is much work to be done. The King depends on me to hold the north yet I fear the people are unsettled. And perhaps they have good cause, if my foolish brother's reckless talk has reached their ears. Most assuredly they will know of Oxford's insurrection and these matters create uncertainty. I must take steps to reassure those who look to me that the crown remains steady on Edward's head."

Stopping, he ruffled his hair and grinned at us, evidently undaunted by the task ahead of him.

"And you, my friends, will help me. James, I am glad you are returned to Middleham instead of idling your life away at Gipping. Yes, yes, I know I sent you there but now I believe you are of greater use to me here. I need you to ride out to the gentry; visit them in my name, take them gifts of game, and assure them of my goodwill. If any have young sons, retain them on my behalf whether they look promising or no. The fealty of the fathers will be worth the bother."

Tyrell nodded eagerly and Dickon turned to me.

"As for you, Francis, over the coming weeks I would have you call on the most influential people in the towns and villages hereabouts. Go to the Metcalfes at Nappa, William Clerionet in Richmond, the Widow Pennicott in York; all persons of that ilk, you will know who to visit, I have no doubt. At Nappa, say you are come to recruit more of their sons into my service. That will be no hardship to me for the Metcalfes always make good foresters and swift messengers. As for the merchants, Anne will give you a list of goods and provisions that we require from them."

I should have bridled at the prospect of running petty errands to shopkeepers while Tyrell called on the gentry, had I not known my lord of Gloucester so well.

"And the true purpose of these visits will be...?" I prompted.

"To encourage these people to speak openly of their concerns. You must find out what the gossips have been saying, Frank. Then refute it with all your powers of persuasion. Let it be known that all is well. Tell those you visit that I know them for my true friends and that

I hold them in the highest esteem. And remind them that their continued prosperity is dependent on the stability of this realm, and that is something only my brother Edward can provide."

As his words caught up with me I realised that I was, after all, to pay another call on Mistress Pennicott. The thought lacked appeal yet I knew my duty. As for the other visits Dickon desired me to make, they would be pleasant enough. It was never a hardship to call upon wealthy merchants in their comfortable houses and drink their expensive wines. As for the Metcalfes, they amused me. A large, bawdy tribe, they were notoriously fecund and therefore always had a lad or two ready to be placed in service at Middleham.

"What of you, my lord?" I asked the Duke, secure in the knowledge that he would excuse my familiarity.

"I shall be wooing the lords," he replied. "We are to hold a great feast for some of them here; that is what you will be shopping for! And before that, Anne and I will ride over to Bolton to remind Lord Scrope where his best interests lie."

"I think you are wise beyond your years," Tyrell ventured, "and for my part I shall enjoy the work."

Having paid this compliment, he yawned ostentatiously and Gloucester took the hint, telling him to get to bed lest he drop asleep on his feet like a horse. As Sir James withdrew I lingered, anxious for a private word with Dickon about Eleanor. Once we were alone I wasted no time in broaching the subject.

"You would travel abroad to search for her? This girl you hardly know, whom you would make your wife?" he guessed when I had finished.

I hesitated, reluctant to commit myself so completely. Then I thought of what I had lost with Margaret and knew I would be a fool to squander my chance with Eleanor.

"Aye, I would," I assented. "Dickon, I do not say I love her yet. Certainly not as you love your lady. It may be that I never will. But she is a fine girl and I believe I could be happy with her and she with me."

"Then you must go. You know that Anne and I have long wished to see you wed and Mistress Vernon would seem a fine catch for you. And Jesu knows that your going after her would please my belle-mère as nothing else could. She has never ceased moping for her lady since the moment she arrived here."

I frowned, thinking how little I wanted to ask my next question. Happily for my pride, Dickon pre-empted it.

"I shall finance the endeavour, of course, for you will be doing me a service in recovering her."

Although this was what I had been hoping for, I was humbled by his generosity.

"Father John at Beaulieu has also promised to help me," I told him, "so you need not shoulder the entire burden."

"That is good of him, though unnecessary. Unless you mean to travel in high style the cost will not be so great. And believe me, my friend, I will hold every penny well spent; until your lady is found, I do not believe Anne will know a moment's respite from her mother."

He smiled thinly and I wondered if having Proud Nan under his roof was proving more of a strain than he had anticipated.

"But Francis," he continued, "I must ask you to delay your departure until things are more settled. I know you are eager to get started but I need you here. I'll not deny there are others I could trust to visit the townspeople for me but none are liked by the commons as you are. Your impudence and flattery charms them. I think it will do much to secure their loyalty."

I wondered about that. I was popular with the Metcalfes, it was true, because like many of them I was a lusty young man, skilled in swordplay and dalliance. And I could not deny that I was a favourite with the womenfolk of the York and Richmond merchants; they always made much of me, lavishing me with compliments and thrusting their simpering daughters in front of me with their bosoms pushed high. But did that mean I was better placed to bind their husbands to my lord of Gloucester than any other trusted retainer? I thought not. My guess was that my noble friend had been made uneasy by Clarence's increasing hostility towards him and in consequence wanted me, his foster brother and oldest friend, close by his side as a token that some boyhood ties were unbreakable. For that reason, I accepted that Eleanor's recovery must wait a while longer.

Chapter Fifteen

For the next few weeks the Middleham stable lads knew no peace from the comings and goings of the Duke's messengers and emissaries. Tyrell and I rode forth almost daily, oft-times returning just as darkness fell, our horses spent but our spirits high from the overwhelmingly positive response to our overtures of friendship. While word of Clarence's discontent had indeed spread far into the Duke's domain, we uncovered none that were sympathetic to his complaints. He was judged unsteady, a cardinal sin in the eyes of most northerners, and overly fond of intrigue. Gloucester, in contrast, was thought of as a benign overlord, interested in administering justice and dealing fairly with the complaints of all. The sober merchants I visited spoke with admiration of his renowned piety while their spouses praised him for the kindness he had shown in giving a home to his wife's mother. All spoke of their affection for him and their joy that God had blessed him with an heir. In many quarters, the fact that this heir carried Neville blood was seen as a distinct advantage, Middleham having been held by that noble family for over two hundred years.

While Sir James and I spent our days securing the loyalty of the local populace, others amongst the Duke's confidants had different roles to play. Some made up his retinue when he paid formal calls on the neighbouring nobles; others carried constant messages between Gloucester and the King who continued to perambulate through the Midlands, ever watchful for news of Oxford. Then there were those despatched by the Duke on matters not pertaining directly to the current crisis. One such was young James Metcalfe, an offshoot of the Nappa Metcalfes who had been in Gloucester's employ for several years. Due to his boundless energy and an enviable ability to coax the last drop of endurance from any mount, Metcalfe had the reputation for being the Duke's fastest messenger. Thus it was to his swift hands that Dickon entrusted a letter touching closely upon my own interests.

In the autumn of 1470, Dickon and the King had been exiles in Burgundy following Warwick's treacherous pact with Margaret of Anjou. Margaret's addled husband, the pitiful wretch the Lancastrians called King, had been reinstated on the throne with Warwick working as the power behind it. It was during this painful time that Anne Neville, Warwick's youngest daughter, had been forced into marriage with Henry and Margaret's unpleasant son, Edward of Lancaster. Before its calamitous reversal of fortune, the House of York had been no friend to the powerful traders of the Hanseatic League but in exile the ever canny King had begun to see that an alliance with them might serve his interests. Before long he had established contact with them and, with skill and patience, managed to broker an agreement. One of the first merchants to accept Edward's offer of friendship, an influential man called Albrecht Giese, now lived in London. There he enjoyed considerable trade advantages, his reward for having provided fourteen ships for the King's invasion fleet when he re-claimed his throne in the spring of 1471. It was to Giese's house in the Steelyard that young Metcalfe carried a letter from Dickon.

The gist of the Duke's letter was to ask Giese to make enquiries about Eleanor among his Hanseatic trading colleagues.

"Anyone with contacts in Danzig are of special interest," I reminded him as he dictated the letter to his secretary, John Kendal. From time to time I scribed for the Duke but never when penmanship of high quality was essential. In those instances, Kendal or one of his assistants would be summoned.

"Remember, it was a Danzig ship that took Eleanor away, according to Andrew Coterel," I continued, anxious to make this point clear.

It troubled me to think of Eleanor lonely and afraid, praying every day for a rescue that never came. In my head I spoke to her, telling her to hold on. I will come, I told her. Sweetheart, I will come, just give me a little more time.

Though Dickon winced as I mentioned Danzig for the hundredth time that morning he forbore to rebuke me. Perhaps conscious that my concern for Eleanor was making me stupid, he simply agreed with me.

"Yes, Francis, I shall make sure enquiries are made in Danzig. And now, is there not a visit you have to make today?"

Accepting my dismissal, I thanked him for the trouble he was taking and headed for the stable. As I was mounting my palfrey I spotted Metcalfe taking his ease as he waited for the letter he was to carry to London.

Blessing my luck, I entreated him to make special mention of Danzig to the letter's recipient and paid him a handsome bribe to ensure that he did. Then I left to go about my business, well aware that my behaviour in this matter made me seem unhinged but quite unable to alter it.

The endless summer dragged on. July became August and the weather turned muggy and oppressive, or perhaps that was just my state of mind. Towards the end of the month the Duke and Duchess hosted a magnificent banquet for the high and mighty of the region. While preferring to live as quietly and simply as their royal status allowed, my friends could make a fair pass at splendour when they deemed it necessary. As the castle was made ready, I saw that Anne, in particular, knew how to dazzle and was reminded that her late father, the Kingmaker, had been famous for his ostentation.

To explain his sudden urge to entertain on such a lavish scale, Dickon announced the feast as a belated celebration of the birth of his son and heir. The day before the banquet this became a double celebration when word reached us from Shrewsbury that the Queen had been safely delivered of a second son, another Richard. Now the House of York had cause indeed to celebrate; with two male heirs in the nursery and more like to follow, surely now the succession was secure. The Duke's honoured guests fell to the task of rejoicing with gusto, gorging on the immense quantities of roast and stewed meats that had tested the Middleham kitchens to the limit, the men quaffing Gloucester's finest Rhenish and the ladies sipping hippocras from exquisite enam- elled beakers procured at great expense from York. The highlight of the feast was a pie the size of a cartwheel, decorated with gold leaf and shaped like the King's emblem of a sun in splendour. On either side of this vast sun were two smaller ones, likewise tricked out in gold; a play on words, these lesser pies represented Edward's young sons. As the extraordinary edifice was borne into the Great Hall by three sweating cookboys, Dickon rose and proposed a loyal toast to the King and Queen and all their children. I wished that the traitor Oxford could have been there to hear the approving roar reverberating throughout the hall as the men of the north echoed my lord's salute.

After the greasy remnants of the banquet had been cleared away there was music and dancing. My lord had wisely brought in professional players but since my official position at Middleham was personal minstrel to the Duke, I could not reasonably refuse to play and sing when badgered to do so by a group of red-faced matrons. Obediently I coaxed a few passable tunes from my lute but found no pleasure in the exercise and made my excuses as soon as was decent. Studying the women in their damasks and silks, I envisioned Eleanor dressed in filthy rags, scrubbing floors in some dismal foreign tavern. And that was the best I could imagine for her. Small wonder that for once I found it impossible to flirt.

Escaping to the blessed privacy of my chamber with a flagon of wine for company, I sat on my bed and thought about the bewildering ways of women, specifically Margaret and her mercurial moods which never failed to wrong-foot me. I had delayed obeying Dickon's instruction to visit her until the very last, reluctant to experience anew the biting scorn of this woman who once had adored me. Braced for the worst, I had greeted her with cold formality and been utterly unprepared for her reaction.

"Why so frosty, Francis?" she had teased, her tender mouth smiling sweetly at me. "Surely we are still friends after all we have been to one another?"

The audacity of the woman took my breath away. When we had last met, scarcely four months previously, she had made her disdain for me abundantly plain. When she had told me she would never be my wife I had been stung as never before and had determined to encase my heart in iron so that it might not be wounded a second time. Then I had met Eleanor Vernon and had learned to hope that marital happiness was still within my reach.

Sensing that my thoughts were far from her, Margaret had seized my hands and pulled me towards her.

"I was cruel last time, I know it. I did it to repay to you the hurt you gave me when you shilly-shallied over marrying me. And I stand by what I said. I do not wish to be your wife, Francis, for I find I like being a widow. I have status here in York – can you imagine that? Rich men come to my house and discuss business affairs with me! Their wives treat me with respect. Me, little Meg Smithkin who used to run bare-legged to the guardroom with messages for her father."

She made a sweeping gesture with her arm, indicating the opulent comfort of the parlour we were standing in.

"If I agreed to marry you I would have to give this up," she said. "You would find a buyer for the house and the business and then it would be back to Middleham for me. Where people would remember who I was before, not who I have become! There would be no more Widow Pennicott of York, just little Margaret Cranley, the jumped up sergeant's daughter who somehow tricked the Duke's bastard friend into marriage."

She scowled as she spoke, and pulled her hands away from me.

"Well, I won't do it!" she remonstrated, unnecessarily since I had not repeated my proposal and had scant intention of doing so. One rejection is enough for any self-respecting man, yet belatedly it occurred to me that I had not given Margaret the reason for my visit. The truth was that she had scarcely given me a chance to say anything before she had launched into her speech. Now I realised that she imagined I was there to plead again for her hand.

During the awkward silence which ensued I wondered if Margaret had been drinking too much wine, so peculiar did her behaviour seem to me. Trusting that Dickon would never know of my dereliction, I was about to take my leave without another word when she surprised me again.

"But I will be your mistress," she had offered, reddening as she made the wanton suggestion. "I do love you, Francis. Once I thought I could be happy as your wife, that loving you would be enough for me. Perhaps it would have been, had I never known the joy of managing my own affairs. But I cannot undo what has happened, nor unlearn what I have learned. I will never surrender my freedom to you but I will surrender my body. So there is my offer. I will be your lover, if you will have me, but not your wife."

I had left her then without an answer but returned two days later to accept her terms. As I lay in her arms afterwards, basking in the warmth of her soft embrace, I had told myself to savour and remember every detail.

I had said nothing to Margaret about Eleanor, not wishing to poison our happiness. Nevertheless, I knew with stone cold certainty that I would give up Margaret the moment Eleanor Vernon became my wife. I owed her nothing less.

Sitting in the solitude of my chamber, I wondered why it was that matters of the heart never ran smoothly for me. With a loud sigh I pushed the flagon aside, aware that the wine had lost its savour. Snuffing out my candle, I stretched out upon my bed and waited for drowsiness to claim me. Some hours later my slumber was disturbed by a noise I could not at first make out. Then, as my wits became less sleep-fogged, I realised that what had woken me was the sound of loud, cheerful singing, coming from the foot of my bed.

"Matthew, you knave, are you drunk?" I asked quietly.

The singing ceased as my servant considered the question.

"Aye, master, I believe I am!" he replied after a moment. "Are you not?"

"No, boy, I am not. I am asleep, or at least I was until you woke me with your infernal caterwauling."

At that he chuckled a little and then, gathering confidence, developed the chuckle into a full-bodied guffaw which threatened to rouse the castle.

"Hush your noise!" I barked. "I will not have my lord of Gloucester's guests disturbed by my addle-pated servant."

"There's no chance of that, master. Most folk are still about, drinking and dancing and hustling into corners with their doxies."

Again the chuckle, though more softly this time.

"It's a night for pleasure, master. Only an old moody-boots like you would wish to sleep on such a night."

An old moody-boots. I had never thought of myself that way. I knew I should reprimand him for his drunken insolence but could not summon the requisite sense of outrage. Good luck to him, at least he has enjoyed this night, I thought, before dropping into a mercifully dream-free sleep.

†††

In the days following the Middleham feast I began to prepare for my journey overseas. Thanks to the Duke's great diligence, the loyalty of the men of the north was assured. If trouble was coming, they would be ready to rise for Edward. And trouble was coming, of that we remained certain. As to when it would come, that was unknowable. In these circumstances, Dickon concluded that he could delay my departure no longer. Guessing that I was haunted by visions of Eleanor in terrible straits, he assured me that he could manage without me and pressed me to leave for London at the beginning of September. There, his friend from the Hanseatic League would be able to tell me what, if anything, he had managed to discover about Eleanor's whereabouts, and help me find a vessel to take me wherever I needed to go.

As the last days of August slipped away, I found many pretexts to visit York, always leaving Matthew at Middleham so that I might enjoy a few hours with Margaret without his knowledge. Her servants knew, of course, as servants always do, and I fretted about that. She insisted that my anxiety was needless, explaining that she paid her people generously in order to ensure their absolute loyalty. I affected a reassurance I did not feel, knowing how often malice and spite can overcome self-interest. I was also troubled by the thought that Margaret might conceive my child, though when I voiced this concern she had laughed and said she knew how to prevent such a thing from happening.

"There are herbs that can help," she had whispered, tickling my chin with a lock of her abundant honey hair. "My maid knows a wise woman who grows them and she swears to their efficacy."

I frowned, unwilling to entrust my love's safety to an unsavoury potion brewed by some crazed old crone. Margaret caught my frown and sought to lift it.

"In any case," she had joked, "I should have thought it would please you were my belly to grow big, for then I would have to wed you, like it or no!"

I should have told her then that I was preparing to marry another. It was the right moment, even though in so many other ways it was the wrong one. Our contentment would have been shattered by angry recriminations and since I was to leave very soon, I wanted to drain the last drop of happiness from our encounters. So I held my tongue about Eleanor, telling Margaret only that I would be gone for some time on a confidential matter of some importance. She assumed that I was undertaking another mission for my lord of Gloucester and, by failing to contradict her, I connived at that assumption.

One day before I was due to leave Middleham, the Duchess and her infant son fell ill. The attending physician was sanguine about their recovery, calling their indisposition a slight summer fever that would pass in due course. This was no comfort to my noble friend. Having known Anne as a child, Dickon was aware that her health had never been robust. Furthermore, he knew it had been severely tested during the turbulent years immediately prior to their marriage. Her father's unthinkable betrayal of the House of York, a forced marriage to an unlikeable youth who viewed her with disdain, the slaughter at Barnet and Tewkesbury and her subsequent abduction by Clarence – all these events had left their mark on her. Though the last fifteen months had done much to restore her strength and spirits, Dickon was always anxious on her behalf and now he was convinced that child-bearing had brought her low again. As for the precious babe, no son was ever loved more tenderly by his father than Edward of Middleham. Small wonder, then, that Gloucester spent the greater part of that day on his knees in the chapel, praying for the swift recovery of his dear ones.

In the face of his anguish, I could not countenance leaving my friend. Until I knew that both the Duchess and her son were well, my proper place was by his side, offering such support as it was within my power to give. Happily, the physician's prediction proved accurate and within a week both Anne and the babe were on their way to recovery. Then the bells rang out across Middleham and Dickon returned to the chapel, this time to thank God for sparing his beloved family.

Once again I prepared to leave and once again I was forestalled, this time by the arrival of a messenger from the King. Oxford's invasion was believed to be imminent and Edward was calling upon his brother to array the men of Yorkshire.

Chapter Sixteen

Drear November found me camped out on the sands
at Marazion in Cornwall, serving with a mostly
local force summoned to oust Oxford from his island
toe-hold of St. Michael's Mount, half a mile offshore.
Thanks to the intelligence so expertly coerced from
Jigger by Berkeley's torturer, the King had been fore-
warned that Cornwall was the likely target for the Earl's
latest experiment in insurrection. The news had come as
small surprise to Edward who tended to hold a low opinion of this most south-westerly corner of his kingdom.
According to Dickon, his brother had once described it
as the back-door of rebellion, largely on account of the
undependable nature of some of the Cornish gentlemen.
Whichever house they served, Edward believed that their
first allegiance was always to their own advantage.
Despite this generally disparaging view, the King had the
highest confidence in the loyalty of Sir John Arundell,
the Sheriff of Cornwall, who also happened to be the
father of my friend Tyrell's young bride. Acting on the
King's orders, Arundell had put his county on high alert
in order to foil Oxford's treacherous endeavour.

That he had failed was not in any way his fault. While
all eyes had been fixed on the coast, scanning the seas
for an invasion force, Oxford had crept in by stealth.

Disguised as a pilgrim he had arrived at the island fortress of St. Michael's Mount and made his way to the cliff-top monastery. Cowled and shuffling, he and his small band of similarly garbed companions had roused no suspicion until it was too late. Throwing off their disguises, they had drawn their swords and made short work of the handful of guards who came at them once they realised they were under attack. Then, to the shocked dismay of their hosts, pilgrims who had been lodging at the monastery for several days already revealed themselves to be Oxford's followers. Within minutes the island was taken by a force of no more than eighty men.

All this had occurred on the last day of September but word of it had not reached the King until well into the following month. As it happened, due to an unforeseen turn of events I had been standing within feet of him when he read Arundell's apologetic missive. In the heightened emotion of the ensuing moments, I had been well-placed to beg royal permission to join the force that would, inevitably, be sent to besiege the Mount. Knowing I had a debt of my own to settle with Oxford, Edward had readily given his assent before turning his attention to matters more pressing than the personal vengeance of one of his brother's adherents.

That I was at Leicester with the King when Arundell's message arrived was due in no small part to my lord of Gloucester's tender conscience. When word had come to Middleham of Oxford's impending invasion, he had needed his most able men about him as he acted to preserve his brother's realm. Though he knew I was impatient to set out in search of Eleanor before bad weather made sea travel inadvisable, his preference was for me to stay. Yet, being Dickon, he left it to me to make my choice.

"Do we go south, my lord?" Tyrell had asked as the Duke's friends and advisers gathered in his privy chamber to lay plans.

"Not yet. For now my brother requires me to gather an army and hold it in readiness."

Only now did I truly appreciate the Duke's shrewdness in bolstering the allegiance of the King's northern subjects. All the flattery, patronage and entertainment of the past few weeks had been in preparation for this moment. He had made certain that when the moment came, the north would rise for him, giving him an army to bring to Edward's aid.

First, though, that army had to be raised. Though the people would answer his summons to arms, someone had to take it to them. The responsibility for that fell to those of us gathered around the map hastily pulled from a chest by John Kendal. Conyers, Tunstall, Pudsey, Markenfield, Tyrell and more; each in turn they received their orders from Dickon, bowed and made a speedy exit, eager to be on their way. One by one they left until only Kendal and I remained, though there were many places still to be visited.

"These must wait for now," my cunning friend told his secretary, indicating several outlying locations on the map. "Make a list of them, and issue new instructions to each of my summoners as they return."

"What of me, my lord?" I had enquired with a note of asperity in my tone. "Am I not to ride out?"

Dickon gave me a guarded look that at first I could not read.

"Frank, I cannot ask you to delay your departure any longer. I have kept you from your lady too long already, as my mother-in-law never fails to remind me.

And who knows how long this business with Oxford will last? If you stay, you may not be free to leave for many weeks."

Though he spoke cagily, I understood his hidden message. My friend was telling me that it was for me to choose whether I left now, as planned, to begin my search for Eleanor, or remained to play some small part in putting down Oxford's rebellion. However, should I decide to stay, he would expect me to remain for as long as it might take to vanquish the traitor and restore peace to the realm.

Without hesitation I pointed to John Kendal's map.

"Show me where you need me to go," I said, leaning over the secretary's shoulder to get a better view. My reward was immediate; from the corner of my eye I caught the relief and gladness in Gloucester's face. It was enough, just, to make bearable my anxiety for Eleanor's safety.

For three weeks Gloucester's closest companions had known no rest as we rode to and from Middleham, bringing the call to arms to all the able-bodied men of the county. By the Duke's order, in every community large and small a local leader was appointed and tasked with preparing a fighting force that would be ready to march at a moment's notice. With no massed mustering required as yet, the men were able, for the most part, to remain in their homes, tending to their farms and trades until word should come that they were needed.

By the end of September my lord of Gloucester was satisfied that his army would be able to march south within a day of receiving the King's call. Now all we had to do was wait. As we soon discovered, that was the vexing part. With our blood stirred by the frenetic bustle of the preceding weeks, we were eager to engage with the enemy. Instead, we sat at Middleham, our eagerness subsiding into frustrated boredom as, day after day, the looked-for summons failed to arrive.

Having put the recovery of my intended bride on hold in order to fight beside my friend, I found the inactivity harder to bear than the others. Tense and angry, by day I paced the battlements, scouring the horizon for signs of a messenger while by night I vented my frustration on the hapless Matthew. Not even a few stolen hours with Margaret could cheer me, so conscious was I of the interminably slow passage of time. Since I made no effort at concealment, Dickon soon became aware of how severely I chafed at the enforced waiting and sought to find a solution. Calling me to his privy chamber one day in early October, he had instructed me to prepare for a journey. He was sending me, he told me, to follow the King in his extended progress throughout the Midlands. Attached to the court as his trusted emissary, I would carry between Gloucester and his brother any messages they preferred not to commit to writing.

Although I recognised the move as a thinly disguised ruse to give me some purpose, I was grateful for my friend's thoughtfulness. Quite apart from giving me something to occupy my restless mind, he was bestowing on me an honour far above my rank. From time to time I had gone to court in Dickon's retinue but never in any official role and certainly never without him. This posting changed all that; it gave me access to the King together with the status due to the Duke of Gloucester's personal representative.

From the moment of my arrival at Leicester the King had treated me with kindness, keeping me on the fringes of his inner circle at all times. He did this as a favour to Dickon who, I suspect, had written to him something of my predicament. I believe that Edward, who fancied himself a chivalrous prince, regarded me as a tragic suitor denied his one true love by cruel fate. As long as I played this part to his satisfaction, he was happy to have me about him despite my lowly status. It helped that Earl Rivers, his wife's illustrious brother, was not at court, having recently left to establish a household for the young Prince of Wales at Ludlow. The Earl and I had good reason to mistrust one another and had he been at the King's side, I knew my welcome would have been cooler by far.

When Sir John Arundell's message about Oxford eventually reached court, Edward's response was to issue a commission of array. Arundell was tasked with raising a large body of Cornish gentry to take back the Mount.

"And, Master Cranley, since you are so keen to be part of this action, you can have the honour of carrying the commission to him," he told me with a gleam of amusement in his eye.

"Gladly, Your Grace, but what of my lord of Gloucester?" I dared to ask. "His force will be ready to march within a day's notice, and is comprised of loyal Yorkshire men. Why not send them to deal with Oxford?"

As Edward's florid face hardened and his blue eyes turned wintry, I feared I had overstepped myself. Preparing for his onslaught, I remembered how Fat Nell, my vicious old nursemaid, had always scolded me for not knowing when to hold my tongue.

"A flapping tongue will trip you," she had been wont to say, cuffing me about the ears to make the lesson more memorable. Well, I had never learned and now it seemed I was to trip indeed.

Bracing myself, I ventured to stem the King's fury with an apology but was interrupted before I had half begun.

"If only my other brother were as reliable as Dickon," he sighed, and I realised with unmanly relief that his anger had not been directed at me at all but at his brother of Clarence. "Conceited, stupid and puffed up with pride! Why does the fool continue to be a thorn in my side?"

This time I managed to stay silent and after a long moment the King turned his attention back to my question.

"Clarence has made allies of my enemies before now. There is reason to believe he may have done so again. Thus, until I can be sure of George, Dickon must remain at Middleham. While he holds the north, I have nothing to fear from that quarter. And Oxford has only eighty men!"

Clapping a beefy arm about my shoulders, he gave a short bark of derision.

"It is not so great a threat after all, eh? De Vere must have lost his charm if this is all the support he can muster. Arundell and his Cornish friends are more than capable of squashing him, they will need no outside help. Apart from you, Cranley! You may stay and fight once your message is delivered. I know you thirst to punish Oxford for his treatment of your lady, and so you shall. Never fear, I shall send word to Dickon to explain what you are about."

So it was that, accompanied only by Matthew and Arundell's messenger, I had left Leicester on the 27th

October and ventured into a part of the country I had never hitherto visited. Now, sitting in my tent on the shore of Mount's Bay, waiting for the day's orders, I wondered if the King had indeed been wise to leave the matter in Cornish hands. Arundell himself was loyal and able but there were many in his service that I did not trust. Chief amongst these was one Sir Henry Bodrugan. With his piratical appearance, uncouth manners and reputation for brutality, I found him more brigand than gentleman. When I had voiced these doubts to Arundell, he had shrugged them off.

"Bodrugan a brigand!" he had laughed. "Well, perhaps he is, but what of it? He and his men are fierce fighters. We have need of their sort if we are to win back the Mount. Try not to worry, Master Cranley. I know how to keep Bodrugan in check."

I hoped he was right yet I had a niggling feeling that the campaign was slipping away from us. Lately we had found out that Richard de Vere, one of Oxford's brothers, had managed to escape to France where he intended to seek help from King Louis. Elsewhere, we heard that the Earl's friends were wandering freely about Cornwall, doing their utmost to stir up support for his rebellion. If either endeavour should prove successful, this minor uprising would rapidly become a major embarrassment for Edward.

Dwelling on these gloomy thoughts, I was glad to be distracted by a familiar voice hallooing for me outside my tent. Rising swiftly, I pulled open the flap and strode outside.

"John Knewstubb!" I called, catching sight of Tyrell's trusted retainer. "Whatever brings you to these parts?"

"Sir James's orders, master. Sent me and Tom Brankin down here to join in the fun."

I glanced about for the absent Brankin and Knewstubb rushed to explain.

"Tom's seeing to the horses. We fell in with your rascally servant when we arrived. He told me where to find you, and promised to guide Tom here when he was done."

Re-entering the tent, I gestured for Knewstubb to follow me.

"Well, it is good to see you!" I told him with fervour. "Matthew and I have been feeling quite the outsiders. I fancy the Cornish do not care overmuch for strangers."

Knewstubb chuckled, a grin spreading wide across his rock-hewn face like a river that has burst its banks.

"It is the same everywhere, master. Newcomers are always regarded with suspicion. I've been places where strangers are lynched for no greater crime than speaking different."

"Then it's lucky for us they don't do that here," I quipped. "Most of these Cornish speak a tongue all their own, like nothing you've ever heard. And even when they do speak English I find it hard to comprehend a word they say.

"But why did Sir James send you?" I continued, more than a little perplexed. Though I knew that Tyrell had many trusty men at his command, I also knew that Brankin and Knewstubb were his particular favourites. I could not imagine why he would be willing to part with them for more than a day or two.

"Two reasons," Knewstubb answered.

"One, we bring you a letter from the Duke. He wanted it delivered by trusty hands, to make sure it reached you quick-smart. And two, Sir James wants us to stop here and fight, to show support for his father-in-law. He cannot come himself on account of the Duke wanting him, so we are sent in his stead."

My spirits rose at his words. Fighting alongside Brankin and Knewstubb would be the next best thing to having Dickon and Tyrell beside me.

"Well, give me this letter then," I ordered, making my voice gruff to hide my pleasure. "Then get some rest, for Arundell will be wanting us soon enough."

Taking the letter he proffered, I strode outside again to read it where the light was better. Breaking the Duke's seal, I saw he had scribbled three lines for me in his own hand.

I have received word from Albrecht Giese; his enquiries have borne fruit. In Danzig there is no trace of Mistress Vernon but in Rostock he has heard of a gently bred English girl said to be lodging with a decent family. Francis, I believe we have found your Eleanor.

Chapter Seventeen

The day of Brankin and Knewstubb's arrival was the day our campaign began in earnest. Hitherto we had done little but watch and wait, hoping to starve Oxford's band of renegades into submission, although as yet this strategy had shown little success. Now, however, one of Arundell's observers brought word that a small party had emerged from the cliff-top fortress and was venturing down to the harbour where a fishing boat was being unloaded. We had been doing our best to discourage the locals from supplying the rebels but with too few vessels at our disposal, it was not possible to mount a total blockade. Nevertheless, Arundell's policy of hanging anyone he suspected of trading with the Mount and leaving their bodies to rot on the gibbet had thus far proved an effective deterrent. Not so any longer, it seemed, though the news appeared to delight Arundell.

"We are to see some action at last, Master Cranley," he called to me as I intercepted him striding towards the horses, clad in an old-fashioned combination of padded coat and mail but no plate armour. "A rebel party is making for the harbour. Just a handful of them, but it's a start. Let's make them pay dear for their fish supper!"

Catching his good humour, I sought to strengthen it by telling him of Brankin and Knewstubb's arrival.

"Sent with Sir James's compliments," I told him. "I'm sure you will find them more than useful. Both can handle themselves as well as any men I know and Brankin is uncanny with a bow."

Unknowingly I had said the wrong thing. Sir John was a proud man and far from being gratified that his son-in-law had sent help, he expressed high indignation.

"God's bones, I do not need his aid! I shall flush this traitor from Cornish soil without interference from Tyrell or any other foreign interloper. And that includes you!"

Scowling, he struggled onto his horse, in his temper kicking aside his hapless squire before leaving me without a word of farewell. The lad stumbled and I caught his elbow to steady him. Shrugging me away, he sprang onto his own mount and trotted after his master but stopped when he had gone a few paces and glanced back at me over his shoulder.

"Your pardon, that was churlish of me. And my master spoke hasty. He will regret it, I know, but for now you had best not follow."

Then he was gone, leaving me alone to curse the bad luck that had led to my exclusion from the first real fighting of the campaign. Later, when we saw what befell Arundell and his men, I had cause to retract that curse. It had been a trap all along, another of Oxford's clever ploys.

Charging at the head of his pitifully small sortie along the shingle bank that appeared at low water, Arundell had been far from the shore when the snare was sprung. As he bore down on the small group at the harbour, the fishermen threw off their smocks and drew weapons, moving to stand alongside the rebels. As first blows were exchanged, yet more heavily armed men emerged from behind bushes and carts until Arundell and his lads were seriously outnumbered. Straining our eyes from the beach, only now did we understand what was happening. Aghast, I scrambled to join the band of reinforcements but the bloody skirmish was over before we were halfway there. With the treacherous assailants once more in the safety of their fortress, all we could do was retrieve Arundell's broken body and those of his fallen comrades and carry them back to Marazion. Among them, I was grieved to see, was the young squire who had spoken to me with courtesy before riding to his death.

That night, a man came to my tent with a dagger. As it turned out, it was my own rondel dagger which I had dropped as I stooped to examine poor Arundell for signs of life. Even in the darkness I recognised the stranger from earlier that day; he had been one of the men who had helped me with the Sheriff's corpse.

"I saw it fall," he explained as he handed me the dagger, "but said nothing at the time, knowing you were otherwise occupied. So I picked it up to bring to you at a more opportune moment."

From his speech and dress I knew him as one of the Cornish gentry. Thanking him for his civility in returning the dagger, I invited him inside the tent to share a cup of the local metheglin with me, the available wine being fit only for soaking my soiled linen.

"My name is Francis Cranley," I told him. "I'm a servant of the Duke of Gloucester, sent here by the King because I have a personal grudge against the Earl of Oxford."

The man laughed softly as he took a sip from his beaker.

"I know who you are, Master Cranley. Everyone knows you and that odd-looking lad of yours. How could we not? You are the only foreigners here, saving those two friends of yours that arrived this morning. And what grim harbingers they turned out to be! Better, perhaps, that they had stayed away."

Though I understood this deep-rooted suspicion of strangers, I could not have Brankin and Knewstubb branded as unlucky. In warfare, such notions can foster fear and mistrust of a fellow. Tyrell's lads deserved better and in heated terms I told my visitor as much.

"Well then," he answered, unruffled by my vehemence. "You vouching for them will serve for me. I saw you this morning; you did not tarry when the cry went up to aid Sir John. For that alone, I am glad you are here."

Warming to the man, I sketched him a bow and expressed my gratitude for his friendly words.

"With poor Sir John slain, I fear there are few enough who share your sentiment," I added. "But who do I have the honour of addressing?"

Clearly amused by my mock formality, he answered me in similar fashion.

"Kylter. William Kylter, from the manors of Constantine and St. Keverne on the Lizard peninsula."

The first name meant nothing to me but the second was familiar. Raising my candle, I studied Kylter more closely. Of middling years, he had curly dark hair, greying at the temples, and a handsome, weather-beaten face. While it was possible that he was connected to the one other soul I knew to have come from a place called St. Keverne, I could not be certain since that person's face had been in a state of decay the one time I saw it.

"Forgive my asking," I began tentatively, "but did you have a natural son called Peter?"

It was an impertinent question and had I been wrong, I would not have blamed William Kylter for knocking me to the ground. Instead, he gave me a sad nod although his eyes registered wonderment that I should know about Peter.

"Peter was my boy, my bastard. My poor wife is barren so I have no legitimate issue. Is it any wonder I loved the lad and raised him above his expectations? But Peter was a scrapper, forever into one misdeed or another. I always did what I could to extricate him but in the end my only recourse was to send him away."

"You sent him to the monks," I said flatly, hoping there was no trace of the reproach I felt in my tone.

"I did," Kylter agreed. "The church and some fields at St. Keverne belong to the abbey at Beaulieu, though the rest is mine. I had Peter raised there within my reeve's household but when the boy fell foul of the villagers one time too many, I feared for his life. The St. Keverne monks came to me with a solution; they were travelling to the mother house with their revenues and would take Peter along for protection. Once there, they would use money I gave them to obtain a novitiate for him. It was imperfect, I knew, but with angry peasants baying for his blood it was the best I could contrive. At least he would be alive. Yet I was proved wrong. Even as a novice he found a way into mischief and this time he paid for it with his life."

His account more or less agreed with the version I had been given at Beaulieu.

"What do you know of the circumstances of his death?" I asked Kylter.

220

"Only what the Netley abbot, Father Marmaduke, wrote me. That Peter was murdered by a local carpenter in retribution for despoiling his daughter."

"This was all he told you?" I probed, curious to know if Kylter had been told about the child in Alys Aldis's belly.

"All? What more was there to tell me? That my one son was licentious and wicked? This I know already."

I was not fooled by the man's bitter words for I read regret and pain on his face, pain so raw that it moved me to tell him the truth about Peter's death. First, though, I described to him something of the lad's wretched life at Netley, to help him understand why Peter had strayed. I spoke of Father Marmaduke's excessive abhorrence of anything approaching immorality and the beatings Brother Walter gave him in a muddle-headed attempt to save him from worse. When I saw how this grieved him, I told him that Peter's death would have been so sudden that he could not have known pain. And then I told him about Alys and the genuine affection that had existed between them.

"It is my belief that your son would have put away his wildness had he been able to wed the girl," I told him gently.

Kylter bowed his head and wept silently for a while.

"Thank you for telling me this," he said when he could speak again. "It is some small comfort to know that he was not all bad, and that he knew some joy before he died."

Again I remembered Fat Nell remonstrating with me to hold my flapping tongue. There was more I could tell William Kylter but would he thank me for it? I was on the verge of saying nothing more when a vision came into my head. I saw Eleanor arriving at Netley on the cart that fine morning in May. Lurking nearby was Peter of Keverne, burning her with the intensity of his gaze as he willed her to see him and take his letter. But she was wrapped up in her thoughts – thoughts of me, perhaps – and did not see him. Had she noticed him, I knew she would have agreed. Though I had not known her long, I had sensed something in Eleanor, be it a quality or a flaw, which would always incline her to respond to pleas for help. That certainty decided me.

"My friend, perhaps I can offer you a greater comfort. It may be that as we speak you are a grandsire. I know nothing of the dates but when I met with Alys Aldis, she was carrying Peter's child."

William Kylter and I drained many beakers of metheglin before he left my tent that night. As he staggered out into the chill night air, he joked that he had brought me a dagger and in return I had given him a family. After he had gone I smiled into the darkness, thinking of the life of ease and plenty that awaited Alys and her babe. Once our business here at the Mount was concluded, Kylter meant to find the girl his son had loved and the child she had borne him out of wedlock. Should she prove willing, and I strongly suspected she would, he was going to bring them home to Cornwall and recognise them as his kin.

†††

The day after Arundell was cut down, Sir Henry Bodrugan assumed command of the Cornish forces. Distrusting the man, I was unhappy about this happenstance but realised I could do nothing about it. Not only was

I a stranger here in Cornwall, I was a man of no standing, my presence tolerated by the local gentry purely on the basis of the King's careless favour. Only to Kylter did I share my misgivings, having formed a warm bond with the man since speaking to him about Peter. After listening to me, he admitted that he shared my reservations but cautioned me to speak of them to no one else.

"Bodrugan is not generally well-liked; he has raided too many homes for that to be possible. Nevertheless, he is a Cornishman. In a contest between you and he, none but I would side with you and, truth to tell, even I might waver."

I knew that he was jesting but I took his point all the same. It would have been the same in Yorkshire. However unpopular a man might be, he would always have more local support than a stranger. So I muzzled my concerns and turned my attention to winning Bodrugan's trust. At first it seemed as though my doubts about him were unfounded. I recognised that he brought to the siege a vigour that had been lacking under Arundell's command. Discipline was increased. Regular drills were organised and public floggings held of men who had slunk away to their villages once the novelty of the siege had waned. Bodrugan bribed their comrades to betray the deserters, then forced the same comrades to wield the lash and afterwards wash the tattered flesh on their backs with sea water. I had no issue with these brutal measures, knowing them necessary if we were to maintain our numbers. What bothered me was something that was harder to pin down, an instinct that something was awry with the campaign.

Our forces had begun skirmishing with the enemy immediately after Bodrugan took command. I should have been pleased but instead I found myself confused, unable to fathom why Oxford would choose to ride out from his lair to confront a force many times larger than his. Nor did I understand why Bodrugan responded to these charges with a handpicked band of followers that exactly matched the number of Oxford's men. When one of his Cornish lieutenants asked him this very question, Bodrugan replied with a jaunty laugh that there was no glory in overcoming a foe with superior numbers. Superior fighting power, that was how he intended to take back the Mount, he declared.

The answer satisfied many but by no means all. Gradually our days fell into a familiar pattern. Oxford would ride out, Bodrugan and his chosen few would meet him, blows would be exchanged and then the rebels would retreat or, rather, be allowed to retreat as I soon came to see it. A few days of inactivity would follow, and then it would begin again. One evening, judging that the time was about right for another of these curiously inconclusive episodes, I called Brankin and Knewstubb to my tent.

"If Bodrugan leads his men out tomorrow, I mean to go with him," I told them. "He'll not like it, but if he voices an objection I'll invoke the King's name."

Knewstubb coughed and spat.

"You believe our brave leader is up to some trickery?" he suggested.

"I do. My guess is that the fighting we witness from a distance is half-hearted at best. I think Bodrugan's assaults are a sham, mounted to persuade us of a determination to oust the Earl that he does not truly possess."

"You suspect him of collusion with Oxford?"

I considered before giving my reply.

"It is the only thing that makes any sense. Otherwise, why is the Earl able to retreat every time, and why are his casualties so few? And why does Bodrugan not bring our full force to bear upon the Earl's sorties?"

Brankin sucked his teeth.

"If you're right, I don't fancy your chances if you insist on riding out with him."

I grinned but made no other reply and Brankin exchanged a long look with his friend. I could not read what passed between them but the outcome was all I had wished for.

"Well then, you'll be glad of some company."

The next morning, as I had predicted, Oxford again emerged from his fortress, accompanied by thirty or so of his adherents. At once, Bodrugan and a similar number of men rose to meet them.

"You are not needed, Master Cranley," Bodrugan called to me as he saw me striding towards my horse. "My lads and I have the measure of the traitor."

"I do not doubt it, but I grow weary of inactivity, Sir Henry. I know you will not begrudge me the sport," I replied.

Bodrugan scowled, tugging at his long, unkempt hair.

"The King expects it of me, you know," I added, giving Bodrugan what I hoped was a winsome smile.

"As you will," he snapped, shooting me a look as black as his locks before giving the order to mount.

Matthew had ready the fine charger loaned me by the King. Climbing into the saddle with as much agility as my mail would allow, I fell in with Bodrugan's party, paying scant heed to their bristling hostility. When I sighted the rebels at the end of the causeway, I felt my blood surge and for a moment I forgot everything except the desire to meet my enemy. Riding hard towards them, the salt air whipping my face and men-at-arms thundering at my side, my only thoughts were of blood and vengeance.

As we neared the island of St. Michael's Mount I began to discern the features of my prey. I was reaching for my sword, intending to raise my arm aloft in a feral salute when I caught a sudden movement to my left. Turning my head, I saw that one of Bodrugan's henchmen was riding far too close to me and as our eyes met I watched his sword cleaving through the air towards me. Instinctively I wrenched my body to one side, ducking out of the saddle to avoid the slicing blade. Unbalanced by the force of his failed attack, my assailant lost control of his mount for a few moments, giving me a precious chance to recover. Hauling myself back into the saddle, I veered to the right to put distance between me and my unknown enemy, and found a second attacker swinging his sword towards me. Though I had time to take in his face and recognise him as another of Bodrugan's close associates, there was nothing I could do to avoid the blow. The sharp blade was arcing towards my neck when its owner's charger stumbled and then folded inwards onto the shingle, pitching the rider over its head to be trampled under the hooves of the oncoming horses. Twisting my head, I glimpsed John Knewstubb now galloping beside me, a snarl on his face and a blade in his grip, dripping red from the blood of the horse whose hock he had slashed to save my life.

My own mount kept its head better than I, never once faltering as the mingled screams of the fallen man and horse rent the air. Now we were nearly upon the rebels but before I could give them my full attention, I needed to take care of my first attacker. Glancing about for him, I realised that he had taken fright and ridden away from me. No matter; I had seen his face and would deal with him later. A split second later and I was among the enemy, slashing the first in the thigh and then finishing him off with a thrust to the throat. As I removed my sword I read surprise in the dying man's eyes but took it for the shock every man must feel when he meets his mortality. Readying for the next onslaught, I noticed that the bulk of the fighting was off to one side, away from where Knewstubb and I were laying into our meagre opposition with grim intent. So concentrated was I on the work that it took me several minutes to see the action between the opposing forces was as harmless as a practice tourney. Little blood was being shed and any that was came from flesh wounds that would likely heal.

Knewstubb and I grasped the situation at the exact same time, putting down our swords as our opponents fell away. As we had suspected, Bodrugan's skirmishes with Oxford were indeed a sham, performed to convince the watchers on the shore of his diligence. He was in league with the traitorous Earl, there could be no doubt of that, but to what end I could not yet guess. More pressing at that precise moment was the deadly predicament Knewstubb and I found ourselves in. Bodrugan's hastily forged plan had been to have me slain on the causeway, to prevent me from discovering his connivance with Oxford. That the plan had failed was due solely to Knewstubb whose presence had not been anticipated. Now there were two of us to kill. Any moment now the pretend battle would halt and we would be set upon by thirty or more vicious fighting men. Accepting the situation with fatalistic calm, I edged my horse towards Knewstubb. There had been no time for gratitude on the causeway so I thanked him now for saving my life. Then we positioned our horses side by side and prepared to die.

As if they had been waiting for us, Oxford and Bodrugan's men disentangled themselves from their half-hearted fight, lowering their weapons and regrouping in opposing lines. Then from behind the rebels' line a black destrier emerged and I recognised the handsome face of John de Vere beneath his open sallet helm. As he trotted his horse towards me I saw irritation and contempt in his eyes; here I was again, the troublesome nobody attempting to upset his schemes. Knewstubb shifted in his saddle and I guessed what he was thinking: one of him, two of us. We could at least have the satisfaction of killing the arrogant bastard before we were cut down by the rest. Fortunately, someone else had a better plan.

As de Vere raised his right arm, his gaudy sword glinting bright in the weak November sun, an arrow flashed out of nowhere, piercing the vulnerable mail in his armpit. Disbelief flashed on his face and then he slumped forward onto his destrier's neck. In the mayhem that followed, Knewstubb backed his horse up to a broken section of the harbour wall from behind which, to my confusion, Tom Brankin rose up like a sea spectre, his sleek yew bow hanging from his shoulder. Scrambling onto the saddle behind his friend, he gave me a complacent wink before grabbing on tight as Knewstubb kicked the horse into action. Following their lead, I exhorted my charger to fly like the wind as we began our journey back along the causeway. As we galloped

I strained my ears to hear what was happening behind me; above the shouts of dismay I caught snatches of orders, snarling accusations of treachery and a heartfelt cry of "He lives!" which I guessed came from one of Oxford's brothers. Soon we were too far to hear more so I risked a swift look over my shoulder. What I saw made me urge my mount forward ever faster. Bodrugan and his men had begun their return and I knew that if Brankin, Knewstubb and I were to survive, I had to reach the encampment before they caught up with us.

My plan was simple and, rarely enough for a plan of mine, it worked. Arriving on the sands where a crowd of gentry and men-at-arms had been watching for our return, I flung myself down and began heaping praise on Bodrugan's leadership.

"Thanks to him, Oxford is wounded and many of his company slain!" I yelled, brandishing my gore-smeared sword to prove the point.

Taking my cue, Brankin and Knewstubb joined in, wiping their brows and hailing Bodrugan the most fearless commander they had ever served under. As the Cornish started cheering, glad to have their leader lauded by outsiders, I searched for and found Kylter's face in the crowd. My one friend amongst the Cornishmen. I hoped I could rely on him now.

"Time to celebrate, William Kylter!" I called to him. "What say we drain a flagon at your tent?"

Kylter gave me a penetrating look but answered as I had wished.

""Aye, of course, Master Cranley. You and your brave lads must come with me."

From the press of men Matthew emerged to take my horse and lead it to the stabling.

"Let it be, lad!" I commanded, anxious for him to be included in the tenuous protection I was weaving. "You shall come with me and have something to warm your innards before seeing to the beast."

My servant frowned, knowing how particular I was about caring for my horseflesh, yet he did as I ordered and, walking the charger through the masses, followed us to Kylter's bivouac. Peering across the sands I could see that Bodrugan had now arrived at the encampment with his murderous band and was being hailed for his heroics. I had little time to make this work.

"Sir Henry is in league with the Earl," I hissed to Kylter who had a companionable arm draped about my shoulders. "His men tried to kill me on the causeway and when that failed they feigned a fight, as they have been doing these last weeks, until Oxford himself came forward to do the job. Luckily for me, Tom Brankin was ready with his bow and when he stuck Oxford with an arrow we were able to break free. But Bodrugan will not let us live if he thinks we are wise to his treachery."

Kylter's countenance grew wary and I knew he was wondering just how much I expected of him, our friendship being new and as yet untested.

"My charade just now has bought us some time," I hurried on. "William, I must ask you to go now to Bodrugan and convince him I am a fool. Tell him I fear he has had two traitors in his midst, men who tried to murder me on the causeway. One was thrown from his horse and killed but the other escaped. The next part will be more difficult. Bodrugan must believe that I thought the battle genuine, that when Oxford came at me I trusted he was going to come to my aid. And lastly,

William, he must believe that I have no idea who fired the arrow that struck Oxford."

"What if he chooses not to believe?" Kylter parried without agreeing to do as I asked.

"Then he will kill me but no one else if I can help it."

Turning to address Brankin and Knewstubb, I bade them get away at once.

"Ride hard and ride fast. Go to the King," I instructed. "Warn him he needs a new Sheriff of Cornwall since Bodrugan is not to be trusted. And while you have his ear, tell him we need more men and more ships if we are going to vanquish Oxford."

They heard my orders and obeyed without hesitation. I thought they might have tried to make me go with them but they did not. Men of the calibre of Brankin and Knewstubb did not waste time on sentiment. Matthew was a different matter.

"Go with them," I ordered him. "Get on that charger and get as far away from here as fast as you can. While Bodrugan is in charge, Cornwall is a dangerous place for my friends."

For a moment I thought he was going to obey. Clambering in his ungainly fashion onto the charger, he spurred it on a few paces until he had caught up with Tom and John on their shared mount. Then he slipped off the horse's back and handed John its reins.

"Be a more comfortable journey with a horse a-piece," he grinned at them.

Silently they accepted the gift and then put spur to flank.

"Seems like the lad is staying," Kylter murmured to me.

"Seems like he is," I agreed.

Chapter Eighteen

Kylter justified my faith in him by doing exactly as I had asked. He found Bodrugan in his tent, surrounded by the sweat-stained men who had taken part in the action as well as many of the more trustworthy members of our company. Explaining my absence, Kylter told Bodrugan that I had taken a slight injury which was being attended to by my servant. He then span the yarn I had concocted in a rush. When he reached the part about the traitor in Bodrugan's midst, Kylter noticed the Sheriff exchange a furtive look with one of his lieutenants. Seconds later this man slipped stealthily from the tent, leaving Kylter to draw the conclusion that he had been one of my assailants.

At this mention of a traitor, the honest Cornishmen became vocal in their outrage, demanding I should be dragged from Kylter's tent and made to account for the slur. Before they could act on the suggestion, however, Bodrugan surprised Kylter by intervening in my defence. Pretending he had been harbouring suspicions about two of his men, he said those suspicions had been confirmed in the recent action. After that it was easy for Kylter to finish. As a northerner I was unpopular but since I was in Cornwall at the King's behest, none of his loyal subjects could wish me dead. The interview concluded with more back-slapping for the Sheriff and a grudging promise from the gentry to ensure there were no further attempts on my life.

When Kylter had returned to his tent I asked him if he thought Bodrugan had believed his story.

"Not a word," he answered, raking his thick, greying curls with his fingers. "But he decided it was politic to pretend he did."

"So now he knows me for an enemy. And probably takes you for one, too. Kylter, I am sorry. I knew I was endangering you when I asked for your help."

"Aye," Kylter sighed, "I knew it too. Well, what's done is done. We had better hope Bodrugan trusts us to keep our mouths shut. If he thinks we will talk, he'll have our throats slashed without pausing to consider."

I shuddered, remembering poor Ralph Abney; a blade flashing though the darkness, a gurgle of blood and then his life ebbing into oblivion.

"What if we did talk?" I wondered aloud. "With your support, would the gentry listen to me, do you think?"

Kylter considered my question.

"Some, aye. But most would want better proof than the word of an outsider before they would believe us."

"Then all we can do is wait for reinforcements from the King, and trust that God will keep us alive until they arrive."

††††

I lived the last days of November on a knife edge, avoiding encounters with Bodrugan as much as possible. This turned out to be easier than I might have expected. The skirmishes ceased immediately after Oxford's injury at the Mount but in their place came endless parleys. Day after day, the Sheriff and his chosen few rode across the well-worn shingle bank to the island, meeting with Oxford's representatives at the harbourside. After the first of these parleys, a boat carrying the Marazion barber was permitted to land at the Mount, Bodrugan insisting to his astonished peers that this was necessary since the King wanted the Earl taken alive. We all knew this to be nonsense. Edward's first priority was to suppress the upheaval in his kingdom. Knowing warfare for a bloody business, he would accept Oxford's death as a necessary consequence of quashing his rebellion.

Following the barber's visit, further boats were given leave to land. From our vantage point on the sands we watched in horror as barrels of wine and sides of meat were unloaded onto the quay. Again Bodrugan was questioned and again he dissembled, arguing that using starvation as a weapon was a coward's way to win a fight.

Little by little, Kylter let it be known that he was dubious about the Sheriff. A word dropped here, a hint dropped there, and soon he had a slow stream of disgruntled Cornish gentlemen meeting in his tent. All voiced the same concerns: why was Bodrugan parleying so often with the enemy, and why did he allow so many provisions through?

One day in late November a new worry rippled through the ranks of the disaffected gentry. Messages were reaching them from loved ones at home, telling them of raids on their houses and farms. Money and goods were stolen, barns set alight and, in the worst cases where there were none to protect them, wives and daughters ravished. While it was impossible to prove the raiders acted under Bodrugan's orders, their methods were identical to those he had been known to use before. Then, however, the outraged parties had had recourse to the law, taking their complaints to the Sheriff. With Bodrugan holding that post, this option no longer remained.

Finally I understood what Bodrugan was doing. Though he had no love for Oxford or his cause, he connived with the Earl to prolong the siege out of self-interest. With the fighting men of Cornwall camped out on the sands at Marazion, his brigands were free to roam the county, striking wherever he ordered and seizing anything he fancied. For as long as the siege continued, his lawlessness would carry on unchallenged.

Now that I understood what lay behind Bodrugan's irrational behaviour, Kylter and I judged it safe to start telling a chosen few the truth about the skirmish in which Oxford had been injured. Word spread and soon we had a significant number ready to oppose the Sheriff next time he arranged for supplies to be taken to the rebels. It would be risky, for we could not guess which way the majority would turn when the time came, but with a fair number of Cornish knights and gentlemen on our side we reckoned we did at least have a chance of success.

In the end it did not come to that. One afternoon in December, as Kylter and I were squatting outside my tent sharing a dish of pickled herring, we heard a cry go up. Hurrying to see what the fuss was about, we stared in amazement at the sight of four ships making graceful progress through Mount's Bay. My first thought was that French Louis had answered Oxford's plea for help but as they came closer I saw that they were good

English ships. Aboard them, I soon discovered, were nine hundred men sent to reinforce the Cornish besiegers under the command of Sir John Fortescue, one of the King's Esquires of the Body. With the arrival of Fortescue, a man who stood high in Edward's favour, Bodrugan's reign of deceit and brigandry was ended. Without raising a voice in dissent, the Cornish gentry accepted the King's man as their new Sheriff, leaving the ousted Bodrugan to skulk back to his estate, there to await his punishment.

I was relieved beyond measure by the arrival of the King's reinforcements and overjoyed when I spied Tom Brankin and John Knewstubb among the new Sheriff's entourage. From them I heard of the King's fury when they had delivered my message about Bodrugan's perfidy to him.

"Mark you, we very nearly never got to tell him," Knewstubb had chortled. "When we first pitched up at court, filthy and stinking from the road, the preening shitbag who controls access to the King told us to be off before he had us whipped for impudence."

"Johnny did not take kindly to that," Brankin interrupted, "so he seizes this oily lickspittle and lifts him clean off his feet, ready to barge past him. Only our way is now blocked by several men-at-arms looking ready to knock our heads off if we venture any further, for all that they are smirking to see Lord Lickspittle handled roughly."

When I had sent them with my message for the King I had not considered the difficulty Tom and John would have in gaining audience with him. In fairness there had been no time to dwell on such details but I now realised the enormity of the task I had given them. While Edward maintained a whimsical fondness for the common man, his courtiers preferred them to keep their distance. Had the lads carried a letter from me they would have been granted grudging admission but with just my verbal message to deliver, there had been no way for them to prove their credentials. It was small wonder they had encountered difficulties.

"What happened next?" Matthew demanded to know, eavesdropping as usual on my conversations when he should have been attending to his duties.

"A good soldier knows when to retreat," Knewstubb answered. "So that's what we do. We retreat to consider our next move. Lucky for us, at that moment Sir James arrives with a letter for the King from the Duke of Gloucester, him having taken on that particular role in your absence, Master Cranley."

He paused to cough and Brankin seized his chance to carry on with the story.

"What brings you two reprobates here, the master asks us, casual-like, more amazed to see us there then he cares to let on. So we tell him the whole sorry tale, and he glowers like he's fit to have a seizure when we say that you are in peril and very likely dead already. Then he barks a few orders and before we know it we're grovelling on our knees in front of King Ned."

"With Sir James to vouch for us, the King believed our tale all right," Knewstubb continued, his coughing having abated, "and his rage at hearing of Bodrugan's dealings with the enemy was something to behold. We were dismissed from his presence soon after that but Sir James came and found us later in the kitchens, scrounging the first hot bite we'd had in days. He told us that the King was sending men and ships to Cornwall."

He stopped abruptly, as though unwilling to say more. Brankin didn't notice and finished the story for him.

"Sir James said we could go back with him to Middleham now we'd delivered the message. But Johnny and me, we said if he had no objection we'd like to come back and look for you and Matthew. See that you had come to no harm without us to mind your backs but if you had, to take vengeance on the buggers that did it. Then Sir James says, aye, I'll square it with the King for you to go back, and I would come with you if my duty to the Duke did not prevent it. So here we are."

"You talk too much, arrow-boy," Knewstubb growled at his friend, discomfited in case I should embarrass him with a display of thanks. Aware of this, I told them that I was glad to see them and left it at that, though both understood the depth of my gratitude.

Fortescue had been in command less than a day when it became apparent how high my stock had risen following my timely warning to the King of Bodrugan's unreliability. At his behest, as he met with the highest ranking gentleman to discuss strategy, I was summoned to deliver my view of the situation. It gratified me to find my counsel listened to as closely as that of Edward Brampton and William Fetherston, staunch supporters of the King who had accompanied Fortescue to Cornwall. My first suggestion, to use the four newly arrived ships to cut off the Mount by sea, was already being acted upon. The next, however, was of more use; I suggested to Fortescue that he should initiate a systematic assault on Oxford's support by promising royal pardons to those that came over to our side of the causeway, supposing he had the authority to do so. Assuring me that the King had empowered him to use any means necessary to defeat Oxford, he told me that he would give my suggestion serious consideration.

Two days later the penultimate parley of the siege took place. It was a formally conducted affair, very different to Bodrugan's shambolic parleys. Only Fortescue, Brampton, Fetherston and I rode across to the Mount but on the shore serried ranks of mounted men waited, ready to charge into lethal combat at a signal from the Sheriff. Still nursing an injury, Oxford himself declined to appear, sending in his stead his brother George and several other men of rank. This proved his undoing. In the Earl's absence Fortescue was able to make his offer of pardons with only a small amount of indignant interruption from George de Vere. Before riding back to shore, we gave warning that the full wrath of the King was about to fall on the rebels.

This was the twenty-second day of December. The next morning we began besieging the Mount in earnest. It would be a lie to pretend we had it all our way after that; for all his faults Oxford commanded the loyalty of his men so that only little by little did we wean them away from him. In the meantime we pursued the siege with all the vigour we could bring to bear. It was slow, frustrating work but we stayed resolute, sensing that the tide had turned in our favour. By early February, reports told us that fewer than ten supporters remained with Oxford and a few days later a messenger rode out from the Mount to make terms. The mighty Earl of Oxford himself was suing for pardon. Though I wanted the siege over, I harboured a secret hope that Fortescue would refuse him pardon and insist on fighting to the end so that I might have the satisfaction of meeting Oxford in battle. It was not to be; on the King's orders Fortescue offered the Earl his life in return for his surrender. Thus, on the fifteenth day of February, John de Vere gave himself up to the King's men and was sent a prisoner to Hammes Castle near Calais. The long siege at the Mount was over.

March was well advanced before I saw Middleham again. At Fortescue's request I had remained by his side until the siege was ended and then, just when I thought I was free to please myself, I found myself ordered to court to give the King a firsthand account of Bodrugan's misdeeds. This I did with relish, my anger at Sir Henry's perfidy having become inflamed anew by the many months' worth of provisions we found when we took possession of St Michael's Mount. Without Fortescue and his reinforcements, the siege might easily have dragged on until summer or beyond.

At court I learned that war with France was looming. With Oxford's insurrection crushed and the Earl pining for his freedom in a dank castle, Edward felt secure enough at home to advance his ancestral claim to the French crown. It would take time to find the money necessary for such a bold undertaking but the court whisperers were sure that it would happen. This made me all the more impatient to rescue my future bride from foreign shores and thus, having made my report to the King, I begged his leave to depart for Middleham the next day. He smiled his dazzling smile and refused my request, giving no reason save that he had need of me a few days more. A week passed by, during which I kicked my heels with ill-grace, until at last one morning a page summoned me to the King's audience chamber. Had I known what was about to occur I would have taken greater pains with my appearance. I entered the King's presence as Francis Cranley, a landless bastard of small significance; leaving, I was Sir Francis Cranley, newly knighted by the King for my loyal services at the Mount. More astonishing even than this, I left as a man of modest property. As I rode north, concealed beneath the folds of my jerkin close to my heart I carried a document giving me legal title to my father's old estate in Surrey. When he had died with no legitimate heir it had passed to the crown but now Edward was returning it to Cranley hands. Bestowing the gift, he warned me that the estate was small and its revenues smaller, hence his willingness to part with it a time when he was milking richer estates dry in order to finance his French campaign. For the past two decades the manor had been maintained by a bailiff who, the King's clerks advised him, was either incompetent or corrupt. He would need to be replaced if I intended, as the King correctly presumed I would, to remain most of the time with Dickon at Middleham, venturing to Surrey only on rare occasions. The house was in disrepair and the coffers sparsely filled. Nevertheless, the Cranley estate was mine. I had title, I had status and I had a home of my own. Now all I lacked was a wife.

Chapter Nineteen

Nearly a year to the day since I first set eyes on Eleanor Vernon at St. Leonard's Grange, I found myself loitering by the famous astronomical clock at the church of St. Mary in Rostock as I waited for her to arrive. It had taken far too long but at last, after many delays, I was making good the promise I had made to the Countess of Warwick and to myself to bring her lady safely home.

In the end, finding Eleanor had proven as easy as seeking a favour from a friend. It helped, of course, that the man asking the favour had been the noble Duke of Gloucester while the man to whom he turned for help was Albrecht Giese, one of the most powerful merchants in the Hanseatic League. While I had still been ankle-deep in seaweed, flushing out traitors on a soggy Cornish shore, Giese had ventured north to Middleham to share in person with my lord of Gloucester all he had gleaned about Eleanor Vernon. That he put himself to this considerable trouble was an indication of the esteem in which he held my lord of Gloucester. It also betokened the immense favour he expected to receive from the Duke in due course.

"The most important news is that Mistress Vernon is safe," Dickon had hastened to reassure me when we spoke in his privy chamber soon after my triumphant return to Middleham. Anne and her mother sat with us, both with needlework in their laps though I noticed that the Countess plied her needle with greater diligence than her daughter.

"She is living in the town of Rostock in a respectable house," my friend continued, "and is well-treated according to Giese's informant who keeps a close watch on her now he knows of our interest."

"But how did she come to Rostock?" I burst in. "By his own admission, I know that the ship Oxford had her put aboard was bound for Danzig."

Ignoring my bad manners, Dickon gave me a wry smile.

"Very true. The ship was bound for Danzig. I believe you made that point many times. But its master, one Karl Warsitz, is a Rostock citizen. He sailed from Southampton to Danzig but when the voyage was complete he returned home, taking Mistress Vernon with him."

I glowered, not liking the sound of this, so Gloucester hastened to settle my concerns.

"Giese tells me the man's motives were pure, Frank, and I am inclined to believe him. By all accounts Warsitz is a decent young man of sober disposition. When Oxford's chief ruffian brought Mistress Vernon to him, he refused at first to take her. Even his fear of losing Oxford's custom could not persuade him. We are told that he only relented when the wretched Jigger said he would slit her throat if she remained in Southampton. And I think we can be sure Warsitz laid no hand upon her, for as soon as he brought her to Rostock he took her to the house of his betrothed."

"Poor Eleanor!" the Countess fretted. "Passed like dirty linen from murderous brutes to low-bred foreigners who do not even speak her language! I cannot bear to contemplate what she must have suffered."

The Duchess put down her sewing and clasped her mother's hands between her own.

"Be easy, mother," she exhorted. "Master Giese assures us that Mistress Vernon is with good people, as we have told you before. As for language, Warsitz speaks English well enough and Eleanor has learned enough of the Duringers' native tongue to make herself understood by them."

She glanced at me, her pale, pinched face made pretty by the sweetness of her expression.

"Isolde – that is the name of Warsitz's betrothed – is the daughter of a craftsman famed far and wide for his skill, Francis! Hans Duringer was born in Nuremberg but the people of Danzig hired him to create their wondrous clock. It is such a marvel that they prize it above everything."

"So much so that once his clock was complete they blinded poor Duringer to prevent him going elsewhere to build another," the Duke commented with a hard look upon his face. I had no trouble guessing what my fair-minded friend thought about such a barbarous act.

"So how did he come to Rostock?" I enquired.

"It was thanks to Isolde, the daughter," Anne explained. "She was acquainted with Karl Warsitz. He was pressing her to marry him but she wanted more time to consider. Then, when her father was blinded she told Warsitz she would be his wife if he would help them escape from Danzig. So he brought them to Rostock. See, Francis, this is how I know him to be a good man. Your Eleanor could not have fallen into safer hands."

Stopping, she turned to gaze fondly at her husband who had given a mild snort of derision at her words.

"My lord husband thinks I see too much good in people. In this as in so little else he is wrong. I know better than many the darkness that can corrupt a person's goodness."

A shadow crossed her face and I knew she was thinking of her father.

"But I also know that a man in love will not take a girl he has dishonoured to live with the object of his affections."

As she finished Dickon laughed, acknowledging that Anne had for the moment bested him in the argument.

"Indeed he will not, I cannot fault your thinking. But, sweeting, what you fail to consider is that not all matches are lucky enough to be founded on the same deep affection as ours. It may well be that Warsitz wooed his Isolde because he loved her. For the sake of their marital felicity I sincerely hope that it is so. Yet is it not equally possible that he wanted her because the good burghers of Rostock desired an astronomical clock of their own? And did not Warsitz know they would reward the man who brought Duringer to them? By courting the clock-maker's lass, he made sure he was the person she turned to when her father needed help."

Clucking mildly at her husband's cynicism, the Duchess turned her attention back to her needle.

"And has such a clock been built?" I asked, intrigued by the tale in spite of my eagerness to hear more about Eleanor's circumstances.

"It has. Giese says it was completed a few months ago, built to Duringer's instructions by local craftsmen since the poor man has been robbed of his sight.

Apparently it is a thing of great ingenuity and beauty. In return for his labours he and his daughter are allowed to live free in Rostock for the remainder of their lives, in a house provided by the town."

"So this is where Eleanor now lives," I murmured, picturing her quiet life with the blind clockmaker and his daughter. "Well, it is not what she was born to but I daresay it has served her well enough. At any rate, I am glad she has had a woman to see to her comforts."

At this Anne's eyes flew up from her sewing so suddenly that she stabbed her finger with the needle.

"You are clumsy, Anne," her mother chided her pettishly. "Now there will be blood on your work. Small wonder your stitching is not as fine as mine, nor even as good as your poor sister's."

I saw Dickon bristle at these unkind words but Anne seemed not to heed them.

"Francis, there is something we have not yet told you," she said softly. "Isolde and Warsitz married soon after Mistress Vernon arrived in Rostock. They have set up home a few doors from the clockmaker's house."

"Leaving Eleanor to care for the decrepit old father," her mother added indignantly. "The poor child! A virtual prisoner, alone and friendless in a strange land!"

Anne sighed heavily before replying.

"Not friendless, mother, nor even alone. Yes, she undertakes the care of poor Master Duringer but Giese's informant says she seems to do so gladly, out of gratitude for the kindness Isolde and her father have shown her. He believes it was at her urging that the young couple wed so swiftly, that she might be useful to them. She has even been heard to joke that while she lives beneath his roof she is the clockmaker's second daughter!"

Although I had been listening as she spoke, my mind had been troubled by a bothersome worry that refused to go away.

"Forgive me, my lady, but there is something I do not comprehend. You say that Giese's Rostock associate watches over her and is certain she is not held against her will. But if that is the case, why has she not sent word to us, her friends at Middleham? I understand that she lacks the money to arrange her own passage but surely, if she is free to move about as she pleases, she could find a way to get a letter to us? Surely she wishes to be brought home?"

I stopped abruptly, concerned that I sounded plaintive and unmanly, and was grateful when Dickon stepped in with a possible answer to my question.

"As to that, she may think it too dangerous to return. Remember, Oxford's cut-throat warned Warsitz he would kill her if she remained in England. He will have told her of her peril, if only to justify abducting her. Very likely she does not know that Oxford is no longer in any position to harm her, and thus may be too frightened to return."

"What folderol!" the Countess cut in, speaking to the mighty lord of the north as though he were no more than a humble page in her household. "You do not know Mistress Vernon. She has courage in abundance, far too much to cower overseas because of some imagined threat to her life."

Though I disliked the way she voiced it, I could not disagree with Proud Nan's opinion of her lady.

"Then I have no answer as to why she does not write," the Duke remarked, looking with mild reproach at his mother-in-law. It was apparent to me that since her arrival at Middleham, Dickon's domestic life had become less harmonious than it had once been. Happily, there was no diminution of affection between him and his Duchess – indeed, since the birth of their son it seemed stronger than ever – but I could tell that he found Anne of Warwick's presence unsettling. Not that he was alone in this; it was no secret that her ceaseless barbs and complaints were making life a trial for many at Middleham. This puzzled me. She had always been a woman of indomitable spirit; haughty, certainly, with no time for fools and flatterers. Yet while she had always been ready to speak her mind, she had usually spoken with courtesy and consideration for the views of others. Even at Beaulieu, where I had found her altered by the calamitous reverses she had suffered, she had still for the most part been reasonable and pleasant. Now she was a different woman, prone to soaring into a passion without provocation or dissolving into sudden melancholy. I could only conclude that her sufferings had unbalanced her mind and comforted myself with the thought that Eleanor would know how to soothe her.

As I had been reflecting on the sad alteration in her mother's disposition, the Duchess had been considering the reasons for Eleanor's silence.

"I think she is angry," she offered at last. "I think that is why she has not written."

This notion made the Countess incredulous.

"Angry? What nonsense! Other than the Earl of Oxford, with whom could she possibly be angry? What reason has she to be angry?"

Anne's face remained passive but I heard the feeling in her voice as she replied.

"What reason? None, save that she is a young woman whose life has been torn asunder by forces over which she has no control. When her father and brother met a brutal death at Barnet she lost not only her family but also her home. Well, you will say, that is sad but it is the lot of many women. But her misery did not end there, for following the death of those she loves she spent three wearisome years in virtual captivity, taking tender care of a woman whose heart had been broken by her husband's treacherous folly, with only a gaggle of fusty monks to lighten her days. And then what happened, just as time her in sanctuary was set to end and a brighter future was dangled before her in the guise of marriage to a personable and considerate man? Why then, through no fault of her own she was pitched into terrible danger. Snatched away from those she cared about, abducted to a foreign land and left to live among strangers. Oh yes, I can very well believe she might be angry."

After she had spoken we all fell silent for a moment, uncomfortably aware that the Duchess had been thinking of her own experiences as the helpless pawn of powerful men. Then a terrible thought occurred to me.

"Will she refuse to return to England?" I asked, aghast at the possibility that the woman I had envisioned pining for me these many months might not want me after all.

Anne gave me a pitying smile.

"Foolish one! Of course she will not refuse," she said, her gentle tone removing the sting from her words. "I said she is angry, not witless. Eleanor may be smarting that you have not yet come to rescue her; perhaps it is unreasonable but I know that was how I felt when I was held in captivity by my lord's brother of Clarence. Every day I prayed Dickon would come for me and when each day ended and he had not come, a tiny sliver of doubt would enter my heart, whispering that perhaps he would never come because he did not want me. Your Mistress Vernon may be feeling something of this but have courage, Francis! All her anger and doubts will be forgotten when she sees you."

Rising, she went to stand behind Dickon's chair, letting her small hand rest lightly on his damask-clad shoulder. He raised his eyes to her face and though no words passed between them, their love was plain to see.

†††

Though I had delayed long enough already, there was one last task I had to complete before I could start my journey to Rostock. On the pretext of wishing to choose a betrothal gift for Eleanor, I rode into York and put up at my usual inn. Giving Matthew a few pennies to waste on idleness, I left him and made my way to Margaret's house. When the manservant answered my knock I loudly declared my wish for an interview with the mistress. Though I had been to the house in secret several times before, on this occasion I wanted nothing furtive about my visit for I had come to York with the express purpose of ending my illicit relations with Margaret.

To begin with she had not taken me seriously when I said I could never lie with her again.

"As you will," she had chuckled, putting her soft arms about my neck and resting her head against my chest. Steeling myself, I had grasped her shoulders and pushed her away.

"No, my love," I said, endeavouring to keep my voice steady as I prepared to break her heart a second time. "I mean it. We must do this no longer."

This time she listened. Summoning her dignity, she moved away, patting into place a strand of her honeyed hair that had come loose when she embraced me. Only when she was satisfied that her appearance was tidy once more, did she speak.

"Why, Francis? Whatever has happened?"

The bewilderment in her wide brown eyes was almost my undoing. Feeling myself falter, I forced myself to remember her scornful reply the first time I had begged her to marry me. Even the memory of her second refusal carried a sting, when she had misinterpreted my motive for visiting her; assuming I had come to plead once more for her hand, she had declined honest matrimony, finding it preferable to be my paramour in order to retain the freedom granted her by her widowhood. Dwelling on these memories gave me the strength to complete what I had come to do.

"I have found someone for whom the idea of marriage to me is not repugnant," I said harshly. "Eleanor Vernon is from a good family yet unlike you she is willing to be my wife."

Margaret stared at me, flushed with anger and confusion, and then her expression cleared and she laughed.

"You have my felicitations," she said. "I am sure you will make her a wonderful husband. But Francis, this need not be the end for us. Marry the girl by all means and be kind to her, as I know you will be, but cease this foolishness! There is no call for you to stop visiting me. I will not object to sharing you with her, for I know I have your heart."

There it was, the offer I had been dreading: Eleanor for my wife and Margaret for my mistress. It was a tempting proposition – oh, sweet Jesu! how I yearned to accept it – yet I knew I must not. For Margaret was right, she did own my heart. All the same I was determined to make Eleanor Vernon my wife. Since I could not give her my love, at least not yet, I knew that I must give her something equally precious, my fidelity. From this moment onwards I intended to be true to her as I knew she would be true to me.

I explained this to Margaret as gently as I could and then left her house at once. I could not let her see the tears in my eyes, brought there by the certainty that I would never again experience the unequalled bliss of holding her in my arms.

†††

Three days after my return from York, Matthew and I set out from Middleham yet again. We were travelling south once more only this time our destination was London. Months ago, when Albrecht Giese had visited Dickon with his news about Eleanor he had offered to give me passage to Rostock aboard one of his vessels whenever I was ready to bring her home. That time had now come.

For part of the way we had Sir James Tyrell, Tom Brankin and John Knewstubb for company, enlivening the journey with their bawdy talk and amiable spirits. When we parted company at Nottingham, they to take the road to Gipping while Matthew and I continued London-bound, I was sorry to see them go. I consoled myself, however, with the thought that we would meet again soon enough, Tyrell having pledged to return to Middleham in order to drink my health at my wedding. Somewhat to my astonishment, he also promised to bring his own young wife north in the fond hope that she and Eleanor might form a bond.

"If we make quick work of filling their bellies, our brats can share a nursemaid," he had grinned as he tendered me a cordial farewell.

"And mayhap in time you and your good lady will honour us with a visit to my house in Surrey," I had riposted, savouring the moment as for the first time I invited a guest to a home of my own. "I will find it the greatest pleasure to entertain you under my roof."

It was left to Matthew to deflate my pomposity.

"Hold up there, master!" he butted in. "Better fix the roof afore you go inviting company."

At that moment I could not decide where my anger was best directed: at Matthew for his cursed impudence or myself for not knowing better than to confide in him about the urgent repairs that were needed before the house could be counted habitable.

†††

In London I lodged at Albrecht Giese's house in the Steelyard, hard by the Thames. Hanseatic merchants had been in possession of this separate walled community since the reign of the first Edward. Due to their restrictive trading practices they had not always been welcome in London and four years ago much of the Steelyard had been destroyed. Since the King's recent rapprochement with them, however, there was a new veneer of acceptance for these powerful traders; even so, I thought them wise to keep to themselves as much as possible behind their stout walls. Fortunately for me, as a trueborn Englishman I was exempt from the suspicions of hostile Londoners and was therefore free to roam the city without fear. This was good, since I would not be sailing for several days. I found my host absent on business when I arrived but he had left careful instructions with his household servants to see to my comforts and facilitate my passage aboard the next vessel of his to leave for the Baltic.

With empty days to fill, I sought out a goldsmith recommended by Giese's steward and chose the betrothal gift for Eleanor that I had failed to buy in York. I was tempted by a pretty golden brooch in the shape of a heart, set around the edges with tiny seed pearls. As I studied it, it brought to mind something Eleanor had told me as we rode together in the Great Close at Beaulieu. She had spoken about having to trade her dead mother's betrothal brooch for a knife when she and the Countess were left unprotected after Barnet. That, I recalled, had also been heart-shaped. I knew she would be moved if I were to present her with a similar token but in the end I could not bring myself to give her a symbolic heart while my own still hankered for Margaret. Despising myself, I opted instead for a simple gold ring set with turquoise, a stone known to protect against drowning. It seemed appropriate, given that I would be bringing her back across the sea, but scarcely the sort of romantic gesture that would fill a young bride with delight. Aware of this, at the last possible moment I returned to the goldsmith and had him inscribe the hoop of the ring with the words, 'I am wholly yours'. In terms of fidelity, it was a pledge I could make in good conscience.

The day before sailing I called upon Tyrell's whore, Joanna, at his house in Hosier Lane. Visiting her at my friend's behest, I gave her a sum of money and a message that he hoped to enjoy her company again before too long. To my unfathomable astonishment, she in turn had something to give me. In all that had happened to me during the past twelve months, I had completely forgotten the seafarer I had commissioned to make enquiries about my mother. Yet he had not forgotten about me, and now I learned that the man's enquiries had been fruitful. Not only had he discovered the whereabouts of the convent my mother had entered, he had found out that she was still alive. This was a great shock to me. Even greater was the news that she had heard about my search and had sent a letter for me. The captain had left it with Joanna at Hosier Lane, knowing that Tyrell or I would visit there in due course.

Back in my quarters at Giese's house I stared at the letter for a long while before reading it. Then, warning Matthew not to disturb me unless he was anxious for a beating, I broke the seal.

Chapter Twenty

The first thing I noticed was that the letter was written in a fair hand, far better than my own if I am truthful. The letters were formed neatly and carefully and there were none of the ink splodges that marred much of my correspondence. The second thing I noted was the length of the letter. My mother, it seemed, had much to say to me.

My dearest son, she began,

You may wonder at my temerity in addressing you thus, given that I deserted you when you were little more than newborn. It is my profoundest hope that once you understand my reasons for this most unnatural action, you will be able to offer me the comfort of your forgiveness. You must understand that I never thought to hear from you; indeed, until recently I did not know whether you had survived infancy. When I learned that you were alive and grown into a fine, healthy man, I beg you to believe that I wept tears of joy.

To begin then, I must tell you of my inauspicious start in life. Of my parents and my first years I know nothing, save that as a very young child I was abandoned outside the great Abbey aux Dames in Caen, the same place where I now live out the last years of my life. I have the good nuns to thank for my survival; they took me in and saw to my upbringing. Naming me Mathilde after the noble lady who founded their house, they clothed and fed me, teaching me all the while to fear God and be useful. They planned for me to become an abbey servant once I reached womanhood but as I grew their scheme altered. Little by little, the nuns became enchanted by my dainty prettiness. Making a pet of me, they pretended to themselves that I showed unusual cleverness and piety; in short, they became convinced it was their duty to give me an education so that I might take holy orders in due course.

I cannot pretend that I did not enjoy their attention for it suited my temperament to be feted and praised. As for my lessons, learning to read and write was no hardship and because my efforts were invariably rewarded with treats and caresses, I worked hard to please. However, I was certain from an early age that a life in the cloisters was not for me; after all, what was the point in being beautiful if I was never to be loved by a man?

I must have been about fourteen years of age when I rewarded the nuns' kindness by running away from the abbey. A troupe of jongleurs had come to Caen; I watched them perform and became fascinated. One day I begged them to take me with them when they left town. They agreed, for the price of my maidenhead. I travelled with those jongleurs for many months, eventually crossing the sea with them to England. By then I had begun to tire of their company and wasted little time in attaching myself to the first decent man who showed interest in me. That man was your father, Sir Francis Cranley.

Believe me or not as you will, my dear son, but I speak only the truth when I say that I came to love your father truly. He was handsome, kind and honourable and I swear that I would have stayed with him forever if Our Lord had spared him. I will not overburden you with the details of our time together; it is sufficient to say that he took me into his care when he found me starving and friendless, at first refusing the only payment I had it in my power to offer him. His intention was to find some honest position for me as a serving wench but in this he failed, since everyone he asked mistook the situation, assuming I was a whore he was discarding. Nobody wanted to take on a French girl of immoral character and so I stayed with him, preparing his meals and washing his clothes. Eventually the inevitable happened and I began to share his bed. Then a miracle occurred, for love blossomed between us. To celebrate our new life together, your father determined that I should have a new name. Mathilde was too solid for a slight creature like me, he insisted; from now on I was his Fayette.

Well, you know what happened next. When I knew I was expecting his child perhaps I should have been filled with shame and fear but in fact I was happier than I had ever been. As for your father, he was overjoyed by the news. I knew that although he was a knight he was poor, though not in the way that I understood poverty. In service to the great Duke of York, he was obliged to follow his lord from place to place but he wanted his child to be born at his manor in Surrey. A scheme was duly hatched; I would be escorted there by one of his trusty men and your father would join me as soon as the Duke could spare him. Alas, fate can be cruel. My travails began earlier than we had expected so that I was still sharing his cramped lodgings when I gave birth to twins, a beautiful son and daughter. The delivery was a terrible ordeal for me and I became delirious for a time, so I cannot remember every detail of what followed. Yet I swear by all the Saints that this is true: your father was so moved when he saw you and your sister that he vowed to make me his wife whatever the world said about it, so that his children might take their rightful place as his heirs.

Before he could act on his pledge, he was called away on some errand for the Duke, in the course of which he and his men were set upon and slain by a group of Lancastrian supporters. That was when my nightmare began. With my dearest love dead, I stood alone and friendless. His men would have rallied to help me but they had fallen at his side. Turning to others, I found no comfort from his associates. I had always known that I was despised for the twin crimes of being French and a wanton, yet I had not understood how deep the hatred ran until your father was killed. Then the whispering started; I was accused of being untrue to your father because I had borne twins. A gossiping nursemaid spread the lie, saying it was well known that twins were fathered by different men and therefore I was doubly a whore.

I thought people would disregard her vicious slur but I was wrong. Without your father to protect me, I became a target for suspicion and hostility. No one came to the house, so in my weakened state I was forced to carry both babes when I went to the market for food, ducking my head against the barrage of abuse and rotten food that was hurled at me. When the small amount of money your father had left in our lodgings was spent,

I knew I had to take action. First I tried appealing to the Duke of York for help, knowing him to be a decent man who had held your father in high regard. Three times I attempted to gain an audience with him and three times his lackeys turned me away before he even knew I was there. In despair, I offered myself to a disreputable man of some rank who had made plain his infatuation with me while your father was still alive. Then I had spurned his attentions but now I went to him and begged him to help me return to France. He agreed to pay my passage; my dear son, I do not need to tell you the price he extracted for his favour.

So now my reputation was blackened further but at least I had enough money to take me home, though I had no idea how I would survive when I arrived there. At once the reality of my situation bore down on me. I was virtually penniless with two hungry babes at my breast. I planned to pass myself off as a respectable widow in France but the nursemaid's slander rang in my ears. What if the common people at home shared her superstitious prejudices about twins? More worrying even than this, however much I hated the thought, I knew that to survive I would have to attach myself again to a wealthy man. But what man would be willing to take on a mistress with two bastard brats?

The night before the cart came to carry me to the coast, I reached a terrible conclusion. I had a slim chance of finding a new protector with one child but none at all with two. Therefore, I had no choice but to leave one of my babies behind. It was the darkest moment of my life yet I did not falter. I chose to take your sister and leave you, not because I loved you less but because I believed a boy child had a better chance of survival than a girl. I understood what the English would say; without my corrupting influence, poor Cranley's son might be worth the bother of raising him. The girl, though – pah! A strumpet's daughter, why take the trouble to save her?

So there it is, my son. I chose your sister over you and have lived with the guilt of it ever since. As I had hoped, I did indeed find a foolish man willing to marry me for my beauty and treat my daughter as his own. A tavern-keeper, he was vulgar and low but kind in his way. I rewarded him with coldness and contempt. As for your sister, I loved her but my guilt forbade me to show it; how could I lavish affection on this bright, chattering child whom I had chosen over her brother? Every motherly embrace I gave her was one I should have given you. I could not bear it. Eventually prayer became my sole consolation. When my husband died I returned to my childhood home and have lived here ever since, spending the greater part of each day begging the Lord's forgiveness for my sins.

And now I know that he has heard my prayers. God be praised, you are alive! It is enough for me, my son. I do not ask you to visit me or even write to me but I will continue to live in hope of your forgiveness.

Your ever loving mother,
Mathilde of Caen

Chapter Twenty-One

When I had finished reading I tossed the letter aside and called upon Matthew to bring me some wine. As I raised Giese's jewelled goblet to my lips I saw that my hand was shaking with some emotion I could not name. The depth of my feeling confused me. As a boy I had never wondered much about my mother, accepting the story I had been told, that she had been a low woman who had absconded with my father's meagre fortune soon after his death. Only recently had I learned of the existence of a twin sister. This knowledge had sparked a new interest in my mother but only in so far as my male pride demanded to know why she had preferred my sister to me. I had never considered her as a person in her own right. She was just the woman from whose womb I had slithered. Her letter changed things, it made her real. Whether or not I believed her words, I knew I would never be able to banish her entirely from my thoughts.

Reaching for the letter again, I cursed the curiosity that had prompted my search for this stranger who claimed to think of me as her dearest son. Well, she was not my beloved mother. Dickon had been my brother for as long as I could remember and since his marriage to Anne, I had been blessed with a sister, also. Soon I would be adding a wife to this family. I felt no need for any other kin, especially not the wretched woman who had abandoned me to the charity of strangers.

Thinking these thoughts, I confronted and then accepted the depths of my resentment. My mother's explanation had angered me yet taking a dispassionate view of the situation I could not truly fault her actions. I could even recognise that in her own way she had done her best for me; after all, by abandoning me she had made possible my upbringing with Dickon. Had she stayed, I might never have met him and even if I had, we would never have formed such a strong bond. So why did the letter make me so uncomfortable? I concluded that it was because I disbelieved much of her story, sensing falseness and self-justification in every well-crafted sentence. If Mathilde of Caen was hoping my forgiveness, she would have to hope in vain.

Disgusted, I was about to discard the letter a second time when I caught sight of two lines scrawled some way beneath the signature. I had not seen them before, perhaps because my mind had been in too much turmoil. Reading them now, I struggled to comprehend their meaning.

Since penning this letter it has come to my knowledge that you grieve for one you think lost to you forever. My son, I would have you know that hope remains; I dare say no more for now.

Here was a conundrum. For whom did she think I grieved? My first thought was Margaret, my true love who was indeed lost to me forever. But was it possible that my mother, living a cloistered life in a foreign land, could have knowledge of my ill-fated romance with Mistress Pennicott? No, I concluded, it was not.

So, then, perhaps she referred to Eleanor. Yet just as she could not know about Margaret, it was equally implausible that she could know about my plans to marry Eleanor Vernon, or her subsequent disappearance. These facts were known to a handful of people, none of whom were likely to be in secret communication with a woman who had once been a notorious whore. As hard as I tried to fathom the puzzle, I could think of no one else for whom I might be thought to be grieving. And then, with a seething surge of nausea, it came to me; those last words, *"I dare say no more for now,"* gave away her meaning. I had met my twin sister without knowing her true identity and soon afterwards she had died in a way that still haunted me. Only after her death had I learned that she and I had shared our mother's womb. Now my mother seemed to be hinting that my twin had somehow cheated death. It was too much for me: a mother emerging from the murky legends of my childhood, a sister rising from the grave. Though they were my kin I could not cope with their tangled deceptions. Maybe I would feel differently when Eleanor and I were wed but for now, finding space in my affections for a bride was enough of a challenge.

When Matthew and I sailed for Rostock the next day I willed my thoughts towards Eleanor. The voyage was much as I expected it to be, which is to say uncomfortable and wearisome. The crew aboard the hulk in which we sailed were competent and affable and my panelled cabin was fitted out with many conveniences. Even so, I found it a sore trial living in close proximity with so many people, most of them unwashed, and when the sea turned rough the terracotta urinal beside my bed overflowed with Matthew's vomit. Then the stench in the cabin became unbearable and I longed to go above but instead stayed with my ailing servant, strumming my lute to distract me from his heaving. We both gave heart-felt thanks to God when we reached our destination, though not without a shudder that soon enough we would have it all to do again.

Giese's associate, Steffan Kornherr, was waiting for us as we disembarked, a slight, neatly dressed merchant of middling years wearing wooden pattens strapped to his boots to protect their leather from the watery quayside. As he greeted me I was relieved to find that Kornherr spoke English, heavily accented but easy enough to understand with a little effort. He guided us through the orderly streets to his lodgings where I was grateful to find a menial standing ready with tasty food and a tub of hot, scented water. After availing myself of both, I put on fresh apparel and then followed my host to the house of Karl and Isolde Warsitz. As we walked, he explained that my arrival would come as a complete surprise to the couple, Giese having instructed him to keep secret his observation of Eleanor.

"Are you willing to remain with me when I speak with them, to translate what I say?" I asked hopefully.

Kornherr nodded his assent.

"I will remain, yes of course," he agreed, "but you will have no trouble making yourself understood. Karl Warsitz speaks English better than I. As a seafarer he has found it useful to learn several foreign languages."

As he spoke I realised that I knew this already. At Middleham, I had heard Anne reassure her mother that Eleanor was able to communicate with Warsitz in her own tongue. This was all to the good. Communicating directly with Warsitz was preferable to speaking through an interpreter, much as I trusted Giese's man.

We found Isolde Warsitz working in the small, well-tended garden outside her house, pulling weeds from a bed of green shoots. Kornherr spoke softly with her for a few moments and then she straightened, wiping her hands on her fustian apron as she took my measure. She was a short, round woman with a bright complexion and dark brown hair escaping from her linen coif. Though not beautiful, I found her face pleasant enough, or rather I would have done had her eyes and mouth managed to welcome me with a smile. Instead, she studied me with cold antagonism before uttering a few words to Kornherr in their incomprehensible tongue and then disappearing into the house.

"Her husband is inside," he explained. "We are to wait here while she fetches him."

From his neutral tone I could not tell if this was normal behaviour but from my point of view, the woman's reaction to my presence did not bode well. At home, the rules of hospitality would have ensured that, as visitors of some status, we were invited inside and given refreshment while Warsitz was summoned. I could not believe that matters were conducted so differently here.

"Whatever did you say to upset her?" I asked Kornherr, with a half smile to let him know that I was jesting.

He gave an apologetic cough before answering.

"I told her you were Sir Francis Cranley, an honourable knight and close friend of King Edward."

At this over-exaggeration of my importance I raised my eyebrows but gestured for Kornherr to continue.

"You have come, I said, to fetch Mistress Vernon home. At that point the good lady decided to summon her husband."

As he finished he turned and gave me a shrewd look.

"I do not think she is happy that you are here."

I had reached the same conclusion and was beginning to fear another obstacle in my path when Warsitz himself emerged from the house, his wife hovering in the doorway as he strode out to meet us. A compact man with the weather-beaten face common to seafarers, he gave us a genial greeting much at odds with his wife's hostility. Kornherr introduced me again, this time in English. In response Warsitz offered me a small bow and then ushered me towards the house, moving his wife from our path with a reproving word.

As soon as we were settled in the Warsitzs' best chamber, my welcome became much more cordial. Refreshments were produced and when we were seated and sipping politely, Warsitz offered an apology for his wife's ungracious behaviour.

"Please forgive her, Sir Francis. She was unprepared for your coming. We have all become so fond of Eleanor – Mistress Vernon, that is – and will be sad to see her leave us."

Anger flared within me for a brief moment. Here was the man who had abducted Eleanor from her home speaking of her in familiar terms and daring to express his reluctance to let her go. My fists clenched as hot words flew to my lips but I swallowed them, remembering just in time that Warsitz was not really to blame, having agreed to take Eleanor away under great duress.

"Her friends in England are grateful for the many kindnesses you have shown her," I told him through clenched teeth, "but now it is past time that she came home and became my wife."

Warsitz nodded and spoke to his wife who was standing, rigid and set-faced, behind his chair. As he finished she replied in a jumble of furious words. Sighing, Warsitz turned his attention back to me.

"My Isolde reminds me that it was Mistress Vernon who urged us to marry and set up home on our own. She promised she would stay with Isolde's father until he dies so that we need not worry about him being left alone. What are we to do now, she asks, if Mistress Vernon breaks her promise and leaves with you?"

He spoke as though deprecating his wife's stance but beneath his reasonable manner I detected a calculating brain and felt my anger returning.

"Can he not live with you?" I enquired. "Surely it is not uncommon for an elderly father to live out his remaining days in his son-in-law's home?"

This time I did not disguise my feelings and I had the satisfaction of seeing Warsitz appear somewhat shame-faced.

"As to that," he answered after a long consultation with his wife, "naturally we would be glad to have him here with us. But my Isolde is with child now and, alas, her health is not as strong as I would like it to be. I fear she would not cope with the extra work involved in caring for both our infant and her invalid father. Please, Sir Francis, try to understand. We are totally reliant on Mistress Vernon. Without her help, we would need to pay someone to care for the old man and that, alas, we cannot afford to do."

Here it was at last. Warsitz wanted recompense for losing his father-in-law's unpaid attendant. Glancing about their clean and cheerful chamber, I saw no evidence that money was in short supply yet I could not doubt his meaning. In truth, his venality came as no surprise to me. Warsitz was not a bad man but it was a rare soul that would pass up the opportunity to wring advantage from a situation such as this. Anticipating this very eventuality, Dickon had given me two purses before I left Middleham, one heavy with coin and the other only slightly less so. The lighter of the two was to cover expenses incurred on the road to and from London but the other was to be used for any bribe or ransom that I might need to pay.

Producing this purse, I informed Warsitz with cold composure that its contents would be his as long as he agreed without demur to my demands. The effect was instantaneous, as if a sorcerer had cast a spell upon the man and his wife. Wreathed in smiles, they gave their assent to all that I asked and with breathtaking gall assured me of their happiness that their dear friend would finally be going home.

"Isolde is so very attached to Mistress Vernon," Warsitz gushed, seemingly unaware of my growing distaste for his company. "Bidding her farewell is bound to hurt, they have become almost as sisters. But her pain is eased knowing her friend is making a fine match with a man such as you."

Privately I wondered how close Eleanor could have become to a woman whose language she hardly spoke but wisely I kept this thought to myself. Pleading tiredness after my long voyage, I managed to refuse an invitation to share the Warsitzs' dinner and made good my escape back to Kornherr's lodging.

A little before the appointed hour the following morning, I made my way to the town's largest church, the brick-built Marienkirche. Entering, I took up my position by the splendid clock constructed by Isolde's father. I had chosen this sight for my rendezvous with Eleanor for two reasons. I preferred not to be reunited with my future wife under another man's roof but since we are all God's children, I had no objection to meeting her in His house. That was my first reason. The second was curiosity; I had heard so much about Duringer's clock that I wanted to see it with my own eyes and I knew that Dickon and Anne were also interested in this marvel and would be sure to question me about it.

Standing with Matthew inside the cool church, I gazed up in wonderment. Easily the height of eight or nine men, the clock was constructed in three parts. As I endeavoured to take it all in, the hour struck and I watched dumbfounded as a series of small figures began to move at the very top. Kornherr had told me about this, explaining that the procession of figures represented the Apostles. As they moved they crossed in front of another figure, this one representing Our Saviour who blessed them as they passed into Heaven where they would remain until the clock struck the next hour. Fascinated by this mechanical marvel, I noticed that just before the final Apostle could enter into Heaven, the door slammed shut against him.

"That must be Judas," I explained to Matthew, awed at Duringer's powers of imagination and skill. "He is shut out because he betrayed Our Lord."

"Serves the bugger right," Matthew snorted.

The middle section of the clock was the largest. Studying it, I realised I could make no sense of the gleaming mass of numbers and symbols upon its face though I knew they showed the time, the month and the phases of the moon. More perplexing yet was the bottom section, set slightly in from the middle one, which Kornherr had told me was a calendar capable of giving an accurate date for centuries to come. As a spectacle the whole edifice was magnificent but utterly beyond my understanding. Nonetheless I did my best to commit its appearance and features to my memory so that I would be able to describe it in detail to my lord of Gloucester.

When Matthew had taken his fill of gazing at the clock, the strangest thing he claimed ever to have set eyes upon, I sent him outside so that he could watch for Eleanor and warn me of her approach. I had made Isolde and her husband give me their solemn promise to keep Eleanor ignorant of my presence in Rostock. To ensure they kept their word, I threatened to reduce their payment by half if I judged they had played me false. I took this step because I wanted to surprise Eleanor, to see in her face if she was truly glad to see me. Unconcerned with my reasons, Warsitz readily agreed to keep quiet about me and so it was decided that his wife would bring Eleanor to the Marienkirche the next morning on the simple pretext of desiring her company.

Now the time had come. Matthew darted back inside the church, coughing twice as we had arranged to signal her approach before disappearing into the darkened recesses of the transept. Trembling, I stood facing the clock as Isolde Warsitz guided Eleanor towards me, drawing back when she was within three feet of where I stood. Turning, I looked into Eleanor's face and noticed how pronounced its hollows and planes looked in the flickering candlelight of the church. With a tug at my heart I saw that she still wore the tired blue gown she had been wearing the day we first met. One day soon, I promised myself wordlessly, she will wear nothing but the finest silks and have a fine new gown for every season. Still I looked at her and still I stayed silent, taken aback by her loveliness that was so much greater than I had remembered.

I had seen Eleanor stagger a little when she recognised me, her cheeks flaming with strong emotion. Nevertheless, she recovered her composure before I recovered mine. Gazing directly into my face, she spoke.

"You have come, then," she said, her voice devoid of emotion but her eyes shining with tears.

Historical Note

A lthough this is a work of fiction, some of the events described in it are known historical facts, such as the Earl of Oxford's attempted landing at Chich St. Osyth in May 1473 and his seizure of St. Michael's Mount later that same year.

After the Battle of Barnet, the Countess of Warwick did seek sanctuary at Beaulieu Abbey; since it is not known where she was accommodated, I have lodged her at St. Leonards Grange. She remained in sanctuary until June 1473 when Sir James Tyrell brought her north, the Duke of Gloucester having obtained permission from the King for her to live out her days at Middleham. Tyrell's father-in-law really was Sir John Arundell, Sheriff of Cornwall.

Sir Henry Bodrugan was an unreliable character who is suspected of prolonging the siege at St. Michael's Mount to suit his own purposes. When King Edward became suspicious of him, he was relieved of his duties and replaced by Sir John Fortescue.

Hans Duringer built astronomical clocks in Danzig (now Gdansk) and Rostock. According to some sources, he was blinded by the Danzig authorities to prevent him from building another clock.

Glossary

Belle-mère : mother-in-law

Braies: medieval breeches

Carrack: a large merchant ship

Cellarer: the person in a monastery responsible for provisions

Cellarium: the storehouse in a medieval monastery

Cog: a single-masted, clinker-built vessel with steep sides and a flat bottom

Conversi: monastery lay-brothers, usually responsible for the agricultural and manual work

Crayer: a two or three-masted cargo vessel

Hanseatic League: a powerful economic alliance dominating medieval trade along the coast of Northern Europe

Hippocras: wine flavoured with sugar and spices

Hosteller: the person responsible for a monastery's guesthouse

Hulk: a three-masted trading vessel favoured by the Hanseatic League

Infirmarian: the person in charge of a monastery's infirmary

Keeper (of the castle): the official responsible to the King for a castle's governance

Kitchener: the person responsible for serving meals in a monastery

Lauds: a service of morning prayer traditionally said at daybreak

Metheglin: spiced mead

Nones: a monastic service held at 3pm

Palfrey: a saddle horse with a smooth gait

Prime: a monastic service held at 6am

Rondel dagger: a stiff-bladed steel dagger with a long, tapering point

Rouncey: an all-purpose horse

Sacristy: the room in a monastery where vestments, sacred vessels and important records are kept

Sallet helm: a light war helmet with a back-flaring brim

Sumptuary laws: laws introduced to ensure people dressed according to their rank

Lightning Source UK Ltd.
Milton Keynes UK
UKOW06f0031060515

250955UK00007B/131/P